SPECTER

CIRCUIT: BOOK 1

LACEY DAILEY

To Jacob:

For that one time in fifth grade you shoved a crayon up that poor girl's nose because she wouldn't stop picking on you.

You're a badass.

THE HEAVY KNOCK on her door should've woken her up from a deep sleep. It was six in the morning and she was wide awake, staring vacantly at a brightly painted wall. The yellow she'd chosen was vibrant and reminded her of sunflowers. That is what she told her husband when he'd come home from work and found her rolling the rays of the sun on their wall.

It was vibrant. Overwhelming and way too much. Guests looked shocked when they'd seen it, and her mother had scolded her, insisting she'd ruined her chances of reselling one day. Nobody would ever want to buy a place with a yellow wall. But it didn't matter because she loved it. And that meant he did too.

Her wall of sun had since lost its vibrancy. It may as well have been sprayed jet black. It did nothing to make the room lively, and frankly, she was sick of staring at it.

She forced one leg in front of the other when the knock sounded again. She glanced down at her outfit, noting the same purple peplum dress she'd put on five nights ago when she sat down on the couch to wait for her husband. When he didn't return, she kept waiting. After the third night, she knew he wasn't coming back and cried until her eyes were dry.

She looked through the peephole of her front door, spotting a large man with lips pressed together and impatience splashed across his face. The long dark braid that fell down his back would've given away his identity if he didn't already have the eyepatch to do it for him.

She knew who he was, what he did, and why her husband needed him. She didn't agree, but there wasn't anything she could do. This man had connections to a bigger man. One who supplied her husband with what doctors couldn't give him. She slept a full night's sleep only after reminding herself the man behind her door had helped her husband walk.

Now, all her brain would put out is the idea that the man behind the door was the reason her husband was dead.

She backed away from the door, turning and heading towards the bay window that overlooked the porch. She pulled back the curtains and used trembling hands to push the window upward. Even with the screen and absence of the sun, the sticky, Miami heat hit her like a slap in the face. She gasped once, pulling pieces of hair off her sweaty cheeks.

"Mrs. Clemmons?"

She'd made a sound to confirm it was her and kept a firm grip on the handles of the window when she heard the heavy sound of his footsteps that told her he was approaching.

"Good evening, ma'am."

She'd snorted at his greeting. He spoke as if he were a gentleman greeting her for dinner rather than a criminal standing on her doorstep in the early hours of the morning.

"Mrs. Clemmons, I'm here to pass along a message."

"He's dead, right?" She cleared her throat and spoke the words again. The first time she'd rasped them, they were barely audible. Sounded like sandpaper on gravel. She wet her tongue, blinking rapidly at the familiar moisture filling her eyes.

"I'm afraid so, Mrs. Clemmons." He dipped his head. "I'm so sorry for your loss."

He wasn't sorry. She knew that. Her husband was just another man to collect money from. Another customer to keep business booming.

"How?"

He clapped his hands in front of him, widening his stance. "The FBI performed a drug raid. A handful of my men went to prison. My boss included. Many shots were fired. Your husband was collateral damage."

"Are you trying to insinuate a federal agent shot my husband? In a room full of bad guys, you're going to expect me to believe it was the good guys?"

His muscles stiffened. A low snarl came from between his lips. She knew she'd said too much. Took it too far and made the man with a gun strapped to his waist angry.

But she just couldn't bring herself to care.

"Listen, princess. Me and my men ain't in the business of making house calls. You think if we killed your old man, I'd be on this porch? Hell no."

His phony facade was long gone. He wasn't the polite gentleman he was a few minutes ago. Though she'd instigated his switch, something told her it didn't usually take much to flip it.

"If you aren't normally one to make house calls, why are you here?"

"Because!" He spat, as if the mere thought of her not

understanding enraged him. "Them Feds shot your husband! Your so-called good guys are killers! Me and my men is busting our asses every day to help your old man and we're still considered bad guys! You got your shit twisted, lady."

They were bad guys. Despite the fact they consistently helped her husband, they were bad humans. She knew it down to her bones. And she wasn't so sure she believed a man who smelled of liquor.

"Where is his body? Why isn't the FBI here telling me about his death?"

He thrust his finger at the screen. "They ain't here because my men took him. Shit happened fast, princess. Them pigs shot your man and kept walking. Didn't even check to see if he had a pulse. My man, Frankie, drug his body away. You ask me? You is lucky the FBI ain't here raiding your house for drugs and asking a million questions."

"I want his body."

"I suppose you could have it. Probably rotted up by now."

Tears rolled down her cheeks at the way this man spoke about her husband. Her best friend. The sweet boy she'd met at the age of fourteen. They'd conquered every milestone together.

And she didn't know how to handle his death without him.

Vomit rose up her throat at his vile description. She didn't bother to move her curtains or hold back her hair before she bent at the waist and hurled everywhere.

She heaved for a long time, gasped for breath in between sobbing and hurling. She was surprised when she sat back up and found the man still standing on the other side of the screen.

She rolled her head, miserable eyes meeting his. "Why are you still here?"

"Them Feds killed your man, girl. Didn't even think that there might have been people inside that house that wasn't working. He was in the way and they took him out when he got scared and started to run. You don't think that's fucked up?"

She did. She thought it was on high levels of fucked up. She knew what her husband was doing was wrong. Knew he could've faced jail time and got mixed up with some bad people. But he didn't deserve to die.

And she had no chance to say goodbye.

"It's fucked up." She rasped, swiping at her face. If that's what he wanted, her to admit the precious police had fucked up, he could go now.

"Ain't it? That your husband is dead. Four of my men are dead. My boss is in jail after being shot and barely surviving. All that damage they did and they were still on the news made out to be some heroes who took down a drug ring. I dunno 'bout you, but that don't sound like some heroism to me."

It sounded like absolute bullshit. Her husband was a firing target for a couple of officers who had their eyes on a bigger picture. She couldn't deny what he did was wrong, but there would be no mention of his death. No apology. No talk about all the good he did or the suffering he endured after his accident.

He was suddenly nothing. Just gone.

She'd wake up tomorrow and it'd be like he never existed. He was nothing to the FBI while the man who sips his flask before the sun comes up is making him out to be something.

Rage filled her petite body. She threw her back and screamed. Wild and unrestrained. Screamed while hot tears barreled down her cheeks.

She was pissed.

And broken.

And conflicted.

"What they did ain't right." The man spoke, wiping his mouth with the back of his hand. He screwed the lid back on his flask. "And my men? We done with it. We got a plan to expose what they did. Show the public their superheroes ain't so damn high and mighty." He leaned close to the screen, alcohol assaulting her nose. Her stomach churned, and she swallowed down the rising vomit. "We could use a hand. You in?"

Her eyes nearly fell out. "In with your plan? No. My husband is dead. I'm alive."

Barely. But she was. And if her husband were here, he wouldn't want her anything but.

The man's laugh surprised her. "All due respect, lady, you ain't exactly someone we're looking to have on our team. We don't ever have to have more contact than an email. Just need someone to tie up a loose end. Your career could come in handy."

And his house call suddenly made sense. This man felt no sympathy. He had justice to seek for his friend. And agents to rain revenge down on. He didn't have time to visit widows.

Unless it benefitted him.

"I can't help you."

"You sure? It'd be real easy. Your pretty self would just go about a normal day, sending an extra email every once in a while. Once our plan is complete, you'll never hear from us again and the Feds will be exposed for the rat shit they are."

She went over his words. Her mind was an internal battle of right and wrong. But the line between the two was blurred long before this moment. The group of people who were supposed to always do right had done wrong. And there would be no consequences for their wrongful actions.

Her husband paid for his actions with his life.

It enraged her, drove her wild and forced another agonized shout from her chest.

"What would I have to do?"

He grinned, slow and menacing. "Your normal job."

"What's the agenda here?"

"Told you. There's a piece to our plan that don't fit. We need to keep an eye on it, make sure it won't go rogue before we can put it back the way we want it. You'll act as a distraction, send some words if they start acting up or talking funny. I'll fill you in on the trip."

"Trip? Are we going somewhere?"

"All part of the plan, girl. Start packing." He stood up, popped his neck, and adjusted his belt. "You ever been to Arlington, Virginia?"

8 months later

I STARED into my paper cup, eyes fixated on the lone ice cube that was fighting not to become another reason why my Diet Coke went from fizzy and delicious to lukewarm and flat. It floated towards the top, not much thicker than my fingernail at that point but I had to give it credit for being the last cube floating.

In the end, it would perish.

Just like the other twelve cubes did.

I lifted the paper cup off my desk, using the sleeve of my fleece sweater to wipe away the ring of condensation it left on the wood. I was extra careful not to swallow the ice cube warrior.

His defeat would come.

But I wouldn't be the reason for it.

Watching ice melt was an exceedingly underwhelming way to spend an afternoon. But it was how I spent all of them. My undeniable addiction to Diet Coke was a topic of conversation every time I visited my mother. She was positive my Coca-Cola intake would result in a cancer diagnosis.

What type of cancer I'd get was still unknown.

But according to her, each time I took a sip of the stuff I was one step closer to death.

So I sipped it slowly. Prolonging my good health and impending cancer diagnosis. But giving up Diet Coke all together was something I could not do. The Aspartame in that one cup was like Nicotine to a smoker. It got me through the day.

When I was offered the position to be head of Tech Support for a start-up company pegged to make six figures in their first six months of business straight out of college, I'd thought I hit the motherload. Turns out, head of Tech Support for a recruiting firm was more mundane than watching ice melt. I was rarely needed. When the services I spent four years perfecting at DeVry University were requested, I used them long enough to shuffle down a hall and into an office to plug in a power cord that somehow fell out of the power strip located on the bottom of somebody's desk.

Then it was back to my ice warrior.

Don't get me wrong, SevTeck paid me well. So well I often felt bad for spending hours on end naming small blocks of ice and watching them die. My mom told me having a job that pays well and barely lifting a finger to earn those wages was every man's dream.

It's why I stayed and spent my time plugging in power cords for aggressive headhunters instead of stopping servers from crashing like I thought I'd be doing.

SevTeck must be pretty damn hooked up in the Tech

department for not having one serious crash in the last two years.

Wonder who programmed their system.

Oh, wait.

It was me.

SevTeck was comprised of three owners. One owner was a man who stood at almost seven feet tall. Had to have his three-piece suits made specially. He played college basketball until he tore his ACL and was forced to take his education seriously. He owned a third of this company and asked everyone who works for him to call him Hal. Why? I had no damn idea. His name was Craig.

One owner was a baker turned badass recruiter who wore jeans and untied tennis shoes to run an internationally successful company every day. Kate was the exact same age as me. In fact, I was pretty certain we were only a few weeks apart in age. And you can bet your bottom dollar she has no idea what watching ice melt can do to a person's will to live.

The third owner was a hot-headed tigress who scared the living shit out of any new employee and would rip their skin off their body if they even thought about making a mistake. She was the sole reason I was given this job. Her name was Lilah Wilder, and she was my older sister.

How the hell Craig, Kate, and Lilah became friends was truly beyond me. Lilah claimed it started with her and Craig back in college bonding over a study group. They stayed in touch after graduation and spent their monthly catch up meetings in a bakery Kate's family owned. Long story short, they were all bitching about their boring ass jobs and decided to start a company.

I wondered then if I started whining about how boring my job was if there was anybody who'd run into my office with a million-dollar idea. I could start a business. My last cube had melted. What else did I have to do?

"You don't look like you're working very hard."

My sister's pursed lips and stormy eyes compiled with her sleek red dress and sky-high pumps would have sent a lesser person running. Me? I wasn't afraid of her business persona. The badass bitch spent her nights in pajama pants with kittens on them and screamed at the TV while she watched The Bachelor and stuffed herself with cookie dough.

"That is entirely untrue." I argued, spinning in my leather desk chair. "I've been watching ice melt and killing myself with Diet Coke."

Her eyebrows raised as she scanned the paper cup filled with dark liquid. "Can't you just drink water?"

I groaned, flopping back in my chair, arms flailed outward like I was shot in the chest. "Not you too! Lilah, water has no taste!"

"It does so! It tastes crisp and refreshing."

"Crisp and refreshing?" I snorted. "You just described a cucumber."

"So get some cucumber flavoring and pour it into a bottle of water."

"Or." I sat up in my chair, pushing my glasses back up my nose and clapping my hands together like a brilliant idea just struck me. "I could keep sucking down my Aspartame."

Her dark eyes rolled deep into her head, her heels clicking against the hard floor as she made her way into my office. She shoved some papers aside and made herself a home on the edge of my desk. "Are you going to be at brunch on Sunday?"

I leaned back in my chair, propping my Adidas covered feet on my desk. "You came in here to ask me that?"

"Well, I clearly wasn't disrupting your workday."

"There is no work to be done."

She sighed. Low and deep, drawing air into her lungs at a slow speed and letting it out just as slow. I felt bad for bringing it up. Complaining about my job when she paid me so damn well. "Wren, I've said time and time again you can quit. My feelings won't be hurt. I know your brain cells are shriveling due to boredom. I only offered you the job because-"

"Because I have Circuit." I finished. I knew the reason why. As achingly normal as my nine to five day job was, once the sun went down and I took off my khakis, I sat down at a desk in an outdated building that appeared abandoned and used my skills to do some good. Not that having a hand in the success of my sister's company wasn't good, it was just... flat. Dull compared to the work I did at Circuit every night, working my fingers into arthritis until the sun found its way back into the sky.

I considered looking for another job almost every day the last six months. But truth was, I knew I'd compare every job to the work I did at Circuit.

"You can quit, Wren." She reassured me, her brown eyes meeting my green ones. "I promise I won't shave off an eyebrow in your sleep."

A laughed popped out of me. "I would replace your shampoo with hair remover."

"And then I would kill you." She deadpanned, lips flattening and eyes narrowing. If I didn't know her so well, I'd think she was serious.

"I'm not gonna quit, Gracie." I said, using the version of her middle name only I used. "Every job is gonna be like watching paint dry compared to Circuit." I nudged her waist with the tip of my foot. "Besides, I need to be here when this place comes crashing down. Craig is gonna fuck something up. I'm calling it right now."

Before I could even think about extracting my leg from her personal bubble, she pushed up my pant leg and twisted the shit out of my leg hair. "Craig is not gonna fuck something up! Do not give us bad ju-ju."

"God damn it!" I howled, spasming in my chair and yanking my leg back with so much force, I almost fell out of the damn thing. "Christ! I was joking."

"I don't do jokes." She brushed her red curls behind her shoulder and dusted her hands as if she were proud of herself. Because I knew her so damn well, I was positive she was. "Back to Sunday. Are you going?"

"Probably." I shrugged, still rubbing at my leg. Her long, fake nails had a bite to them. "I don't see why not."

Sunday family brunches were held bi-weekly in the Wilder family. Because Lilah and I lived together in an overpriced flat she mostly paid for in the center of the city, our parents rarely saw us. They were both retired and lived thirty minutes out of the city with a St. Bernard they named Paulanka. Lilah had the idea to start Sunday brunch as a way to keep our parents from packing Paulanka in the back of their Prius and ditching their little house for an apartment with a quarter the personality as their home all in an effort to stay close to their only children.

"Why do you ask? You aren't going?"

She brought her bottom lip between her teeth and started chewing. It was her tell. And I knew right then she was feeling guilty about something. "I can't go."

"Why not?"

"Craig and I are going to Atlanta to help a client."

"Okay?" I didn't see the problem. But to my big sis, missing one family brunch to help her still developing company was practically a federal offense. We both took family seriously. But Lilah was attached to our parents in a way I often envied and didn't understand.

Don't get it twisted. I loved my parents with all I had to give. But Lilah would take down a third world country for them, and I didn't know why. I strongly believed it had to do with the fact that she was a control freak and made herself sick trying to perfect all the pieces of her life. Making sure our parents felt loved even though they weren't needed twenty-four seven was only one piece.

"Gracie, missing one brunch is not a huge deal. Don't fret."

"Just make sure you remind them I love them and I'll for sure be at the next one."

"I will."

"Promise me, Wren." She shot daggers at me, her upper lip curling into a snarl.

I promised her again, crossing my heart. I was certain she'd call them Saturday night and again Sunday morning. That's just the way she was, and I loved her for it. Though Lilah was five years older than me, and I had no interest in playing with a single Barbie growing up, we were close. I'd even go as far to say she was my best friend.

But I'd never admit that to her. Or Ace, my actual best friend who'd put my nuts in a blender if he thought I was trying to replace him.

The sound of my phone buzzing against my desk forced a sheepish grin onto my freckled face. Lilah looked down at my phone and lifted it, showing me the screen though I already knew what it said.

It was an alarm. Set for 5 o-clock with the note "Purgatory is over. You are free."

I flashed her a sweet smile and took the phone from her

grasp, grabbing my messenger bag and plopping a kiss on her cheek in one swift motion.

"You can quit!" She called after me as I slipped from my office and headed towards the elevators.

"I'm good here!" I hollered back, not sure if she heard me or not.

The steel doors slammed shut and descended down into the lobby of the sky rise that held SevTeck. I pushed out into the warm summer air, inhaling car exhaust and pepperoni from the deli down the street. The apartment I shared with Lilah was a whole two blocks away. She chose the location because she knew she could walk to work without having to worry about traffic making her late to work. Me? I would've walked no matter how far the distance. I liked walking. I always have. I didn't even get my license until I turned eighteen because I enjoyed shuffling around the streets, watching people and learning the town.

Also, it was a necessary form of exercise. When I wasn't asleep in my bed, I was behind the screen of a computer. All them pepperoni subs I ate had to go somewhere. And it wasn't gonna be my gut.

My walk lasted all of four minutes before I was striding into my building and stepping back onto an elevator. I rode up to the ninth floor in silence, watching the numbers above the door light up and stepping swiftly off the car when it made a pinging sound on number nine.

I unlocked the door and pushed inside the two-bedroom apartment I shared with my sister. At some point, I'd be an actual grown up and move out. But my thought was, why waste extra money on rent when I could buy another monitor or a third laptop?

I spent next to no time in my apartment. I was there long enough to slap together a sandwich, shuffle to my room, and change into jeans and an old T-shirt from high school. I turned and headed right back out the door, down the elevator, and back onto the street. I shifted my body and took a bite of my sandwich, licking mustard off my top lip. I headed in the opposite direction of SevTeck, crossing the street.

In the time it took me to finish my sandwich, I was pushing through the front doors and stepping onto yet another elevator. As soon as the steel doors shut, a keyboard extracted from the wall. I typed in my password and began my descent into my own personal Wonderland.

Ladies and gentlemen, welcome to Circuit.

[2]

WREN

THE AVERAGE PEDESTRIAN walking down the street or driving down the road looked at the old building that housed Circuit and thought that's all it was.

An old building.

I doubted even one of them wondered why the building had seemingly been under construction for more than two years. There was thick brown paper covering the glass doors and windows, caution tape and do not enter signs every few feet. The ruse only heightened once the front doors opened. Behind them lay the shell of an old credit union, all the furniture pieces ripped out ages ago. The whole place was gutted, covered in a thick layer of dust and dozens of footprints. The old scaffolding and empty paint cans were all part of the scheme to make the place appear as though it was being transformed into something bigger, better, newer, and brighter.

It was my belief that's all people saw and thought about when they passed the old building that was sandwiched between two brand new ones. Soon, they'd get something shiny and new to gawk at and take part in. I knew for a fact they had no idea the run-down credit union was home to a ring of hackers. People just weren't as observant as they thought they were.

The elevator inside wouldn't even open without hitting the up and down arrows in the proper sequence. Even then, there was no ding or lights that signaled when it opened. It simply did. Slid open with an old creak and slammed shut, trapping its passengers inside until they entered their own personal password into a keyboard that extracted from the wall and took their descent.

Once the doors opened, it was like stepping into a very technological, very illegal Wonderland. The beautiful underworld spanned the length of the entire building. There were desks everywhere, strategically laid out to mimic the inside of a circuit board. Though each circuit board was initially different, ours was created specifically and purposefully.

The power cords connected to each of us were spread out across the cement floor like a maze. It looked like complete madness, but there was a reason for it. All thirteen members were connected to the same central processing unit, exactly like a circuit board should. Each member had a duty, sometimes we had separate agendas, but if one of us stopped working or came undone, the entire unit would go down.

And that just could not happen.

A megaprocessor spanned the back wall, built from a shit ton of transistors and bright blue LED lights. The thing stood at six and a half feet tall and stretched thirty-two feet across the building. The first time I stepped inside Circuit and got a good look at the beauty in the back of the room, my mouth dropped open and I drooled.

I swear to the computer Gods, saliva fell off my bottom lip, ran down my chin, and hit the floor.

Not my proudest moment, but I still earned myself a spot on the circuit board.

Not only me, but Ace did too. We stood next to each other, gawking like a couple of people who just witnessed the moon fall from the sky. Ace took off running around the place, waving his hands in the air and screaming in delight. I thought Cruz- our fearless leader- was going to kick us out right then and there.

But rather than kick us out, he did something I haven't seen him do since.

He smiled and gave us a tour.

Aside from the maze of desks and cords, and the megaprocesser that got us all hard, there was a staircase that led to a loft positioned right above the megaprocesser. There were a couple of couches, a few bean bag chairs, a television, a refrigerator, a microwave, and some cupboards that held a good stash of snacks. More than half our members spent most of their days here. Not everybody had a day job, though Cruz encouraged it. We were volunteers. Circuit didn't pay us an ounce of money. We were all here because we wanted to be, and some people had the means to be here all damn day.

I was jealous.

I'd been a member for two years and had yet to take a nap on one of the oversized bean bag chairs or raid the refrigerator for all of August's food.

"Wren!"

I spun at the sound of my name, spotting a hand flying above a computer screen and waving frantically.

"Zelda!" I shouted back, chuckling as I made my way through the maze of desks and power cords. "What's up?"

"Cruz will be M.I.A for a few hours. He didn't say why, just told me to spread the word." She didn't even look up as she addressed me. Her small eyes stayed glued to her screen, fingers covered in silver rings flying across the keyboard. Her eyes narrowed as she stared at the screen, a huge wrinkle across her forehead as if she were trying to make someone explode with her eyes.

"Hell yes!" She slammed both her fists on her desk, knocking over a small Zelda figurine my team and I gave her as a joke. She pushed on the edge of her desk and sent herself flying across the room in her chair. She spun around in glee, clapping her hands deviously. "Take that, bitches!"

"Well, that took her twelve minutes." August tipped back in his chair, propping his feet on his desk and folding his hands behind his head. He was four desks away but there were only five out of thirteen of us present right now. Because of the absent bodies, he had a clear view of Zelda's bizarre happy dance.

"What'd she do?" I shuffled through the room and plopped down into my own chair, firing up my computer.

"Someone was fucking with Josie!" Zelda announced, using Hayden's desk as leverage to launch herself back across the room. "And I just took care of it."

"Does Cruz know?" I asked, lifting the cup I left on my desk last night and taking a generous sip of lukewarm, watered-down Diet Coke.

"Does Cruz know I was helping my girlfriend?" She shot back.

"No. Does Cruz know you're pulling a black hat?"

"I was not pulling a black hat!"

"August!" I shouted. "What's the definition of a black hat?"

"A person who uses hacking for personal gain rather

than activism!" August's definition bounced off the concrete walls and registered in Zelda's head.

She frowned. "These assholes were trying to take down Josie's site. I took down theirs first. That's all. I could've done it with my eyes closed."

Zelda's girlfriend Josie was a freelance photographer. One didn't have to be in the business to know how competitive it is. Any schmuck could buy a fancy camera, take a few pictures of someone in a nice outfit, and call themselves a photographer. Josie's demand for customers was growing rapidly. Especially since everybody took their own photos with their iPhones or other fancy gadgets.

I didn't know the whole story, but from Zelda's ramblings, I'd put together the pieces and figured out another photographer was attempting to put a bug in Josie's site.

What those assholes didn't know was, Josie had a girlfriend who hacks into the secret service database on a regular Tuesday night.

Hell, Josie didn't even know.

"That's all you did?" August asked, shoving his hand in a bag of chips. "Wiped out the corny site they probably made for free with Wix?"

"It was Wordpress." She corrected. "And yes. That's all I did. I was helping an independent business owner."

There were two rules at Circuit.

1) Remain Anonymous.

2) Never use your talents for evil or personal gain.

Zelda helping Josie's business would've broken the second rule if it weren't for the bigoted assholes who started it. Zelda simply ended it in the way she knew how. She stopped a few low-grade hackers from destroying a small business. That was not evil. That was *good*. Because at Circuit, we all wanted to be good.

"I say you're fine then." I shook my mouse, brought my screen to life, and typed in the three different passwords it took to get inside. "It's just different because it's Josie."

"Yeah!" August shouted. "Gotta be careful. Your judgment could get clouded when it comes to your lady friend. Fizzle your brain and all that."

"She fizzles my brain every night, my friend." Zelda winked, turning back to her screen.

"TMI, dude!" August gagged dramatically.

I chuckled and took another sip of my warm pop. It wasn't that bad, and my obsession ensured I could drink Diet Coke anyway I could get it. This old drink tasted more like water than actual Coke but I was not mad.

Why?

Because I didn't watch a single ice cube melt in the six hours I was here last night. I had no time to give them names or watch them take their last little frozen breath. When I was at Circuit, ice cubes were not my friends. And I was not Wren Wilder.

I was Specter. I existed on the Dark Web as nothing else. The people I hacked into, the organizations I took down, the businesses I overrode all cursed the name Specter at night.

IP addresses could not be traced back to me. Hell, they really couldn't be traced at all. Circuit was more secure than NASA or the CIA. The world knew we existed, but they didn't know how and they sure as shit didn't know where.

We were hacktivists, and the average Joe-Schmo would tell you hacktivism was a big hell no. There were headlines all over the internet, warning business owners and internet users of hackers. Our logo was stamped across articles, red Xs slashed through it. The half black, half white circular logo represented the good versus evil in our mission.

We liked to wreak havoc by breaking into a computer system that was supposedly secure. Usually, our efforts were aimed at big corporate suits or government targets. That also included, but was not limited to: terrorists, drug dealers, and pedophiles. We took down scumbags for fun. And oh boy was it fun. We exposed groups who sold illegal weapons and wiped out child pornography and sex trafficking sites on the daily. The biggest head trip of all was our relationship with the FBI. Their headquarters resided just across the river in Washington DC. A whopping fourteen miles away. We were right under their noses, risking a breach and sharing intel. Whether they wanted to admit it or not, we got shit done a lot faster. We had no protocol. No higher-ups to go through or permission to be granted. If we required permission for something, we shouted across the room to Cruz and waited for his grunt in response.

Our relationship with the FBI was typically one-sided. We gave them information and they used it. Just eight months ago, we'd found the home base of a drug ring the FBI had been investigating for nearly six years. Taking down those motherfuckers had been our biggest win yet.

"What's up, Circuit?" Ace came bouncing out of the elevator, dressed in sweatpants, a T-shirt, and a pair of slippers. His thick blond locks brushed his shoulders when he walked. He had a bag of Slim Jims in his hand and held it out as he crossed the room. "Who wants a meat stick? Zelda? Nah, you probably don't."

I rolled my eyes as he plopped in the chair next to me. "What's up, bro?"

"Hey, dude." He thrust his bag at me. "Want to touch my meat stick?"

I pulled one free of the bag and took a bite, chewing with a smirk on my face. "Is it this small? Shame."

He flipped me off and smacked the power button on his machine, firing it up as he chewed his processed meat. I watched him type in his three passwords, a plain background appearing on the screen. He relaxed in his seat, dropping his bag of meat on his desk and popping his knuckles.

"Mischief is gonna create some mischief tonight."

Ace and I chose the names Specter and Mischief in high school. We decided we needed code names when hacking started to become more of a lifestyle rather than a hobby. Some of my team members didn't create a code name until they stepped in the door and were required by Cruz to do so. It basically went hand in hand with rule one.

Zelda's code name was Jo. She decided her real name was too cool to try and one up with a pseudonym. She claimed she didn't want to disrespect the actual Zelda like that. Because to her, video game Zelda was a real person.

August and his twin sister, Hayden, went by the names Apollo and Artemis. On this side of the circuit board, we also had a Titan, a Jester, and a Helios. All different names and all for different reasons.

Ace calling himself Mischief was a no-brainer. That's all he did. Created Mischief. And he had one hell of a time doing it. In all honesty, it really and truly should've been his middle name. Ace Desmond just didn't do him justice. Who cared if Desmond was his grandfather's name? He was born to be and create mischief. The dude got lunch detention constantly in middle school. I doubted he even remembered what the cafeteria looked like. He was suspended so many times in high school, it was a true miracle he graduated. What they say is true, you can have it all. Ace was living the dream. Creating the highest level of mischief possible and nobody yelled at him for it. In fact, it was encouraged.

I chose Specter after one of my favorite DC comic characters. He was arguably the coolest anti-hero ever created and nobody had any idea who he was. It enraged the nerdiest parts of me. He first appeared in number forty-six of the More Fun Comic series when his alter ego was murdered by thugs and his spirit was denied entrance into the afterworld and sent back to Earth. The purpose was for him to eliminate evil.

And that's all I wanted to do as a hacker. I longed to eliminate evil. To wipe out the bad guys by beating them at their own game. And alas, my own version of Specter was born. I kept my old comic inside my desk in case I ever needed a reminder of why I ran on four hours of sleep and a gallon Diet Coke. So far, I didn't need the reminder.

My phone buzzed against my desk. I lifted it, finding my sister's name flashing across the screen.

"Hey, dude?"

I turned to look at Ace, swiping my finger across the screen to open my sister's text. "Yeah?"

"Where's Cruz?"

"Zelda said he'd be back soon."

"He's probably getting another tat. That's like the only reason he ever leaves this place. I'm still convinced he lives in the rafters."

"He does not live in the rafters, you dumb asshole."

He chuckled and slid closer to his desk, nodding at the phone in my hand. "Do something productive."

"Fuck you. How do you know I'm not?"

The thirteen of us could hack into just about anything. Cell phones, ATMs, vehicles, elevators, airplanes, trains, any online store. Hell, we've hacked into a damn Furby before. Just to see if we could. It was all illegal, but damn if you'd ever get me to admit it was wrong. We spent our nights with eyes burning from the light of a computer screen to stop bad shit from happening in a world where bad shit was inevitable. I didn't need my computer to eliminate evil, though it made things a shit ton easier.

"Is that a booty call?" August hollered.

"Does Wren know what a booty call is?" Zelda shouted back.

I set my phone on my desk and held up both of my middle fingers, scanning Lilah's text quickly.

Lilah: I'm on my way to meet with a client. I'm not confident I locked the door. Can you go look?

Me: You want me to walk home to make sure you locked the door?

Lilah: Yes, please. :) you're closer than me!

Me: omfg

Lilah: You're my favorite brother.

I was her only brother, but that wasn't the point. My sister did this at least once a week. If it wasn't her forgetting to lock the door, it was her leaving a curling iron on, the coffee pot still brewing, the refrigerator open. Anything. She was scatter brained, and I meant that in the nicest way possible. She was constantly on the move, never stopped to take a breath. I worried she'd wear herself out, but I'd never seen her with bags under her eyes and never heard her complain.

"Be right back." I stood from my chair and put my

computer to sleep. It wasn't that I didn't trust everybody inside this room. It was just that a dude's computer was like his underwear drawer. There were some places that were sacred to a man. A place he didn't like others to go.

"Where you headed?" Ace asked, eyes on his screen.

"Lilah thinks she forgot to lock the front door."

"Of course she does." Ace shook his head. "That girl needs to stop and smell the roses every once in a while."

I grunted in agreement and headed back towards the elevator, riding silently to the main floor and pushed out onto the street. I nodded politely at a few people who walked passed me and stopped to pet a small dog, adding another reason why I should move out soon.

Lilah wouldn't let me have a dog.

I waved to the doorman of our building and contemplated taking the stairs, but thought better of jogging up nine flights of stairs and slid between the elevator doors just as they closed. I rode in awkward silence to the ninth floor while a couple made out against the wall beside me.

I practically barreled out of the elevator and down the hall to my apartment. As soon as I rounded the corner, spotting the entrance into my home, my feet stuttered against the carpeting. My heart rate increased to the pace of a jackhammer when I spotted the brown box sitting outside my door.

It appeared as though Lilah and I had a package. But I knew right away that wasn't what was happening. Any packages Lilah and I received went to the desk in the lobby. We picked up anything we ordered downstairs. The package perched outside my door was special. And as I approached it, sweat pooling at my temples and dripping down my neck, I saw who it was addressed to.

SPECTER

Shallow breaths escaped in me in quick rotations. I squatted down and got a good look at my name written in permanent marker over the top of a box no bigger than the one my shoes came in and taped shut with packaging tape.

My identity as Specter was kept under wraps for a reason. Fourteen people knew who I was and what I did at Circuit when the sun went down. And I was more than positive this package didn't come from anybody in that fourteen.

I wasn't thinking clearly at all. I forgot about checking the front door and swiped that box off the floor. I took off down the hall and towards the elevator. It could've had a damn bomb in it for all I knew. Yet I took off anyway, my feet flying across the sidewalk at a pace that had me panting for breath.

I held the box tight to my chest, praying to whatever God would listen it didn't mean what I thought it did.

Circuit was compromised.

And somehow, it was all my fault.

[3]
WREN

"Brother, you need to breathe." Ace placed the heel of his hand on my back, rubbing deep circles in my lower back muscles as if I were giving birth. "You don't even know what's in there. Could be panties from your last hookup."

There was a snort I was positive came from Zelda. "What last hookup?"

"Everybody shut up for a second!" Cruz's bark was just as intimidating as my sister's. It echoed off the concrete walls and silenced all thirteen of us in a nanosecond. He'd just returned from wherever the hell he was when I flew out of the elevators, hyperventilating and talking a mile a minute.

"I'm sorry." I rushed out, my gaze focused on the way my knuckles tightened against the back of my computer chair.

"Knock it off, Wren." Cruz clipped, studying the little box. "You did nothing wrong." He took a long breath, dropping down into his large leather chair spaced evenly between two desks, each lined with three monitors and a flatscreen built into the table.

Cruz exuded every type of quality a leader was supposed to have. He was as hardcore as they came. Had a gaze that could make even the strongest of man's knees weak. Ace thought it was his Puerto Rican descent, and all the tattoos that made people think twice before spewing any disrespect at him. Art covered almost every inch of his body. He had large patches of color inked across his chest and back and down his arms. Small words and scriptures covered his fingers and the tops of his hands. He had some type of mantra written in Spanish that wrapped around his neck. Due to an extremely unfortunate situation, I'd witnessed Cruz taking a shower. That's how I knew he had tats covering his thighs and down to his toes. The crazy mother fucker had a tat on his shlong. The only part that wasn't covered was his face.

And though it seemed like he'd spent his life savings putting ink into his body, I thought the badass persona had a lot to do with the way he held himself. During the two years I'd been part of Circuit, I hadn't once witnessed Cruz slouching. He stood tall, shoulders pulled back and chin held high as he stared at his computer screen. When he was sitting in his big chair, his fingers flying across a keyboard faster than the rest of us combined, he didn't get up to stretch or shake out his legs like the rest of us.

Most of Circuit joked he was a Puerto Rican robot, remembering when to blink at certain times so we all didn't become suspicious he wasn't made of flesh. But I knew that wasn't true. Despite the way Cruz seemed to snap at people instead of talk, and had no family to go home to, he was soft.

I mean, yeah, he was tough as nails and wore brass knuckles over his tattooed fingers.

But he was soft when it mattered. And right now, it mattered.

I wasn't sure how the hell I did it, but I broke the first rule.

Remain Anonymous.

"I doubt it has anything threatening in it." Ace offered.

Cruz lifted his gaze from the box and gave Ace a stare that said he was a moron. "That's not the situation here, mano. If this were holding a bomb, we'd probably already be dead. I'm more concerned with how this person knows Wren is Specter and why the hell they know his address."

I swallowed thickly, wiping the sweat off the back of my neck. It wasn't just that something in that box could be threatening to me or my team. It was that I was the one who had compromised us. I put us on the radar of some nameless, faceless person who could have easily followed me here.

The damn FBI could be above us right now, rubbing their hands together, giddy about arresting thirteen hacktivists who've spent years stepping on their turf and breaking the law in order to do some good.

The sound of a knife slicing open the thick cardboard sent a rough shudder down my spine. I didn't normally act so squirrely, but my brain couldn't comprehend the notion that I would be the reason Circuit got caught after more than ten years in production.

I wasn't sure when exactly Cruz took over Circuit from the man who funded it and created it. I did know he was running it long before I came along. As much as Cruz was intimidating, he was even more of a mystery. Nobody knew much about him or how the hell a man whose first language was Spanish, and hacked into NASA for fun, ended up living fourteen miles from Washington DC. All I had the privilege of knowing was Cruz took over Circuit from a man who ran a multi-million dollar company. Who that man was and the name of that company was unknown to every person who was standing inside this room. Mystery man bought this building under a pseudonym, started it up, and did what he could by himself until Cruz came along and found himself a team. Anything beyond that remained a mystery.

There was only one person in the world I could think of that might know more. She lived in my apartment and had the same bright red hair as me. I never asked Lilah anything about the years she spent in love with Cruz. It wasn't my business. If they wanted to make it my business, they would.

But they didn't. Because Cruz couldn't be explained. And he liked it that way.

I forced my feet to move, climbing up the three stairs to get to the platform that held Cruz's workstation. His rightful place was in the center of the rest of us. The central processing unit we were all connected to was him. He held all of us together. If he went down, we all did. So we did our best to make sure he never did.

"Wren." Cruz sighed, sliding the blade of his small knife back into its protective casing. "I think you're freaking out for no reason."

I choked on nothing. "No reason? Cruz, my identity has been compromised. I may have just fucked this whole thing up."

Cruz held up his hand to get me to shut the hell up. A small snicker came from him. "Listen, mano, I've been doing this a long time. You know as well as I do we're prepared to handle a breach. There's no way this is the Feds."

I narrowed my eyes at him, giving myself a death wish. "How do you know?"

He sized me up, looking up and down my lean body with a small shake of his head. "Because Marshall would've warned us." He pointed at the box. "This is somebody fucking with us. So calm down before you piss in your damn pants."

Ace's laughter barreled out of him. He slapped my back, coming to stand beside me so we could peer into the mystery box. Cruz peeled it open slowly. I was pretty sure he did it just to drive me mad. Nobody wanted to know what the hell was in that damn box more than I did. I had almost had a heart attack over it. Almost pissed in the pants I'd just bought.

Cruz's face twisted in confusion when he peeled back both flaps of the box. He pushed it across his desk, my neck craning so I could see what was inside. My whole face contorted when I got a good look at the contents. There was a card, tucked nicely into a crisp white envelope lying next to a pile of gift cards on a bed of blue tissue paper. All to different restaurants and department stores around town. Tentatively, I reached inside the box and lifted the card.

My hands shook with a strange surge of adrenaline as I shoved my pinky finger under the flap and tore it open. My confusion deepened when I pulled out a simple white card, folded in half. Ace let out a sound of impatience and yanked it from my hand, flipping it open. His gaze dropped when he read it and handed it back to me. My eyes scanned the sentence, brows furrowing. I pushed it across the table and watched Cruz's brown eyes read the strange wording.

Tell everyone at Circuit I said thank you.

Cruz stood out of his chair, turning to face the rest of our team and read the card out loud. Nobody said a damn thing. The question was no longer what was inside the box, but rather who the hell was thanking us.

And why.

[4]
SAGE

I woke with ice in my veins and sweat inside my mattress as if it were a sponge here to soak up the aftermath of my nightmare. My hair was stuck to the back of my neck with a glob of sweat, my breaths coming out in quick pants. I pressed my hand to my chest, breathing in for three seconds and letting it out for three more. It took five times of the breathing exercise I was taught in counseling before my heart rate slowed to a healthy pace.

I peeled myself off my bed, yanking off my sheets and stripping from my pajamas. I checked the clock. It was only six in the morning. Which meant I got about four hours of asleep.

It wasn't the amount I should've been getting, but beggars couldn't be choosers. I asked the universe to give me a way out of hell for almost two years straight.

They gave it to me. I couldn't get greedy and keep asking for more.

I slipped into the bathroom connected to my bedroom and flipped on the sink, pressing cold water to my face. My skin was flaming, blood pumping through me at a relentless pace. Still, I was shivering. There were goosebumps along my arms, my body hair sticking straight up as if I stuck my finger in an electrical socket. When I lifted my head and gazed at the reflection I found, I saw it clear as day.

Fear.

It was etched into me like a second skin. I couldn't remember the last time I didn't look like I'd just seen a ghost. Eyes that were supposed to be a bright blue looked like old dishwater. My cheekbones had too much definition and my lips were cracked. I was already a naturally pale person but now it looked as though I was a phantom. A ghost of a girl I once was. And as I splashed more water on my face and slipped into the shower to rinse away the perspiration matted onto my body, I decided I was okay with that.

I asked for an angel and received a handful of them. They did their part, ripping me from a life I'd thought I'd die from. Now it was my turn to put myself back into my old one. Bulk up and show some gratitude.

I was lucky I wasn't dead.

But even as I thought it, I wondered if it were true. I hadn't slept a full night's sleep since I'd been home. I was incapable of stepping outside of the house without someone by my side. I hadn't attempted to get a job or go to school. I had no interest in any hobbies.

I was stagnant.

I went to counseling with Dr. Julie three times a week and said what I felt comfortable saying. Then I came home and didn't do anything worthy of the second chance I was given. But I had no idea how to stop the fear from crawling under my skin.

As if the universe were trying to prove a point, a bottle of shampoo crashed against the shower floor. I screamed like somebody shoved a knife in my chest and threw my hands over my mouth to attempt to muffle it. I whimpered into my palms, falling to a heap on the shower floor and crying softly.

It was suffocating.

The fear was suffocating me. Almost like an overprotective parent or possessive boyfriend. Both of which I've lived with. I knew what it was like when something controlled your life. Took away your ability to make choices and say no. Took away your basic human right to take a breath without trembling.

I was very familiar with what happens when you have to gasp for breath because your life is suffocating you. Pressing on your chest and robbing you of all your air.

I knew what it felt like to have no control. And fear took it all away from me. Took away my ability to even think straight. I couldn't even take a damn shower without losing myself to the panic.

And I was so damn sick of it.

"Sweetie?"

Another scream was blocked by my palms when a knock sounded at the bathroom door. I swallowed the rest of my fear and fought hard to keep my voice steady.

"Yes?"

"You okay?"

My mother thought she hid the worry in her voice so well. I loved her for trying but I didn't think there would come a day I wouldn't see right through the calmness she tried to perceive. "Fine." I called out, untangling my limbs and standing back under the water. "Shampoo fell off the ledge."

"Oh, okay! Do you need anything?"

I needed a lot of things. A good night's sleep and a face

that didn't scream ghost girl were just a start. But as desperately as she wanted to, she couldn't give me those things. So I smacked a smile on my face and said, "No! I'm great!"

I didn't hear anything from her after that, but I knew she was putting new sheets on my bed and taking the old ones to the laundry room. My nightmares happened at least twice a week and everybody liked to pretend it was normal. My mother especially. But I was in no shape to argue her delusion was just that. A delusion. I couldn't tell her the fear she held of me being taken again was irrational. Because I held all the same fears and delusions.

I dried off quickly, slipping on a thick fleece robe and tying the band around my waist. I took my time brushing out the snow-white hair that went to the middle of my back and slid my feet into a pair of slippers. It appeared as if I were about to go to bed. And though I was nothing but exhausted, I couldn't bring myself to close my eyes.

"Good morning, honey!" My mom plastered her fake calm across her face the moment I opened the bathroom door. "Would you like some breakfast?"

"Mom." I said, sitting on the edge of my newly made bed. "You can go back to sleep. I know you woke up because you heard the shampoo."

She made a sound, waving her hand at me. Her eyes went glassy which told me she was about to lie to spare my feelings. "Oh, pish posh. I was just about to make breakfast. Want to help?"

I had nothing better to do. So I stood off my bed and followed her downstairs, working double time to mold a neutral smile on my face.

———

From an outside perspective, the four of us would look like one happy family. Somebody who didn't know my situation would look through the large bay window in our dining room and see two doting parents, sharing a nice breakfast with their son and daughter. They'd see the stacks of pancakes and plates of bacon spread out across a mahogany table with matching chairs. They'd see the orange juice my mom had me make fresh and the bowl of fruit I cut up. What they wouldn't see was the large gap between my brother and I's chairs because I went into a frenzy when somebody touched me. They wouldn't hear the strain in my father's voice when he tried to make conversation with me. The awkward silences would be missed, and they'd only see the perfect picture.

The same picture I liked to see because even though the alternative was the undeniable truth, I couldn't breathe when I thought too much about it.

"So, Sage, do you wanna watch a movie today? Play some video games?" Brett was the kind of older brother every sister wished they had. He was the brother one would find in a Disney Channel show. He never picked on me too harshly and doted on me the perfect amount. His overprotective persona was never overbearing. And then I got kidnapped, and I could hardly stand the way he tried to shield me. I'd already been to hell and back. What more could he have prevented?

"Sure." I mumbled, lifting my shoulders in a shrug.

What I really wanted was for him to go hang out with his friends. Go back to college. Ask someone on a date. I wanted him to live life for the both of us. But I knew as long as I was around, still walking with no actual destination, that just wouldn't happen.

"Sage is going to Dr. Julie today." My mom reminded

him in a tone that was the same one she'd use if she were announcing a trip to the grocery store.

"Cool." Brett said, chewing on a strip of bacon. "After then."

I cleared my throat and set down my fork. "Brett, I wouldn't be upset if you wanted to hang out with your friends."

"No plans today, sis." He said easily. "You and me. Super Smash Bros."

I nodded, pushing pancakes around my plate and excusing myself to go get dressed before my father had a chance to ask me if I'd thought about college and I'd have to entertain the idea that I could handle it.

I was a victim. Through and through. I suffered immeasurable amounts of fear and pain at the hands of Kade Wilson. I took pills for anxiety and spent six hours a week in trauma counseling. I should've been allowed a nightmare or two. Should've been allowed to break down and chuck something at the wall. But I wasn't. Because if I crumbled, my whole family would. So I used any strength I had to hold us all up and keep my shit together.

The only time I allowed myself to lose it was in Dr. Julie's office. She was not permitted to tell my parents about the fears I had or memories that spurred the nightmares. She couldn't utter a word about the reason why I refused to let someone touch me even though my whole family wondered.

And she could never, ever tell them how I'd often wished it was my blood that filled the hallway that day instead of Trish's.

Coffee dribbled down Dr. Julie's chin, a rough cough escaping her chest. "You did what?"

"I left a thank you package."

She looked at me like I'd grown wings and a horn as she took a Kleenex from the box on her desk and dabbed at her chin. "Sage."

All she said was my name. She stared at me, lifting her pen to write something on her pad and then setting it back down again. She did that over and over, shaking her head and mumbling to herself.

I thought I'd broken her.

And then she finally spoke.

"Why?"

"Because." I lay back on the soft couch, pulling my favorite yellow throw pillow to my chest. It was soft, covered in faux fur. If I saw it in a store, I would've considered it a monstrosity. But the past eight months, it's been a piece of sun I could actually reach.

"I wanted to say thank you."

"For having a hand in saving you?"

"Yeah. If it weren't for them-"

"But you don't know for sure if it was them, Sage. It was all speculation."

"Julie, come on!" I huffed, peering at her white ceiling. "Kade was caught because an anonymous tip of his where-abouts was given to the FBI." I recited it exactly like they did in the courtroom seven months ago when Kade and three of his goons were sentenced to life in prison.

"There is no proof it was Circuit."

She made a good point. There was no proof at all. Simply speculation. The group of hackers had been assisting the FBI for years. I'm sure the Feds had brains spinning, fighting whether to arrest them or kiss their feet.

Though the decision was taken out of their hands considering nobody knew where the hell Circuit was or how many people were part of it. For all they knew, Circuit could be hundreds of people spread out across the country.

Circuit didn't want to be found, and they did a damn good job staying hidden.

Finding Specter was absolute luck. Something I thought I ran out of.

"Sage." Julie let out a long, deep sigh. "The people inside Circuit are criminals."

"I spent two years with criminals, Julie." My voice was hollow, my brain focusing only on my words. The last thing I wanted was to get swept away in memories. "Criminals do not take down drug rings. They participate in them."

She said nothing for a long time. How the hell was she supposed to argue that? She couldn't.

"Did it occur to you that Circuit almost ruined your case? The court can't use evidence that wasn't obtained in a moral manner. Gaining intel from an illegal organization is not a moral piece of evidence."

"A moral piece of evidence?" I snorted. I'm positive that's not what the court called it but I knew what she was saying.

"Kade is gone." I reminded her. It was no use talking about the technicalities. It was over. Done with.

"And you still can't be positive it was Circuit."

"True." I agreed. "But who else could it have been?"

For that, she had no argument. So we sat in silence for a long while. I turned on my side and scanned her office. I appreciated how hard she tried to make it feel warm and homey. It looked nothing like the offices one would see on TV. The couch I was laying on wasn't oddly shaped or brown leather. It was gray suede and my body sunk right into it. The chair she sat in was a lavender color with a high back. It was perched behind a wooden coffee table shaped like a sunflower.

Her desk was metal with a glass top. There was not a single drawer in it. I thought maybe she did it because she didn't want her patients to feel as though she were hiding something.

Instead of stacks of papers and cups of pens, she had photos of her small orange kitten named George, and her husband Derek arranged neatly on her desk.

"Do you wanna talk about your nightmare last night?"

"Nope."

"Alright."

I loved Julie because she never pushed me. She accepted my boundaries and my need to process before I talked. Between breakfast and the three-minute car ride it took to get here, I was given zero processing time. My brain didn't know what the hell happened last night. So how could it have formed words?

She tried again with something new. "How about the package you left?"

"What about it?"

"What'd you leave inside?"

"A few gift cards." I mumbled. "A note that said thank you."

Truth was, I had no idea what the hell a group of hackers liked to receive as gifts. So I used the emergency money my parents gave me and bought a bunch of different gift cards. Placing that package outside apartment 905 was the first time in over two years I'd felt like breathing got a little bit easier.

Even if they didn't use a single one, I'd at least done something for the ones who'd given me back my life.

As tough of a time as I had living it, it was far better than the one I was living before.

"Can we back up this gratitude train?"

I chuckled at her expression, watching with a smirk as she blew a lock of brown hair out of her face and tried to tuck it back into her braid. "Are you telling me you went out to a store on your own, bought several gift cards, and then stepped into an apartment building you weren't familiar with all to leave a package for a group of people you aren't even positive helped you?"

I considered her words. "Yes. All of the above is correct."

She squealed. Her pen went flying and she popped out of her chair, bouncing on her pink ballet flats.

I gawked at her, wondering what the hell she ate for breakfast and where she got the electric blue pencil dress she was wearing.

Not that I had any place to wear one. But still, it was really cute and hugged her curves perfectly.

"Sage!"

I blinked. "Huh?"

She shook her head, a slow smile forming on her lips. "You don't even realize what you did. Do you?"

"Uhm, expressed gratitude? Just because I spent two years with bad humans doesn't mean I don't remember how to be a good one."

She went quiet, closing her eyes and taking a slow breath.

"What'd I say?" I blurted.

"I'm not sure you realize how mature you sound at times. I often forget you're only twenty years old."

"I've lived more life than most ninety-year-olds."

She walked around the coffee table, perching on a flower petal and reached toward me, quickly stopping herself before she took my hand without warning. "I'm proud of you, Sage."

I cringed. I despised that sentence. There was nothing I did that warranted someone to feel pride when it came to me. I did nothing. Didn't fight back. Didn't try to escape. Didn't try to call for help.

I simply survived.

And that's something people do every damn day.

"Sage-"

"Thank you." I clipped out. "For being proud."

"You don't believe you deserve it." It wasn't a question. "One day you will."

"K."

She sighed, but stayed up close and personal with my bubble of space. "Can we talk about you leaving the gift again?"

"Why?"

"Because you aren't seeing what I am."

"Then could you enlighten me, please?"

She chuckled at me. "Sage, you left your house alone and went to a building you weren't familiar with. For the first time since you've been home, you did something on your own without feeling fear."

I blinked. And then I did it again. And again until tears were rolling down my face as I considered her words.

"Why the tears, Sage?"

"I don't know." I gasped out, clutching my sunshine pillow to my chest. "I don't know."

"Think about it."

So I did. I laid there and swiped at my tears, trying to understand why they were dripping down my face until only one word came to mind.

"Relief."

"You're relieved?"

"Yeah." I sniffed. "Because I did something without my father or brother acting as my bodyguard. I feel less broken." I admitted, weight sliding off my shoulders. It was only a small amount, but enough for me to notice the difference. "I did something on my own and I didn't freak out once."

"Do you know why?"

"No." I snorted, wiping my face. "Of course not. I'm just relieved I'm not damaged like I thought I'd be forever."

"You aren't damaged forever, Sage. You're healing." She corrected. "And it can happen in several ways. I think maybe you taking the package to Circuit gave you a purpose. Something you haven't felt like you had in a while. You had a mission and a thank you to deliver. There was no room in your mind for fear."

"Why?"

There was always, always room in my mind for fear. I

could not fathom how it escaped me for even a minute let alone the thirty minutes it took me to buy the gift and get to Specter's door.

"Because Circuit is filled with people who saved you. Not hurt you."

I considered her words. I wasn't sure if there was truth behind them, but I also couldn't argue. Julie was right. There wasn't an ounce of fear when I stepped off the elevator and squatted down to leave my thank you on a welcome mat. I don't know what that said about my brain or how it heals. But I wasn't sure it was a bad thing.

Julie wasn't convinced it was Circuit who took down Kade. But I knew it was them. I just had this feeling. It was deep in my bones. Was just as burned into me as the fear was.

And for a moment, it was stronger. And for that reason, I had to keep chasing it.

"I think I'm gonna leave another." I declared.

"Okay." She nodded, studying my face. I wasn't sure what she saw there but I hoped it wasn't fear. "Can I ask something?"

"Sure."

"How did you manage to find a man who works for an organization so top secret the FBI can't locate them?"

A smirk unfolded across my face. I looked her in her wide eyes and told her the absolute truth. "Luck."

THERE WAS a song from 1984 my father used to listen to on repeat and try to do the moonwalk. No, it was not a Michael Jackson song. It was by some dude who called himself Rockwell. I wasn't even sure if the dude had another song or was famous for just the one. Even so, I couldn't get the damn words out of my head. Eighties music wasn't normally my thing, but I couldn't remember a time I'd resonated with the words of a song so much.

I always feel like somebody's watching me.

And I have no privacy.

For the first time since I accepted the position at SevTeck, I found myself feeling grateful I didn't ever do a damn thing. I would've been entirely useless. My brain was scrambled, and I was distracted. I could think of nothing but those lyrics and the haunting feeling that snaked through my bones and up my spine each time I found something new outside my door. I'd gotten four more packages in fourteen days. Each time my blood hammered in my veins and I thought I might explode.

Not of fear.

I was going to explode from the unknown. I despised that this person knew not only my full name and my address, but who I was and what I did at Circuit. It made me want to hurl. They knew something about me I went to great lengths to hide. And they could use it any damn time they wanted. It terrified me and pissed me off all the same. They knew all about me and I knew nothing about them.

It drove me fucking mad.

I was the hacker for shit's sake! I was the one that was supposed to have access to people's personal lives. If I knew the person's first name, I'd be able to print out their phone records, when their last cavity was, and if they're due for an oil change.

And believe me, I tried tracking them down. Each gift I tracked down to the exact place it was bought and what time the transaction happened. Each time I found what made me close to yanking my hair out.

Cash.

My little gift giving phantom paid in cash.

But I was no quitter. And finding out where the gifts were bought was child's play for someone who's been hacking more than ten years. So, I took seven minutes and hacked into the store's security cameras.

Bingo bitch.

I had to wait for the right moment considering two out of the four stores they used didn't have cameras and one didn't even bother to hook them up. Businesses still thought they could use them as a scare tactic to prevent shoplifting. It worked on some level but not enough to warrant not turning the damn things on.

So on the fourth time, I found her.

Yep.

My phantom friend was a girl.

I'd watched her as she walked up to the register at a candy store and purchased one hundred and four dollars worth of candy. I chomped on my breakfast as I studied her movements. She looked young. I'd say too young to know how to be sending candy to hacktivists, but what the hell did I know? I was twenty-three and looked like I was going on twelve. I got carded trying to go to an R-Rated movie.

Still. The girl looked *so* young. The quality on the camera was shit, and I couldn't do much to fix it while I was sitting at my counter in Fred Flintstone pajama bottoms eating Lucky Charms. I didn't like to hack too much on my personal computer. So I shoved more marshmallow goodness in my mouth and dealt with it.

"Who's that?"

I choked on my cereal, milk threatening to come out my nose. "Give a dude a warning!"

Lilah chuckled, looking down at her heels. "I wasn't actually trying to be quiet. You're just focused."

I turned my laptop screen to give her a better view and pointed with my spoon. "This is my phantom friend who left me all that candy last night."

"Oooo. She's pretty."

I rolled my eyes. This chick had been borderline stalking me, and my sister is first concerned with the way she looks. "Lilah, this is the girl who knows all my secrets."

"All your secrets?" Her eyebrows raised as she rounded the counter and towards the coffee pot. "Does she know you pissed the bed when you were fourteen?"

"I hate you."

She burst out laughing, pouring too much sugar in her coffee.

And she gave me shit over my Diet Coke.

"Run facial recognition and figure out who she is then."

She waved her hand, sipping her coffee slowly. "Hurry up before I have to leave. I wanna know who she is."

I gaped at her. "I am not hacking into a facial recognition system on my personal laptop. Especially since I don't know who this person is or what they want. I'm not gonna give them more ammunition if they're working with The Feds. Circuit is a million times more secure." I slurped up my sugary milk and wiped at my milk mustache with the back of my hand. "I'm taking the day off. You want to know who she is? Take the day off too and come with me."

Her face twisted like she smelt something funky. "Never going to happen."

It was easy for her to blame her desire to stay far away from Circuit on not wanting to miss out on a day's worth of work. But I knew it had more to do with Cruz. I wouldn't even begin to pretend I knew anything about the dynamics of their relationship. It was all one big mystery. Fitting. Considering Cruz was half of the relationship.

"Ya know." I said, standing from my place at the counter and placing my bowl in the sink. "You are the only person who has been inside Circuit that isn't actually part of Circuit. You should feel special."

She rolled her eyes. "I am special. Specter is my baby brother."

"Ace has a sister. Polly has no idea Ace spends his evenings as Mischief."

She stared me down, her stormy eyes growing darker. "I don't know where you are going with this."

"Yeah, you do."

She finished her coffee, her eyes never leaving mine. "You'll fill me in later."

"True." I agreed. I'd tell my sister everything. Phantom girl didn't just know where I lived. She knew where my sister lived too. "But it's not as cool as watching it play out on Cruz's forty-two-inch touchscreen monitor."

Her eyes finally left mine. She placed her mug next to my bowl and grabbed her purse off the counter without another word about Circuit. "Enjoy your day off."

"Lord, please don't let today be the day Craig burns the place down."

She flipped me off and headed towards the door. "I sincerely hope you change your pants before leaving the apartment."

"Don't dis my jammies!"

Once the door slammed shut, I fixed my gaze back on my computer and tried to figure out if I knew this girl from somewhere. I doubted she was a former classmate. I went to a small, private high school and knew all the people I graduated with by first and last name. In college, I was a recluse. Ace and I locked ourselves in our crappy apartment and spent our evenings playing League of Legends and hacking into shit.

As I studied her and the way her white hair spilled down her shoulders like a curtain of snow, I decided I wouldn't ever have forgotten her. She was... gorgeous. Plain and Simple. Despite the shitty camera quality, I knew that for a fact. She looked almost angelic with her snow-white hair and skin that reminded me of vanilla ice cream. Her stature was petite and not at all threatening. If she didn't already look and seem enough like a ghost, she wore a long white dress that went down to her feet and draped around her small body. I half expected her to rise a foot off the ground and float right out of Lily and Millie's Wonder Emporium.

I slid off the stool and grabbed my computer, walking the five steps it took to get to the living room and plopped down into a burgundy recliner my sister despised. It wasn't exactly trendy. And didn't at all match the hues of gray and blue my sister had in here, but it's mine. I bought it in college with my first paycheck from my first actual job, and it's been in my possession ever since.

Not to mention, it was comfy as hell. It may be burgundy corduroy, but the cushions were stuffed with clouds.

I sat back, pulling on the lever that engages the footrest and relaxed with my laptop propped on my stomach. I clicked rewind on the screen and watched her as she walked up and down the aisles, packing six pounds of candy into a small basket. I observed the way she kept her eyes from meeting anybody else's and handed the lady at the register the perfect amount of change and didn't bother to wait for a receipt.

If it weren't for the way she lifted her head to brush the hair from her eyes, I would've never seen her face. I wasn't really in the business of talking to people of the opposite gender. Actually, I was pretty fucking awkward and failed epically at it. I had one girlfriend in college. It lasted less than three months, and I haven't had big enough balls to ask a girl out since. I was an introvert, through and through. My last girlfriend dragged me out to bars and clubs, begging me to go to group outings and spend my Saturday mornings going for walks. She talked to so many strangers, it actually made me cringe. I would've rather stayed in and watched a movie. Or played video games.

Yep. I knew how much of a loser I was. And I was okay with it.

Mostly.

Because if my phantom girl wasn't seemingly stalking me, and I'd just met her on the sidewalk or we happened to run into each other in the deli down the street, I'd be all sorts of disappointed with myself when I let her walk away without attempting to learn her name.

My lack of experience with the ladies meant I wasn't great at pick up lines or knowing which words to use when complimenting them. But if I had to choose something worthy to say to my phantom girl for the first time, I'd wait until she lifted her head to brush her hair from her eyes, and I'd ask her if she was okay.

Seeing how I was both a proud introvert and walked everywhere I could, I was an expert at watching people. And the more times I rewound the footage and studied this girl, I noticed she seemed wound up. Jumpy. As if she were terrified of someone or something. The way she scooted a few steps away when another shopper stood next to her and scanned the same small shelf told me she had a hard time around others. There was no missing the way she angled her body to avoid anybody's accidental brush or the lack of her lips moving. It appeared as though she didn't speak once. Didn't even lift her head until it was her turn to pay and it could no longer be avoided.

She reminded me of glass. I'd only been able to see her through the bird's eye view of a low-grade security camera, but she appeared so fragile. Like she'd crumble if I snapped my fingers too loud. And the more I watched her, the more I wondered if she'd already crumbled and somehow, it was Circuit that helped put her back together.

Question after question about this girl filled my head until they spilled out of my ears. I was determined to answer every single one of them. But first, I just wanted to know her name.

Marshall strode into Circuit looking like he was just chewed up and spit out. His normally pressed dress shirt looked like it just came from a fight with the dryer. His tie was crooked and suit jacket missing. Brown eyes were sunken into his face, his lips pressed into a line as he made his way through the maze of workstations and towards Cruz. There was a manila folder in one hand and a coffee in the other. If I had to guess, I'd say that coffee is the only thing keeping him awake.

"She ain't a damn ghost." Marshall clipped, dropping down at his desk and rolling his neck.

Ace trotted across the building, dropping his hands to Marshall's neck and kneading aggressively. When Ace wasn't breaking the law, he was working as a masseuse at a spa. Why? Because he had no idea what to do after high school. The thought of going to a university made him wanna hurl, and he wanted a job that didn't require a suit and tie. He saw a brochure for a program, thought "I love touching people" and signed up.

Marshall made a sound of appreciation, closing his eyes.

Ace beamed, patting the top of his head. "Can't have our little chocolate swirl all wound up."

If Marshall's eyes were open in that moment, they would've rolled to the back of his head. The shit that comes from Ace's mouth is borderline offensive.

Marshall came from mixed parents. His dad was white and mom was African American, making his skin the color of hot chocolate after all the marshmallows had melted inside.

Marshall's membership of Circuit has lasted triple the time mine has though he was rarely around. He was an intelligence analyst at the FBI, risking ten times more than the rest of us. He was the walking definition of a double agent, warning us when the FBI was getting too close, and giving us intel on a new project.

His Circuit name was Judas.

The moment my phantom girl's face appeared on the massive screen built into one of Cruz's desks, we'd both went quiet and called Marshall. I choked on nothing but air while Cruz re-ran the software. I'd witnessed a lot of weird ass shit in my time at Circuit. Cruz probably quadruple that. I was prepared to find out she was a missing person. Or that she'd somehow been in jail and was out now. Maybe one of our hacks had helped a family member of hers. Maybe she wanted to join the organization. I was even mildly prepared to handle it if she were some sort of cop.

What I wasn't prepared to handle was the idea that my phantom girl... was actually a phantom. What Cruz and I found first was a missing person's report filed by Rod and Janice Maddison more than two years ago. That was unsurprising. What was surprising and had me questioning every single move I ever made in life was the death certificate.

Her name was Sage Maddison, and she was dead.

Sage's funeral was announced in The Washington Post five months after she went missing. The article basically told us squat. Gave no more than a picture of her with rosy cheeks and a beaming smile that looked nothing like the girl on the footage, and a few sentences explaining she'd been believed to have died.

If it were a normal day, I would've believed she was dead. It's not exactly hard knowledge that if a person is missing more than seventy-two hours, the chance they're dead escalates to ungodly high percentages depending on the area one lives.

After Cruz and I got a short message from Marshall stating he'd hit the motherload in the FBI's database, we let him do his thing and focused on the three people who were poised in black in front of a church.

We spent the rest of the afternoon learning all we knew and about Sage's family. Her father Rod was a prosecutor that worked at a General District Court here in Arlington. Her mother Janice worked as a middle school English teacher until three weeks after Sage's disappearance when she quit her job. She grew up with a brother. Brett. He was four years older than her and pulled himself out of classes at Trinity Washington University around the same time his mother quit her job.

It seemed like Sage's disappearance should've shaken the town more than it did. Sadly, I wasn't at all shocked the public heard nothing of her. Arlington was a sister city to DC, where bad shit happened more than it should. Sage got filed away like the other runaway teens and nobody thought anything of it. Her parents believed she was gone enough to throw her a funeral.

And by the looks on their faces while they stood at the door of her funeral, Sage's death destroyed them all. Her poor mother had permanent tears on her cheeks as she clutched her son's hand. Brett didn't even open his eyes for the picture. He kept his eyelids closed and chin down as if he were talking to her. And her father? The man looked as though he didn't want to believe it. His face was stone, refusing to crack or show the emotion he had to have been drowning in.

Cruz and I went silent, staring down at the photos and information of her family, attempting to swallow with thick throats and heavy hearts. It's clear by the footage Sage is not dead. And any decent human would find it absolutely gut-wrenching to learn her family grieved her anyway.

And after I learned her name, I was desperate to know why the world thought she was dead.

And that's where our double agent came in.

"Sage Maddison was kidnapped." Marshall announced, standing swiftly out of his chair. He tore off his tie and walked up the steps to join Cruz and I on the platform. He slapped down the folder and pulled a USB drive from his pocket, sliding it into the back of one of Cruz's computers. It took two clicks of the space bar before we were staring into Sage Maddison's life over the last two years.

"Two years ago." Marshall started, smacking the mouse and pulling up a news article on a bank robbery. "Sage and her best friend Trish Summers stepped into Wells Fargo Bank at exactly fifteen hundred."

"Duuuuuude." Ace groaned, dropping into Marshall's chair. "Real people words, please? Some of us didn't care to learn military time."

"Three o'clock." Marshall clipped. "She stepped inside the bank at three o'clock. Four minutes after that, this mother fucker and his band of assholes showed up."

"Kade Wilson." The name left Cruz's mouth with a heavy dose of disgust the moment the man's face appeared on screen. I cringed at his mugshot, tasting bile in my mouth. There was thick, brown hair matted to his forehead, dark eyes rimmed with red as he snarled at the camera. When he turned to give a profile view, the dried blood crusted to his face stood out against his sticky skin. I'd bet my riot points the man was high as a kite when this picture was taken.

And I doubt he went down without a fight. The dude was a monster. As slimy as they came. He ran two major drug rings in the US, changing their location of operation every three years to stay underground. Not only that, he was heavily into trafficking. Took and sold humans of all genders and races to make a quick buck.

The thought that this man had anything to do with Sage made it harder to keep the vomit down.

"Kade Wilson and three other men robbed this bank-"

"Why?" Ace blurted. "He's a God damn drug dealer! Why would he do that?"

"Don't know, man." Marshall rubbed the top of his head, tugging on the short dark strands. "Some say he needed fast cash. My supervisor thinks he did it as sport."

The color left Ace's face.

"It says they killed everyone inside." Cruz rasped, his arms crossed tightly over his chest.

"Everyone except Sage." Marshall cleared his throat. "Kade kept her."

"Kept her?" I burst out. "What does that even mean?"

Marshall's eyes went void, staring directly at my chest

though it was likely he wasn't seeing anything. "I think only Sage knows what that meant, Wren. All we know is that Kade spared her life, threw a canvas money bag over her head, and held her for sixteen months."

"Wait." Ace flew from Marshall's seat. "If she was taken, why did her parents assume she was dead?"

"That's the thing, man. Her parents didn't know she was taken. They didn't even know she left the house with Ms. Summers that afternoon. They were both working."

"And what?" Ace snorted. "There ain't no cameras in a bank that show her being taken?"

Marshall's muscles went taut. "They took them down with a gunshot."

"You're fucking with me."

"Wish I was, man. Footage picked up Kade and his friends walking into the bank. They shot out the lenses the moment they walked through the door. Sage said she and Ms. Summers were coming from the bathroom when they heard the shots firing. Forensics reports Trish died almost instantly from a shot in the chest. My guess is Sage decided to attempt to run and was taken seconds after that."

"Mother fucker!" Cruz spat.

Marshall cleared his throat, rubbing the back of his neck. "I have the footage. If you guys-"

"No." I choked out, a cold sweat breaking out on every surface of my body. My throat felt dry but I knew if I tried to drink water, it'd come right back up. "No. I do not want to see the moment dozens of people die."

Cruz gripped my shoulder, a gesture he meant as comfort. His gaze landed on Marshall. "When was Sage rescued?"

"Eight months ago." Marshall blew out a long breath. "She was rescued eight months ago when Circuit was finally successful in hacking one of Kade's distributor's laptops and traced outgoing emails to an IP address in Miami. FBI found Sage huddled in a cabinet beneath the kitchen sink."

The millions of hair follicles across my body stood up in unison. "We saved her."

"Yeah, Wren. We saved her."

Silence filled the sticky air. If the rest of Circuit were here already too, silence still would've fallen over us like a thick fog. The only sound that could be heard was the low hum of the fan running that kept Cruz's computers from overheating.

We'd all been hacking more than a decade, and we all joined Circuit with one common goal. It was why I became Specter.

To eliminate evil.

I guess we could've been considered some form of vigilantes. Using illegal tactics to attempt to make the world a better place. And for the most part, we did. We helped people. Broke the law to achieve a greater good. And that's what gave us our purpose. But giving a girl back her life?

That's an entirely different processing unit. An entirely different server.

Hell, an entirely different realm.

Cruz clearing his throat lifted the fog. "She's been trying to thank us?"

"I believe so." Marshall confirmed. "She's back living with her parents and brother in the home she grew up in. Doesn't work or attend school."

"How come we heard all about Kade's trial and nothing about Sage?" Ace leaned back against Marshall's desk, crossing his arms over his chest. My best friend was doing his best to keep the tremble in his voice light.

"Sage requested the privacy. She agreed to testify and give up everything she'd heard in the time she spent with Kade as long as her story was never told."

"She didn't want people to know she was kidnapped and rescued after living with a monster?"

"No, Ace. She didn't. And she kept her part of the bargain to get what she wanted. The stories she told lined up with certain timelines the FBI had already worked out. She knew exactly where Kade kept his laptop. She even knew the password to get into it. That one device had all his contacts in it. Not only is Kade doing life in prison, but so are six of his cronies and five of the distributors Kade worked with all because of her."

"And she got zero recognition." I mumbled, shaking my head slowly. She'd spent almost two years of her life surviving behind massive gates when she'd done nothing to warrant being locked behind them. As if she were a wrongfully committed prisoner. Sage had all her power stripped away from her in the time it took for a gun to go off. All her choices and the outcome of her life was put into the hands of another. And the moment her power was dropped back into her lap by the click of a mouse, she'd wanted no recognition for the good she did with that newfound power. I couldn't help but wonder why. And I felt like leftover trash at the bottom of a dumpster when my mind had filed her away as someone who was crazy.

The more my trash brain considered it, the worse my thoughts felt. She wasn't looking for a trophy. She didn't want a pat on the back or a high five for telling the truth. She wasn't vengeful. She was thankful and didn't need strangers coming up to her on the streets with empty apologies and side hugs to feel it.

"I read something back at the bureau about her not

wanting to answer questions or be a miracle story on the news." Marshall shrugged. "Seems to me she just wanted a life."

"And we gave that to her." Cruz squeezed my shoulder before rubbing his jaw. "It makes sense she'd want to thank us. What doesn't make sense is how she found out it was us."

"Ahhh." Marshall wrung his hands together in a slow motion. "The FBI told the court they received information from an anonymous source."

"And?"

"And that they believed the source was Circuit because we'd helped them in the past."

"Aren't we tainted evidence or something?" Ace wondered, tapping his foot like he does when he's anxious.

"Technically, yes. But Sage wasn't. She was a witness, and the shit she gave up about Kade was enough to put him away for life without ever having to consider the shady way his whereabouts were discovered."

"Damn." Ace shoved his hands deep in his pockets. "Holy God damn."

Sage's disappearing act and anonymous gifts suddenly made so much sense. It all became so clear. Like the stormy clouds drifted away and opened up to make room for the sun. We'd given Sage her life back, and she was expressing gratitude.

But there was still something that didn't make sense.

I opened my mouth to ask, but Cruz's conflicted voice beat me to it.

"How does a girl who was held captive for over a year find Circuit and one of its members when the FBI can't even do it?"

"And why me? Why Specter?" I cut in. "Why did she

choose me?" There were thirteen people in Circuit. She had the pick of the litter and she chose me.

Why?

Marshall grunted, popping his neck. "I've dedicated the last eight hours to this case. I've gone through her phone records, went deep into the computers that reside in her home. I've checked out her extended family and went through an old classmates list. I searched the shit out of her brother and looked into Trish Summers. I burnt the fuck out of my corneas staring at the damn screen and could only form one sentence that relates to how Sage found you."

"What?" I burst out, throwing my arms in the air, impatient and anxious and overwhelmed.

Marshall's warm brown eyes hit my frantic green ones, and he cleared his throat before answering.

"I have no damn idea."

"Do you remember that time in fifth grade when Darren Scott was picking on me? We were sitting in the back of Ms. Franklin's classroom, working on our world map project and Darren wouldn't shut up about my skin tone? He went on and on, making cracks about me being albino or the descendant of a saltine cracker. The little shit basically had me in tears while you were fuming from the inside out. Before I could blink out a tear, you grabbed a crayon, lunged across the desk, and shoved the thing directly up his nose. You were so aggressive, blood gushed out of his little nostril in a nanosecond. I'd always known how awesome you were. It's why I clung to you the second I saw we had matching backpacks in kindergarten. But it was the moment you launched your body across a row of desks and shoved a cyan crayon up Darren Scott's nose did I realize that you were an absolute badass."

I sniffed roughly, unzipping the small purse that was slung across my body and pulled out a cyan crayon. I pressed a kiss to it and placed it next to a crown of flowers.

"You were always doing reckless shit that had me quivering in my knock-off Uggs and calculating how long I'd be grounded if I ever got caught sneaking out with you. But I never did. Because somehow luck followed you everywhere. Until one day, it didn't." I wiped a runaway tear with the back of my trembling hand and laid down next to her. "It should've been you, Trish. It should've been you because you would've fought for yourself. You probably would've rewritten Taken, kicked all their asses, and saved yourself before Liam Neeson ever showed up. And what the hell did I do, ya know? I didn't do anything to warrant earning a cyan crayon."

I rolled to my side, propped my head in my hand, and closed my eyes. Instead of the square stone that merely had her name and the day she was forced to turn in her crayon, I saw her. Her round face beamed when she smiled at me, warm hazel eyes meeting mine with a smirk. She shook her head, her short brown hair smacking her in the face. The blunt bangs that went across her forehead swayed with the motion. She threw her head back and laughed when she saw the crayon, lifting it between her rainbow fingernails.

"I brought it because I think for the first time since like ever, I did something that may qualify as badass."

I pictured her eyebrows raising and the quirk of her purple painted lips. She propped her head in her hand, mimicking my position as if she were ready to hear my story.

"You remember how I told you it was an organization of hackers that found Kade? Well, I'm pretty sure I found a guy who's in the organization. At least, I sure hope I found him because if not, I've been leaving random hundreds of dollars' worth of gifts."

I forced a smile. She was the only one I'd ever smile at these days, and she always smiled back.

"I guess if it isn't really him, I wouldn't want to know. Julie says it's a big deal that I've left the house on my own and took the initiative to do this. That's why I brought the crayon. If you were here, you'd say only a true badass tracks down a dude who they believed to be in an illegal organization after they spent sixteen months imprisoned in one." I snorted. "The tables have turned, my friend. And I don't have much to give you as an explanation on why I did it. Just felt right, I guess. To thank the people that helped me. Kind of like I would if someone held the door or stopped if I got a flat tire. You thank people for kindness so that's what I've been doing. It gives me a purpose, Trish. I'm a badass with a purpose to deliver gratitude. What color crayon should I bring for that?"

I could almost hear her loud laugh, cackling over the low sound of the light wind, moving between the trees.

"Ya know." I rolled to my stomach, picking at the grass and tearing it in two. "You're never gonna believe where I found him. It sounds way too good to be true, so I'll remind you now of the spit shake we did in seventh grade after I borrowed those wedges without asking. No more lying to each other. So, here's the truth. I found him in a hospital. Swear on the last pretzel stick, he was right next to me in the ER like six weeks ago. There was one of those flimsy curtains separating us. I was there because, no surprise here, I had a panic attack after a nightmare and clunked my head on the floor when I fell out of bed. My mother insisted I get checked for a concussion. So there I was, laying on a hospital bed for like the fourth time in less than a year, waiting for a doctor to come when all the lights went out."

She rolled her eyes at me like I was making the whole thing up for pure entertainment.

"I promise, Trish. The damn lights went out in the ER. I

was laying there, clutching the edge of the bed while my dad went to figure out what the hell was happening and why generators weren't flipping on. And then I heard it. A girl's voice on the other side of the curtain."

"*Turn the lights back on!*"

"*I can't turn the lights back on, Lilah!*"

"*What the hell are you talking about? You hack into shit in a creepy underworld and call yourself Specter for fun and can't turn on some lights?*"

"*Holy shit, Gracie! You have no chill at all! Will you shut the hell up?*"

"*Oh, relax. Nobody knows what the hell we're talking about. And that's if anybody can hear us. So, get your phone out and get to work.*"

"*First of all, this isn't a hacking situation. This is a walk to a breaker box and flip a switch situation. Nobody in Circuit would attempt hacking into a breaker box. Second of all, shut the fuck up!*"

"*You just said Circuit! Not me! Ha!*"

"*Lilah, I swear to God, shut up.*"

"*Come on, Wren. This place is dead. Lighten up.*"

"*Next time you slice your finger trying to dice a damn onion, you can drive yourself to get stitches.*"

"It was like three seconds later when the lights came back on and their conversation stopped, but I swear to you, I was shivering. My body felt like needles were pricking it all over. I was acutely aware of everything, all my senses heightening just in case he started talking again. He never did, but there was something inside me that was telling me two things. One thing was that his friend should not be allowed to speak in public places, and the second, Specter was a piece of those who saved me."

I was working on nothing but assumption and a conversation behind a baby blue curtain. The guy who lives in apartment 905 may be a janitor and not even know how to use Google, but no part of me wanted to believe that. My entire being was banking on Specter being who I thought he was. When I told Dr. Julie all this, she was undeniably stunned. I thought her eyes would never go back to their normal size. I knew what she was thinking. Her big brain was overheating, thinking that occurrence was once in a lifetime. Something that was luck of the draw and just didn't happen.

Well, people also didn't get kidnapped in a Wells Fargo by a dude who runs a drug ring, but that happened. They also didn't get rescued on the day they were supposed to marry the drug captain. And they sure as shit didn't happen to overhear some girl exposing the man who helped save her by overpowering the FBI.

But that was my life.

Shit that didn't happen to others happened to me. It was one unexpected event after another, and while I was grateful for some of those events, the uneasiness regarding the future was absolutely exhausting.

"I don't know, Trish. Maybe that's why I'm clinging to Specter. Because he's something good that came out of the bad hand I drew in life. And at least with him, I won't get any unexpected events. He doesn't want people to know who he is so he isn't gonna look for me. Things will stay the same, and I've become so desperate for something to be the same as it's always been."

I turned and looked at her. She frowned when she spotted the tears rolling freely down my cheeks. I sniffed and attempted to smile through them.

Her hand extended towards me, and I closed my eyes. I waited for the warmth of her touch and her slender fingers to brush them away. But it never came. When my tears ran dry and eyes peeled back open, she was gone.

And she was not coming back.

I was all alone. This cemetery was filled with souls. Souls that came from people who'd spent a lifetime being loved and cherished. How long each of their lifetimes lasted was unknown. What I did know was that their lifetime wasn't long enough. People leave this earth too early. Life takes those we love before we're ready. And if by some miracle, we know exactly when it's coming, there's nothing that would prepare us for the moment our hearts get ripped in two pieces.

I sat up, eyeing the crayon while I cried softly. Grief is such a bullshit emotion. Nobody knows how to handle it. Not the person grieving and not the people who try to offer condolences. The entire thing was just unbearable and overwhelming. I felt like a crazy person half the time and was so sick of people telling me they're sorry. Sick of people telling me time heals all wounds and that she was in a better place.

No.

Trish's place was here. Her place was at Trinity Washington University where she could be enrolled in elementary education. Her place was inside a classroom filled with dorky posters and screaming children. Her place was here. On Earth. With all her family and the best friend who's clinging to a crayon.

Trish was my best friend since Kindergarten. We were five years old when we met. I spent thirteen years loving her as if she were my twin sister. Thirteen years of memories were inside my brain, and if one more person made another crack about how long it's been since she's been gone, or how long I've been grieving her, I'd take a page from her book and shove a cyan crayon up their nose.

I had thirteen years with her, and it all dispersed with a gunshot and a pool of blood. As far as I was concerned, I should get thirteen years to grieve her. To let go of my best friend.

But even then, I worried it wouldn't be long enough.

"DUDE, WHAT ARE YOU WEARING?"

I stared into Ace's face as he worked double time not to smirk at me. His lips were pressed together, but there was no feasible way I could've missed the twinkle in his eye that told me he was about to say something he probably shouldn't.

"You look like Ken."

I gaped at him. "Ken the Barbie?"

"That's the one."

"Fuck you, dude! I'm a ginger! I do not look like Ken."

"It's the outfit. Not the hair. You look like golfer Ken."

He made himself comfortable on my couch, widening his legs and grabbing for the remote. I looked down at my outfit in horror. I thought I looked *nice.* So maybe most guys avoided wearing canary yellow polos to work, but I liked yellow. It was a happy color. You couldn't look at a dude wearing yellow and give him attitude. The sunshine shirt was like a shield that's purpose was to repel negativity. And when it was tucked into light-colored khakis secured with a dark brown belt, I looked damn professional.

"If I'm golfer Ken, then you're masseuse Ken." I flipped him off and plopped down into my recliner, pulling the lever.

Ace came right from work. His body was slumped into my suede gray couch, covered in bright white pants, a white T-shirt, and a white smock thing that had big black buttons and Tranquility's Spa logo on the right side of his chest. His shoulder length blond hair was tied in a knot on the top of his head, stray pieces falling down his neck. If either of us looked like a goober, it was him.

"Man bun, masseuse Ken." I corrected.

"Tell me, Wren." He shifted his body, flipping off the television and raising his eyebrows. "You think the hotties are more likely to play with a masseuse or a golfer? 'Cause I'm betting on the former. Besides, these locks give them something to hold on to."

It took all my effort not to laugh. "I can't even with you."

He winked at me, heaving himself off the couch. "Want a beer?"

"Yeah."

He headed towards the kitchen, yanking open the refrigerator. "Can I see your ID, sir?"

"Piss off." I barked.

He came back into the living room, cackling as he handed me a bottle and threw himself back on my couch. He popped the top of his beer off and took a long swig, adjusting his junk. "That outfit makes you look even younger. And you wonder why you got carded when we tried to see The Purge."

"What is wrong with my outfit? You're the one who looks like some washed up version of Jesus."

"Yeah but I'm required to wear this outfit. You chose yours."

We stared at each with straight faces for a long time. I kept my gaze neutral while I studied his features and focused on the piercing he had in his eyebrow. If our outfits weren't any indication, Ace and I were like night and day. Black and white. Good and bad. Orange Juice and toothpaste. Anybody could take one look at us and wonder how the hell we've been best friends all our lives. We didn't match up at all. But the thing with opposites is that one can't exist without the other. And life without my brother was incomprehensible. We were different, but completely the same where it mattered.

He licked beer off his lip and let out a loud burp, never breaking his stare. We were both waiting for the other to crack first.

"I hate you." I told him. "Why are we even friends?"

"Because our mamas went to Mommy and Me music class. We communicated through the womb about how awful the experience was."

That was when I cracked. My throat burned as I struggled to keep the beer in my throat and not let my sudden laughter destroy my sister's rug. Our moms met at some class they took when they were pregnant. Apparently, they hit it off right away and started planning playdates the second we popped out.

That's probably why Ace felt like a brother. Because I was forced to deal with him since the day I was born. Even though there were moments I had to sit on my hands not to strangle the shit out of him, I was happy my mom took that lame class.

"You think that's why we're both tone deaf?" I wondered. "Because our moms ruined it for us?"

"It'd make complete sense. I'm amazing at everything else I try. It's only logical the one thing I can't do is because of what my mother did while I was still cooking in the uterus."

"First of all, you are not amazing at everything you try. Second of all, don't say uterus. It's weird."

"Uterus." He blurted. "Uterus, uterus, uterus."

"You're ridiculous." I rolled my eyes and set my empty bottle on the glass end table next to me. There was no coaster, and if my sister walked in the door before I could move it, I was risking losing an arm. It was possibly the most dangerous thing I did in weeks. "Speaking of singing, I've had a song stuck in my head for like two weeks."

"I'm confident you ruined the song entirely."

I cleared my throat and belted the words, my voice cracking as he threw his hands over his ears and groaned. "I always feel like somebody's watching meeeeeee. And I have no privacy."

"My ears are bleeding!!" He shouted, rolling off the couch and hitting the floor with a thud. "Help! 911! A ginger dressed like a Barbie is killing me." His body seized dramatically as he huffed out a few breaths. "Tell my mom I love her." He croaked. "And tell Cruz I want the memorial tattoo he gets of me to be on his ass."

I watched in silence as he seized a couple more times and pretended to gasp for breath. Just when I thought it was over, he kept going, coughing loudly and reaching towards the ceiling like he was seeing the light. There was one last seize when his body finally went limp. I waited a few extra seconds to make sure it was finally over.

"Are you done?"

His eyes peeled open. He stared at me like he'd never seen me before. "Are you an angel?"

"No. I'm ginger, golfer Ken."

He cackled in laughter and sat up, bending his legs so

he could rest his arms on his knees. "You destroyed that song, Wilder. MJ is probably looking down on you with disgust on his face. The second you get to heaven, I'd avoid him at all costs."

"MJ? Dude, that song isn't an MJ song. It's by some guy named Rockwell."

"Yeah but Michael Jackson sang the chorus."

I blinked. "You're fucking with me."

"Why would I lie about that? Look it up."

"He's not in the music video!"

"I know, right? What a load of shit."

One look at his face told me he wasn't fucking with me at all. There wasn't a smirk across his lips or the distinct beginning of a devious twinkle in his eye. He was serious. I flailed aggressively in the recliner. "My whole life has been a lie."

He rolled his eyes at my dramatics and flopped on his back. "So, is it safe to assume your obsession with a certain song has to do with a certain girl?"

"Let it be known, the song was stuck in my head before I knew anything about the person who kept leaving me gifts."

He cleared his throat. "Us. She was leaving us gifts. I'm just as cool as you."

"That's debatable."

He yanked out the knot in his hair and flung the band that held it together at my chest. "Are you still stressing over this? Man, nobody at Circuit feels threatened or is upset with you."

"I know. It's not that."

After hearing Sage's story, peering into the faces of her distraught family, and learning how deeply she wished to stay under the radar when it came to putting away a half dozen criminals, it was impossible to feel threatened by her. Though it was undeniable she possessed immeasurable amounts of strength, she seemed delicate. Almost like a "handle with care" sign should have been hanging around her neck. Which was odd to me considering a person so delicate would've never been able to handle whatever she went through. I'd only ever seen her in the security footage. I watched it a half a million times as if it weren't the same thing over and over. I had no business making judgments about her character or personality. But there's just something in me that says she's kind. If she wanted to give up Circuit, she would've done it by now.

"Then what is it?" Ace sat up, brushing his hair with his fingers. "Still freaking out and trying to uncover how phantom girl found you?"

"Nah. I mean, I'm curious as all hell, but I'm not scared anymore."

"Then what's the issue?"

"I'm just... worried about her." It sounded dumb. I hardly knew the girl. What I did know of her everybody else in Circuit did too. The Feds probably have a better insight into who Sage is, yet here I was, slumped in an ugly recliner and wondering about my phantom girl. "She hasn't been here in eight days."

"You're counting?"

"Ace, she's never waited this long in between gifts."

"She probably got sick of buying them. She spent over a hundred bucks on sugar for us, bro. Marshall said she ain't got a job. She's probably broke."

I groaned. Great. Now I was a douche for wondering where the hell she's been. I had the audacity to be cranky because she'd stop bringing us gifts and I was forced to worry. She's probably run herself out of money spoiling me and my team. What a selfish dick I was.

"What exactly are you worried about, Wilder? The scumbag who hurt her is in prison."

"I know, man. Trust me." After four days with no sign of her, I hacked into Terre Haute Federal Correction Complex's security cameras and spent over an hour searching every one until I found him. He looked like shit. The mother fucker was definitely going through some withdrawals. His large body was taking up the entirety of a twin bed while he sweated profusely into a dingy mattress. There wasn't anybody in the bed next to him. It was just him, staring at the ceiling covered in a ratty orange jumpsuit. His greasy dark hair was long enough to be pulled back into a ducktail at the nape of his neck. I knew that only because during the time I spent staring at him, he rolled onto his stomach and shoved his face in his pillow. And Lord help me, I sat there and wished he would just smother himself. I had no personal connection to him. But killing a bank full of people, kidnapping my phantom girl, and selling illegal drugs was good enough for me.

"You double checked and made sure he's still in the slammer, didn't you?"

My best friend was likely reading my mind. "Sure did."

"Dude, he's in Terre Haute. That's in Indiana. Not anywhere close to here. Sage is fine."

I grunted. He didn't know that for sure, and my issue wasn't that Kade may make a bomb out of the shit they serve him in the cafeteria and blow himself out of his cell so he could snatch Sage again. My issue revolved around wondering if somebody upset her. As if I really had the right to care. I didn't, and I knew that. But after watching how careful she was around others, it was clear it wouldn't take much for someone to upset her. And not knowing if she's okay was driving me bonkers.

"You have to let this go, man. She wanted to thank us and she did. That's all." He stood up and shook out his legs. "It's our night off. Let's go eat somewhere before Lilah comes home and wants to feed us some health shit."

He was right. I had to stop stressing. Sage was not my business. I'd already played my part in her life. "You're right." I stood up, snagging the beer bottle off my sister's fancy table. "Are you gonna change first?"

He snuffed, shuffling to the kitchen and dropping his bottle in the trash. "Are you?"

"Touché."

I followed suit, dropping my bottle in the trash and snagging my wallet from the counter. "Where we going?"

"I dunno. Burgers or pizza?"

"Burgers. And I want some waffle fries."

We both froze when a noise came through the front door. "Shit!" Ace hissed. "Lilah's home."

I chuckled. "We're grown ass men. We can eat whatever we want."

"Yeah but now we are gonna get like a thirty-minute lecture and I'm gonna feel guilty for getting double bacon on my cow meat." He whined and stomped his foot like the big kid he is.

I waited to hear her key sliding into the lock but it never came. "Huh. Guess it was the neighbors." I slid on my Sperrys and ignored Ace when he whispered "Ken" under his breath. Shoving my wallet in my back pocket, I yanked open the door.

I froze, my limbs locking up and hair standing at attention. My feet failed to move past the doorway as I stared directly at the top of her head, snow-white hair spilling everywhere. Her head stayed down, but I knew by the way every single muscle in her body seemed to stiffen, she knew I was there. I didn't move as her trembling hands adjusted the small box sitting on my welcome mat. It was wrapped in bright blue paper with **SPECTER** written on the top just as they all were.

She stayed down there for a long time. I could feel Ace's breath on my neck behind me, and nobody said anything for a long time. It was obvious she wasn't expecting someone to be home. And though I was happy to see her, I had no idea what to do now.

So, I did what I do best.

I made a colossal mistake.

I squatted down next to her, bringing my face level with hers. At an achingly slow pace, her head lifted and bleak eyes met mine beneath long strands of hair. A noise came from her as a small hand reached upward and brushed a lock of hair away from her face.

I tilted my head and looked right into a pair of eyes that screamed fear and asked her, "Are you okay?"

And then, all hell broke loose.

THE SECOND HIS voice made its way to my ears, the bubble we seemed to be in popped. I about fell on my ass and scrambled backward, flattening myself against the wall behind me as I panted for breath. Fear squeezed at my chest, forcing my low breaths to come out choppy. Skin began rising on the back of my neck. I gripped it and wiped at the sweat, dropping my gaze to the floor. I scolded my brain. Told it to get a grip. Nothing about him seemed threatening, but he was still a stranger. And there was something about the way he was studying me that had me terrified he was going to attempt to touch me.

And that just couldn't happen.

I watched through pieces of my hair as he stood to his feet and stumbled backward, hands raised as if he were calling surrender. "I'm sorry." He rushed out, stepping behind the line that separated his apartment and the hall. "I didn't mean to frighten you. My name is Wren. Wren Wilder." He cleared his throat, peering down at the top of my gift. "Specter." He corrected.

I know who you are.

I couldn't bring myself to say the words. My voice was caught in the bottom of my throat along with most of my air. If I could've just brought my feet to work, I would've been running. But the damn things were glued to the simple carpeting and I had no choice but to stand there with my knees wobbling. I knew they'd give out at any point. I just hoped he was already back inside his apartment when I hit the floor.

I worked desperately to even out my breathing and assessed him. He was wearing a shirt that reminded me of the sunshine pillow in Julie's office. The bright yellow did nothing to complement his thick orange locks that were swept nicely on the top of his head. But somehow, it seemed to work. He looked like a sunflower. His head the center of the flower and his body the petals. His skin was almost as white as mine though it was painted in freckles. His face was covered in them and they went all the way down his arms. If I got a marker and connected the dots, there were endless possibilities of what the design would turn out to be.

Below his eyes seemed to be the area where most of his freckles lie though I had a hard time discovering the truth behind that suspicion. Navy blue frames hid a majority of his freckles and wrapped around each of his eyes. His square glasses made him look impossibly clever. I half expected him to start reciting useless facts about space nobody cared about. But he said nothing. He just stood in his doorway, staring at me while I stared at him and waited for my feet to decide they wanted to work again.

Sudden movement behind him caught me completely off guard. I flinched and screamed at my feet to get their shit together. I shook violently, moisture pooling in my eyes. There was no way Wren and the person behind him couldn't smell the fear floating off me in waves. It pissed me off immensely. He'd said nothing scary. Did nothing scary. There was no gun attached to his belt, no eyepatch over his eye, and no tattoos on his neck. He had absolutely nothing in common with the other criminals I'd been around. Still though, my body and my mind had trouble communicating, and I thought I might throw up.

"Sage."

My eyes flew to his.

He cleared his throat. "The person behind me is my friend Ace Jackson. Or you could call him Mischief."

Mischief.

Ace Jackson was a part of Circuit.

Wren tilted his body slightly and very slowly, Ace Jackson came into view. I pressed my body harder against the wall as if he were about to rush me. I scanned him quickly, looking for signs that might have made him threatening. I found nothing. He was about six inches taller than Wren and had shoulders much broader. He had no freckles, and his blond hair was almost past his shoulders.

What I found absolutely strange was his outfit. He was wearing all white. Maybe it was simply because I spent almost two years surrounded by only one type of man, but I found it odd a man would wear such white pants.

I liked it. Odd was good. I didn't know why but odd felt familiar.

Go white pants.

"Hi, Sage." Ace's voice surprised me. Unlike Wren's careful and calming voice, Ace's was smooth, dripping with confidence like we were just hanging out and I wasn't acting like a complete nutcase. "Thanks for the candy. Red Vines are my shit." His nudged his thumb at Wren. "This kid over here wouldn't share the gummy bears."

Wren shrugged. "I'm a slut for a good Haribo gummy bear."

The corner of Wren's lips quirked, and I peeled my body off the wall slightly. "You're... You're welcome."

Wren tilted his head slightly, adjusting his glasses. "Are you okay, Sage?"

Was I? Hell no. My knees were bobbing violently, sweat was crawling down my back, and I was so angry. And frustrated. And overwhelmed.

And when all those emotions mixed with fear, I became exhausted.

"Would you like to sit down, Sage?"

I nodded my head and slid down the wall, my body becoming a heap on the floor. I peered at Wren and Ace, curling in on myself. They were across the hall, behind the arbitrary line that technically said they weren't even in the hallway, but I still hated the way they towered over me.

"Would you like some water?"

I shook my head. I never accepted food or drink from a stranger. My mom cooked most of my meals, and I checked the seal on every bottle of water I purchased.

It was paranoia at its finest, but I learned in the worst way possible that the easiest way to get someone to cooperate was to drug them.

Messing with someone's ability to think straight is hands down the most disgusting thing a person could do to another. And I couldn't fathom why people went to bars and did it to themselves.

Very slowly, Wren crossed the invisible line and sank down to a seated position.

"Can I sit here?"

I nodded. I would've rather he went inside but I was the one who showed up here continuously, leaving gifts and disappearing. God. I probably looked like I belonged in a psych ward, trembling in a vacant hallway with a face that belonged on a ghost. I showed up here willingly and was acting like I was being held prisoner.

Though I suppose I was.

But instead of a human holding me prisoner, it was gripping fear and thick paranoia.

"I'm gonna order a pizza." Ace announced, clicking the door shut.

It became a smidge easier to breathe when I had only one person to watch. Wren crossed his legs and put his hands in his lap. "So, what's your favorite candy?"

I blinked. That was it? I was two shakes away from a panic attack outside his home and that's what he asks? Doesn't wanna know how I found him? Or why I wouldn't leave him alone? Doesn't want to call the cops on the creepy stalker girl?

"Wh... what?"

"Candy. Do you have a favorite?"

"Uhm..." He looks entirely serious. This guy truly wants to know what type of sugar I prefer consuming. "I like gummy bears too. But also Sour Patch Kids."

"Oh, those are so good. When I was a kid, I used to suck all the sour stuff off and just plop the soggy candy back in the bag. My sister lost her shit when she ate one of them. Brushed her teeth like a million times."

He smiled and waited for me to reply. When I said nothing, too stunned he was talking to me like I wasn't a basket case, he peered at the box still on the welcome mat.

"May I open it?"

I nodded and watched him lift the box and set it on his lap. He unwrapped it carefully as if he were trying to preserve the moment though I'm sure it was more about preserving the paper. He set aside the wrapping and lifted the flap of the old shoe box I'd set them in. His brow furrowed as he studied the contents.

Three dozen cyan crayons lay inside.

"I wasn't sure how many people are on your team." I mumbled.

"Thirteen." He said, lifting a crayon. "Would you like me to give one to each person?"

"Yes, please."

"Okay. May I ask what they stand for?"

I cleared my throat. "I equate cyan crayons with badasses. And I believe you and your team to be the most badass of them all."

"Oh boy." He smiled wide, freckles rising high on his cheeks. "Ace's ego might not be big enough for his head when he hears that." He peered at the crayon between his fingers and set it back in the box. "Thank you, Sage. This is really cool."

"Take two. There's enough, right?"

"Right. Yeah." He nodded. "Okay. I'll make sure everybody gets two."

"Th... thank you, Wren."

"No, Sage. Thank you. This is probably the most unique gift I've ever gotten. I'll put it on my desk."

"No." I shook my head and swallowed the ever-growing lump in my throat. Over the course of three weeks, I'd been thanking him in gifts and cards and disappearing tricks. Now I had the chance to thank him properly.

"Thank you, Wren." I stressed. "*Thank you.*"

"Sage." He set aside the box and looked me in the eye. Something started bubbling beneath my skin. I wanted to look away but I simply couldn't. The green eyes behind the thin layer of glass kept my gaze rooted. "Please know that everybody on my team is proud to have had a hand in helping you. Your story reminds us why we do this, and though our methods are risky, we do not regret them because you're sitting here right now. If you ever need anything again, big or small, we would be honored to help you. Okay?"

Moisture pooled in my eyes, and I chalked it up to being exceedingly overwhelmed.

"Are you okay, Sage?"

"You've asked me that three times."

"I've wanted to ask you since I saw you buying candy on a security camera."

I sniffed. "That's how you found me, huh? I thought I was being sly with the cash thing."

"That was smart." He admitted. "But I'm pretty good at what I do."

"I'm proof."

His expression changed. His smile dropped just a little as he regarded me with what looked like empathy. "Anything you need, Sage. I'm not sure how, but you know where to find me."

"No offense, but I'll be forced to believe the universe hates me if I ever need your services again. I already got kidnapped once, I'm at the back of the line."

He blinked, almost like he couldn't believe I was making inappropriate jokes about what happened to me. But I became rather good at it. Julie hates it.

"I meant for anything. Big or small."

I nodded. "Would it be alright if I stay here until my legs begin to work again?"

"Sure. Would it be okay if I sat here with you?"

"Sure."

We went silent for a few minutes. I rested my head

against the wall behind me and took long breaths like Julie taught me. When I looked back at him, I found him twirling a crayon around in his fingers.

"Is blue your favorite color?" He asked.

"No. Yellow is."

"Yeah?" He peered down at his outfit. "What do you think of my shirt? Be honest."

"I think it's quite loud. But also very wonderful."

His smile told me he was pleased with my answer. "Ace told me I look like golfer Ken."

"The Barbie? I think you look more like a sunflower."

"A sunflower? God. That's worse."

"Why is that worse? Don't you want to be bright? Isn't that why you wore the shirt?"

He seemed to consider my question. The twirling of the crayon stopped, and he stared into space for a long moment. "I suppose. I really just bought it because I thought it vomited happiness at people. I guess I like things that feel like sunshine."

"There's this pillow." I said. "It's yellow. My favorite because of that same reason. My life was kind of void of color for a while. It seems like I missed yellow the most."

I was getting deeper with him than I did in some sessions with Julie. Except he didn't know the follow-up questions to ask. Didn't know how to analyze me or every move I made. He didn't even attempt it, and it was such a relief.

"Maybe I should buy Ace this shirt. He could use some color."

"Does he always wear white pants?"

"No." He laughed. There was a faint snort in his chuckle that made it overly dorky and oddly unique. I liked it. "He wears white pants because he works at Tranquility Spa as a masseuse during the day."

"Oh God." Everything inside me repelled with that sentence. "He touches people? And they let him?"

He chuckled again. "And they pay him for it."

"That sounds like hell."

"He seems to like it. I told him today if I was golfer Ken than he was masseuse Ken."

"I think he looks like a strange version of Jesus."

Wren stared at me before hollowing in deep laughter. Snort after snort barreled out of him as he clutched his stomach. Freckles were bouncing on his newly red face, and I was stunned into silence when I felt the makings of a smile on my own face.

"I can't wait to tell him you said that." He wheezed. "He'll crack up."

"Does it take much to make Ace laugh?"

"God, no. Dude is like a giant 10-year-old. He still laughs when somebody farts."

"So does my brother."

"Brett, right?"

I nodded slowly. I wasn't surprised he knew my brother's name. It just struck me as strange he had a key to my past. "You know everything, huh?"

"Not everything." He shook his head. "I know what the FBI does. Just background and facts. Enough so I could be sure you weren't a mole or working in the police force. The thoughts inside your head are safe, Sage. You have my word nobody at Circuit will invade your privacy again."

I didn't realize how much I needed to hear that until what felt like a hundred pounds lifted off my chest. The idea that someone was analyzing me added to the suffocation already induced by fear. Between Julie and my family,

I couldn't handle a group of hackers attempting to learn all the horrors in my head.

"Thank you."

He nodded politely in response, and I had no choice but to believe him. There was nothing that said he was lying to me. He didn't avert his gaze or pull his lip between his teeth. Didn't wring his hands together or grip the back of his neck. Didn't pull out his phone to attempt avoiding my gaze. He simply stared at me calmly with a genuine expression resting on his face. "I appreciate that, Wren."

He smiled softly at me, noting the way my foot was tapping anxiously. It was then I realized my legs felt like they were part of my human body again. In no graceful way, I peeled myself off the floor.

"I should go before my family figures out the figure asleep in my bed is a body pillow and an old American Girl Doll."

His eyes seemed to fall right from their sockets. "You snuck out?"

"It was necessary. Ya know, secret identity and all that, Specter."

"Well, I appreciate that, Sage."

"You're welcome. Is it okay if I keep leaving gifts?"

"If you'd like to. Please don't feel like you have to."

"I would like to." It'd been a long time since I was able to express my emotions in any way. Though leaving a box of blue crayons to express my gratitude was hardly a start, it made me feel so much lighter. It made leaving my home and risking my parents breaking out into a worried frenzy worth it.

For the first time in my adult life, I found a purpose. And I would fulfill it until I found a new one.

"Okay then." He nodded. "I'll look forward to finding them then."

"Okay." I lifted my hand in a wave and kept my back to the wall as I shuffled towards the elevator. He stayed seated, almost like he knew that's what I needed from him.

"Hey, Sage? May I ask you something?"

I froze, nodding slowly. "Sure."

"Could you tell me how you found me?"

I brushed my hair from my face. It only seemed fair I explained how I found him, seeing as how I followed him to both his place of business and his home. "Uhm, it was a girl. I believe she's your sister."

His body jerked like he didn't hear me right. His forehead wrinkled as he gaped at me like I just sprouted a second head. "Lilah?!"

LITTLE BROTHERS WERE NUISANCES. It was easily a known fact. We could be complete little shits, especially when we were younger brothers to an older sister. The possibilities in which we could annoy our beloved sisters were endless. Reading diaries, spying when they talk on the phone, embarrassing them in front of Lonnie LaLone in eighth grade, eating the food in the refrigerator that had LILAH'S, DO NOT EAT written in bold letters. But we could also be loyal little dudes. Covering when they snuck out at night, sliding letters beneath a bedroom door, keeping secrets when the truth would've resulted in a grounding, and tying each other to a chair to stage a sit-in when we refused to go to summer camp with Petey the singing puppet in attendance.

There was a fine line between loyal and little shit.

I usually stood right on the border, if not swaying more towards the loyal side. But the last five days I had been the highest degree of little shit one could possibly reach. Not because I was mad at her, or because I felt betrayed she exposed me to Sage, but because it was really fun torturing her.

It made me giddy.

"Lilah." I crooned, wagging my eyebrows at her from across the table. "Do you think you could get me more water?"

Her eyes rolled deep into the back of her head. She dropped her fork with a clank against her plate and pushed out of her chair in exasperation. She walked around the table with disdain marring her red lips and lifted my empty glass off the table with a low growl before stomping from the dining room and into the kitchen.

"Wren, honey." My mom caught my attention. She was sitting to the right of me, placing her napkin in her lap. "Why is your sister acting as your maid?"

"Ah." I grinned widely. "She lost a bet."

"What bet?" My mother pressed.

"Just a bet."

The grin on my face would likely be there for a few more days. The moment Lilah came home that night, I recited every word Sage told me. Her face grew paler and paler each second that passed by. My sister had given me up in the center of an emergency room while waiting for a doctor to come sew her up. I wasn't really mad, but I definitely didn't pass up the opportunity to give her a lecture on keeping her damn trap closed in public.

She felt awful, and I was milking it for all it was worth. It'd been five days, and I knew she was close to cracking. I was reveling in her doing my laundry and waiting on me hand and foot in an attempt to earn back the trust she'd never actually lost.

"Here you go, brother." My glass hit the table with a

thud, sending water sloshing over the rim and onto the table.

I smiled at her like she'd just given me a hundred bucks. "Thanks, Gracie. You're wonderful."

She cocked her head with a wicked smile and made her way back into her seat, plopping across from me. She placed her napkin back on her lap and stabbed a sausage with her fork, giving me a look that told me she wished to stab her fork somewhere else.

It had me cackling.

"What on earth is going on?" My dad scanned the expressions on his children's faces, clearly confused. "Are you two fighting?"

"I had a secret." I announced. "Only Lilah and Ace knew. And then-" I paused, clearing my throat for dramatic effect. "Lilah told somebody."

Lilah rolled her eyes.

My mother gasped. "Lilah Grace Wilder!"

"It was an accident." She mumbled, giving my mother a tight smile. "A slip of the tongue. I was being careless. It will not happen again."

Lilah flashed me a look, her eyes gazing at me intently. They were pleading with me, not to lighten up on this bizarre punishment, but to believe her when she said it. She *was* sorry. I knew that for certain. Call it younger brother's intuition, but I knew she'd never felt worse in her life.

"I know, Gracie." I said fiercely, nodding. "I forgive you."

She slumped her seat, throwing her hands in the air. "Finally. Get your own damn water next time."

"Do not swear at your mother's table." Dad clipped. "You two are grown adults still acting like children."

"You think we're bad?" Lilah gaped. "You should hear

him and Ace. The two of them were arguing over who looked more like Barbie!"

My dad looked at me, the word "yikes" written across his forehead. He cleared his throat. "Well?"

"Well, what?" I asked him.

"Who looks more like Barbie? You or Ace?"

"Wren." Lilah answered. "I believe Ace said he looked like golfer Ken."

"Aw." My mom swooned. "You loved Ken."

I choked on my eggs. "I did not!"

"You most certainly did! You used to carry Lilah's doll around everywhere."

I took a slow sip of my water, making eye contact with Lilah. "Do not breathe a word of this to Ace."

It wasn't that I'd found joy in playing with a doll. I actually didn't find that hard to believe at all. I was a strange little dude. Would have rather been inside with my sister or Ace than outside with the neighbor boys getting trampled during a game of soccer. Video games and Dungeons and Dragons were my shit. Go ahead. Call me a nerd.

You won't be wrong.

"Why can't I tell Ace?" Lilah smirked.

"Because then we will *both* have to hear about it for the next ten years."

"Touché."

"So, darling." My mom stretched her arm across the table and grabbed my hand, giving it a shake. She didn't have to reach very far at all. The dining room table at my parent's house was just a small wooden square with four legs and a simple chair on each side. It was stained a light color, but still had decade old scratches, paint drips, and faded crayon markings across the top. Infomercials told me there were several products that could have easily removed

Lilah and I's childhood, but my mother was sentimental in all the ways a parent could be. Our bedrooms barely looked like they'd been touched. Still the same as they were when we left at eighteen. Just a small knick-knack here or there moved for cleaning purposes.

"What's the secret?"

I shoved an entire sausage in my mouth. "What secret?"

She swatted my head for talking with my mouth full. "The secret Lilah wasn't supposed to tell anyone."

"It's a secret, mom. I can't tell you."

"Oh, pish posh! Mothers and sons don't keep secrets from one another."

"It was nothing." I shrugged. "Just that I have a secret identity and spend my evenings in a dark underworld fighting crime with my computer nerd friends."

Lilah spat out a gulp of water and choked on her laughter.

Both my parents stared at me, slow smirks marring their faces. My mother let out a loud giggle, and my father patted me on the back with a chuckle.

"Funny, son. Always went wild with the imagination."

"What's the real secret?" Mom asked, wiping her mouth with her napkin and placing it on her empty plate.

"He had a pimple on his butt cheek." Lilah blurted, and I pictured myself strangling her.

"Oh, honey, I have a cream for that."

Of course she does.

"Thanks, mom." I smiled, reverting back to middle school and kicking Lilah under the table. "But it's gone now."

"Could come back. I'll send it home with you."

"Awesome. Thanks."

"Who on earth cares that Wren has acne issues on his ass?" My dad gawked. "Why? Just why?"

"Mooooom!" I threw a finger towards my dad. "Dad just said ass at the table!"

"Knock it off!" My mother clipped. "Both of you!"

"Aye aye, ma'am!" I shouted, saluting her.

She rolled eyes and finished her iced tea, staring lovingly between Lilah and I. Sunday brunch was the highlight of her week. I knew it. Lilah knew it.

We all knew it.

My mother lived for taking care of her family. Doting on her children was her favorite pastime. Having all three of her greatest loves at one table was like Christmas on crack. Personally, I got a kick out of when we all got together these days. We looked like a couple of Cheese Puffs sitting at one table, redheads and freckles all around.

When my parents first tied the knot, people used to mistake them for brother and sister, that assumption based entirely on the matching flames sprouting from their heads. Really, it was mere coincidence. A mutual friend in college set them up on a blind date because he thought it'd be funny to hook up the two gingers in his vast friend group.

Well, joke's on that dude.

Barry and Shannon have been married for more than thirty years. And they had a couple of ginger kids to consummate that marriage. It was some kind of miracle. Two gingers having not one, but *two* ginger children was pretty much unheard of.

My father's orange locks had since faded into a color that resembled an orange peel after it'd gotten stomped on, while my mother wasn't keen on going gray. She kept it died a color that was more red than orange. My sister followed suit, keeping her long locks maintained a deeper red. Me? I was allll nat-u-ral. My locks were the color of cheddar cheese.

And I liked it that way.

"Would anyone like any seconds? Barry?"

"Nope." My dad grunted, slapping his gut. "I'm full."

"Same." Lilah pushed her plate away.

I, on the other hand, smiled at my mom while she loaded my plate with more pancakes.

"I can always count on you to eat seconds." She winked at me. "How was your week? Anything interesting happen?"

I snorted. Finding Sage outside my door was interesting. Sure. But I'd describe it more as an unexpected shock but not at all unwelcome.

Sage Maddison was what one would call an enigma.

It was clear she was devastatingly affected by what had happened to her, though she was still able to make jokes. Highly cynical ones, but jokes. What's more is that she likes the color yellow and gives out bright crayons to show somebody they're a badass. Even when she was living in the dark, she found it inside herself to be bright.

I kept hoping she'd make another appearance, but I didn't receive a gift or see her at all after she told me a story that had my jaw scraping the ground and stepped onto the elevator in my apartment building.

My phantom girl had seemingly turned back into a phantom, though I'd worried less about her. Having two cyan crayons propped on my desk at Circuit was a reminder that I wasn't the only badass in our acquaintanceship. Though panic seized all the muscles in her body, and she seemed to wish she'd fall right through the wall she was pressed against, the strength she possessed was undeniable.

She had a fire in her eyes, brewing in the ocean that surrounded them. Her hands were clenched into fists as if she were ready to throw down at any moment. Her eyes never stopped roaming, scanning her surroundings as though she were committing them to memory.

Though I doubt she believed it, Sage was vastly intelligent, and she was a fighter. I hardly knew her, but I knew that for certain. I spoke a few simple sentences and based my actions on what seemed to calm her. I kept my distance and made sure Ace did too. It was clear as glass Sage wanted nobody near her, and I did what I could to respect that.

I would not be another person who intimidated her.

I was not darkness.

I was her sunshine.

"Why are you smiling?"

"What?" I flipped my gaze and found my dad studying me. "I'm not smiling."

"Sure you are. What's got your face all red?"

"My face isn't red."

"Son, you're redder than a lobster's ass."

"Barry Wilder! Good grief." My mom threw her hands in the air and gathered her dirty dishes, heading towards the kitchen.

"Dad, I'm not smiling at anything."

My dad followed my mom's lead and gathered his dishes, standing up. "I don't believe you." He announced, disappearing into the kitchen.

"You don't fool me." Lilah said, crossing her arms across her chest. Sunday was the only day she dressed so casually. If you counted a flower blouse thing and really nice jeans casual. "You were thinking about Sage."

"I wasn't."

"Liar. Liar. Pants on fire."

"My pants are fine. Ice cold."

"Whatever, Wren." She chuckled, standing up. "Your little nerd brain is filled with thoughts of her. Wait until you get another gift. You'll lose your shit like a 16-year-old girl who just got kissed."

I argued with her, rolled my eyes and told her how wrong she was. I wasn't obsessed. I was proud, honored, and humbled that my team and I made such a profound difference in her life and she was filled to the brim with gratitude. I was excited thinking about her only because I was pleased to know she was safe, doing well, and living a life. There was nothing better than knowing you'd been the catalyst for such a positive change in somebody's life.

It felt good knowing I helped Sage, and I hoped she'd come to recognize me as someone who was good.

And even as I lied to my sister, I refused to recognize I was lying to myself.

And then I got home and was forced to admit it. Lilah and I stepped off the elevator onto our floor, stuffed full of pancakes and arms full of leftovers, when I spotted something on our welcome mat. I took off down the hall like somebody strapped rocket launchers to my tennis shoes.

Right there, on the welcome mat outside my door, was a bouquet of sunflowers. Somehow, she'd managed to find a bundle with thirteen.

I peeled open the card with a grin on my face.

Specter, Mischief, and all their friends- thank you for being a sunflower in a world of weeds.

And then I lost my shit like a 16-year-old girl who'd just gotten kissed.

"Are you sure you don't want anything?"

I gritted my teeth, pursing my lips and attempting not to become an angry little demon. "I'm fine."

My brother licked at his spoon, strawberry ice cream coating his tongue while he moaned in delight. "You sure? This shit is good."

"I said I'm sure, Brett. Like a hundred times."

The room seemed to compact. He dropped his plastic spoon in the paper cup that held his frozen treat and dropped his gaze. "Okay. I'm sorry."

"It's fine, Brett." I twisted my water bottle with two fists, crinkling plastic the only sound between us for several moments. "Finish your ice cream before it melts."

He shook his head, his face slamming shut like someone just closed the shutters. One minute he was smiling and then next he looked like he'd never experienced any form of happiness. "I'm done."

"No, you're not." I argued, using two fingers to push his bowl closer to him. "Finish it? Please? It'd make me happy."

That did it. He lifted his spoon and shoved a mouth full

of frozen yogurt in his mouth, swallowing it without savoring the taste like he did the first two dozen bites. It was my fault his smooth, creamy dessert probably felt like nails going down his throat. Leave it to me to become a raging bitch when all he wanted to do was buy me a cup of some overpriced frozen yogurt.

But the thing was, I didn't want the damn yogurt. I couldn't bring myself to point at what I wanted from behind a glass case and let some stranger scoop it into a bowl for me. Never mind the moment she turns around to add toppings or put it on the scale to weigh it.

The whole experience made me jittery. I knew it wasn't entirely rational, but the three seconds the yogurt lady was spun in the opposite direction was a prime time for something to get plopped into my dessert.

Even as I sat here and watched my brother scrape his bowl clean, his eyes focused and clear the whole time, I just couldn't do it.

And Brett knew that. But still he'd picked me up at Dr. Julie's office, smiling bright and insisting we go out for frozen yogurt. I didn't argue. What was the point? I simply slid into the passenger seat of his Chevy Cruise and placed my hands on my lap, knowing I would only be purchasing a bottled water. I knew I'd disappoint him on this random sibling outing eventually. But at least now he had some dessert to make the blow less painful.

But I knew he'd still ache from it.

He'd wanted to do something fun. Unsurprisingly, I screwed it up.

"You want another water?"

"Uhh." I peered down at the water bottle in my hands, twisted in half and mangled. "No, thanks." I nudged my head at his empty bowl. "You going back for seconds?"

He snorted. "Nah. Let's just go."

"Brett." I twisted the bottle harder, the cap popping off with an air-filled sound. It went flying across the small building and hit the glass case with a clank. I sunk down into my seat, throwing a hand over my face when everyone turned to look at me.

"Sorry about that!" Brett called. "My mistake."

I dropped my hands. "My mistake, Brett. Not yours."

He managed a smile. "Your face is turning the color of my ice cream."

"Shut up!" I slapped both my palms over my cheeks in horror.

His faint chuckle eased the tension that was thick enough to choke on only a moment ago. "Nobody is looking anymore, Sage."

"You swear?" I mumbled through my hands, splaying my fingers so I could see him from between my fingers.

I found his smirk. "I swear."

I dropped my hands back in my lap and cleared my throat. Despite the water I'd just consumed, it felt like sand-paper. "Listen, Brett..."

He held up a hand. "Stop. You don't have to say anything. I shouldn't have brought you here."

"No, Brett, it's not..." I paused, stumbling over the right words. When did it become so difficult to have a conversation with the brother who has spent my entire life doting on me? Out of all the things I'd lost in the last two years, my relationship with my brother is one I'd longed to have back the most. "I'm just not ready, okay?"

"Okay. Yeah. That's cool. I just... I didn't know, Sage. You don't talk about it."

"Its best I don't." I shrugged.

I never talked about it with anyone but Julie. And I

certainly wouldn't start expanding that short list in the center of a frozen yogurt shop. There was absolutely no point. No silver lining to stuffing my brother's brain with all the terrors his baby sister suffered through. Why tell him I'm terrified to accept food from strangers because the last time I did, I woke up on a dingy mattress in the back of a moving vehicle in an outfit that did not belong to me.

Why bring up the spot on the side of my neck that seemed to have a permanent hole the size of a needle, perfect for injecting the contents of a syringe into?

I couldn't, for the life of me, comprehend why it would be some therapeutic revelation to tell my big brother his little sister spent the better part of two years with her face smashed against a glass table, a tight fist wound around her hair that was connected to a voice that ordered her to sniff. The grip tightened until she did it with tears burning deep in her eyes and sobs clogged in her throat.

"If you don't want to talk about it, you don't have to."

Did I want to? No. Hell no. I could barely rasp the horrible truth to Julie. That somewhere along the line, when my face was stuck to the glass with tears and sweat, I stopped fighting so hard and came to actually enjoy it.

And then when I'd finally looked forward to the moment I'd start to fly, I crashed to the ground. Kade had decided during one of his benders he didn't want his girl-friend to be like the junkies and hookers that begged him for a fix. So, I found myself cuffed to a bedpost. The extent to how long I was in that room, barfing and sweating and screaming through the door was beyond me.

Withdrawal hit me like a cold bucket of water. I drowned in it and spent an entirety gasping for breath and screaming that I was gonna die.

But I didn't die. I lived. And more times than not, I found myself asking why.

I shuddered, gripping the small spot on my neck. "I really don't, Brett."

He nodded and shifted his gaze, peering out the large windows that took up the storefront. His eyes looked nowhere in particular, flicking past the couple holding hands during what seemed to be a leisurely afternoon stroll. The mom pushing a stroller with her phone tucked between her ear and her shoulder. The man in a full suit, slamming his fist into a parking meter.

The blue eyes that used to match mine, filled with laughter and mischief, were dull. Void. There was nothing in them.

My big brother appeared so much different than he had two years ago. The blond hair he styled with gel and got cut every four weeks was grown past his ears. The honey color had become the color of coffee when too much cream was added. His fresh face now had rough stubble spanning his cheeks and chin. And his smile? The lopsided one that got him a lot of girlfriends and into a whole lot of trouble with adults was simply nonexistent.

He looked miserable, but the awful kind of miserable where you just wanna scream and cry and punch things and slam a shit ton of doors without really knowing why.

My big brother was in pain.

I did that.

"Are you ready to go?"

I blinked, finding him standing from his seat. "Sure."

"The next time you don't want to do something, tell me to piss off. It won't hurt my feelings."

I wondered if he had any left or if those got taken when I did.

"I like to hang out with you, Brett." I shuffled to the trashcan and tossed my shredded bottle inside, sliding out the door while he held it open for me, angling his body so he didn't touch me. "I didn't mind coming here at all."

His car was parked on the street. We took the four steps it took to get across the sidewalk, and he opened the door for me. I slid inside, clicking my seatbelt while he rounded the car. "I feel like I forced you." He admitted, turning the ignition and looking over his shoulder to check for traffic before pulling on to the road.

"You didn't force me, Brett. I won't do anything I don't want to. I enjoy hanging out with you. I just keep wondering when you're going to hang out with your other friends."

"Why hang with them when I can hang with you?"

That sentence right there confirmed most of my suspicions. He iced them out. The dozens of friends my brother had dwindled down to just me. My lack of strength and ability to fight back had resulted in him losing all of his friends. He seemingly confided in no one after I was taken. A low ache formed in the pit of my stomach thinking of my brother feeling helpless and all alone. I repressed the urge to throw my fist in his dashboard and turned my head to mask the mist in my eyes.

Who had been there for him?

Who had held him when he cried?

Who told him it was okay to get angry?

Who clutched his hand at my funeral?

Nobody did. He did it all on his own, and I envied the way he could still stand so tall.

"You wanna Netflix binge when we get home?" I managed the question without my voice shaking.

"Sure. Sounds cool. I gotta work tonight though."

"Oh. Okay."

"I could call in." He offered, and I suspected he'd quit if I asked him to.

I wondered constantly if my brother enjoyed his job. It was a minimum wage job at a sporting goods store in the mall. He sold Yeezys to rich kids and yoga pants to soccer moms when he should've been inside a lab curing cancer and making six figures a year.

He should've graduated last fall with a degree in biochemistry. My brother's brain reminded me of Mary Poppin's handbag. Each time you reached inside, you came out with something new. The knowledge inside his brain was endless. He graduated at the top of his class, wearing his valedictorian medal proudly. He'd taken forever to choose a major. When he stood in front of all our family and announced he was going into biochemistry to be a healthcare scientist, I had to stop his rant and ask him what the hell that meant.

He explained with the most excitement I'd ever witnessed he'd be helping diagnose diseases and find cures for children and adults everywhere. It was evident to everyone in the room he'd chosen to make a difference in the way he knew how.

I oozed with pride for him that day. Cried when we moved him into his dorm room.

My brother should've been wearing a lab coat with his name embroidered on the chest. Instead, he was selling sweatbands and shoelaces across a counter inside a department store.

I knew on some level that it wasn't, but it felt like it was all my fault.

My brother had everything ripped from him that day. And I'd give *anything* to give it all back to him.

When I was a kid, and people asked me what I wanted to be when I grew up, I shrugged my shoulders and gave them the most mundane answer possible.

I don't know.

They'd cock their head and give me a silly smile, rattling off a list of things I might want to be. Doctor, teacher, dentist, fashion designer, scientist, ballerina, lawyer. All sorts of different careers, some excited me and some didn't. Still, I'd sit there and shrug at every suggestion, telling the questioning adult I had no idea what I wanted to be what felt like a gazillion years from then.

The concept of choosing such a monumental thing when one was merely a child was absolute blasphemy to me. I wasn't a total grinch, I recognized it was supposed to be all in fun, getting kids to dream about a time when they're an adult and making exciting, important choices. But I hated getting asked that question. I was a kid for shit's sake. I didn't want to think about giving up a full day of running around outside with my brother or playing Barbies with Trish for a life that meant dressing up fancy and leaving at breakfast not to return until dinner.

That sort of structured life did not excite me as a child. Even the concept of being a prima ballerina had me going "meh." I maintained that attitude until I got to high school and things started to get real. Adulthood hit me like a brick in the face. I was not ready, and I believed deeply very few people were ready for the moment they had to put down their toys and put on their suit. I wanted absolutely nothing to do with any of it.

I had one semester of a careers class when I was seventeen. The class was supposed to help us discover what we wanted to spend our life doing. It should've set us up with internships, college visits, mentors, and assisted us in applying for college. I got none of that. What I got was a bunch of online tests that told me I should be a florist or a professional athlete based on my love of being outside. It also ensured I received several disappointed looks from my parents when I came home every night and defaulted to "I don't know" when they asked what I wanted to study in college.

It was a giant sack of bullshit if you asked me. Sticking teenagers into a class for sixteen weeks and expecting them to come out knowing what they want to do every day for the next fifty years of their life. Making that heavy of a choice had my stomach in knots. I graduated high school, applied to and was accepted into two different colleges without ever deciding what I wanted to study. I couldn't even narrow it down. I'd decide on something, then consider the idea that I'd be doing it forever and second guess myself all over again. My parents were worried I'd become one of those students who wasted a hundred thousand dollars switching majors every semester because I couldn't make a decision.

And then I got kidnapped, and there was no decision to make.

If that was the universe's way of giving me more time, it was pretty fucked up.

"Sage?" I blinked, focusing on Julie and her calming smile. Her hands were folded in her lap, legs crossed at the ankles. "Would you like to respond to your father?"

"No."

I ignored my father's low sigh and focused on a painting Julie had on her wall. It was an eight by ten canvas of yellow. That was it. It looked like somebody painted yellow as a background and then couldn't choose what they wanted to paint over it so they left it as it was.

I liked it.

It reminded me of Wren. My fingers itched to yank it off the wall and deliver it to him as another gift. Aside from the sunflowers, I hadn't been back in four days. I hadn't really been anywhere except my bed and bathroom.

Some days, it was hard to even move.

"Sage, you do understand your father's push, don't you?"

I licked my lips, squeezing my sunshine pillow to my chest. "No."

Normally, I didn't mind coming to see Julie. I actually rather enjoyed it. This room was a safe zone for me. I could say all I wanted in two hours or say nothing at all. There was no push for me to feel anything more than I was in that moment.

But once a month, we had a family day. My parents and Brett tagged along, sitting across the room so I could keep my couch to myself and express their feelings to me and Julie.

My father's feelings? He wanted me to consider going

to college. He claimed he wanted me to move forward, put the past behind me.

What I think he really wanted was me to pretend it never happened. It was a lovely thought. If I knew of a person who could erase the last two years of my life, I'd happily give them all my money and first born child. But it just wasn't possible, and for him to ask that of me simply enraged me.

"Can I say something?" Brett blurted. He was sitting alone, in a blue plastic chair. I didn't meet his eyes but I could see his feet tapping.

"Sage?" Julie prompted. "Would that be okay?"

"Sure."

"Okay, Brett. Tell us what's on your mind."

I heard him take a long breath. "I think my father needs to lighten up. Whether Sage has been home eight minutes, eight weeks, eight months, or eight years, it doesn't matter. She's not ready. She wasn't ready two years ago before her life was taken from her, so why the hell should we expect her to be ready now? Never mind how hard it is to actually make that choice when one isn't weighed down by whatever the hell happened to her. Sage's mind works differently, okay? She's still Sage, but she's different. She needs time to figure out how to put the old Sage and the new Sage together to make one she feels comfortable being. So, we all just need to step back and let her fucking do that, yeah?"

In that moment, and I suspected in most since I'd gotten home, my brother was my greatest ally. My greatest friend. The captain of Team Sage. And I loved him dearly for it.

"Well." Julie chuckled a little. "I couldn't have said it better myself, Brett. Are you sure your true calling is biochemistry?"

"So you believe not letting Sage choose a future is

what's best for her future?" My father sounded less than pleased. Actually, he sounded incredibly insensitive to my situation, but I knew that wasn't the case. My father had a heart of gold that was dented immensely when I disappeared. He was attempting to rewind time in the way he knew how. One day he'd understand it just wasn't possible. And I was not ready for that day.

"It's not a matter of not letting her choose, Rod." Julie corrected. "It's simply not our top priority right now. Sage's refusal to accept food or drink from those who aren't her mother, and her haphephobia are more pressing matters. It's my belief Sage will come full circle, but that takes time."

"Haphephobia?"

"Her fear of others touching her."

My dad looked away, staring vacantly at the wall. It was his go to look when he wanted to pretend something wasn't happening. My mom, on the other hand, leaned forward in her seat as if she were about to take notes. "Does she discuss it with you?"

Julie's lips pressed into a firm line. I knew she was wishing I'd go home and confide in my mother, but I just could not do it. I would bring myself all the way to her room, lift my fist to knock on her door, and take off running in fear I'd destroy her like Kade destroyed me.

"Sage does discuss her fear with me, yes."

"Do you know what causes her fear?"

"There isn't a known cause of haphephobia, I'm afraid. Some say people are born with it or a change in brain function plays a role. My professional opinion is that Sage's fear was developed due to the trauma she experienced."

My mother nodded and set her hand on my dad's thigh, obviously seeking the comfort he could not give her. I wished so desperately I was strong enough to stand up and hold her hand myself. But the mere thought of her skin on mine had sweat pooling at my temples and running down the sides of my neck. The feeling was overpowering. There was a distinct pain whenever another body brushed mine. It felt like all my bones were crushing under the weight of even the lightest touch. If my mother were to hug me, I'd spiral. My heart rate would accelerate to dangerously fast beats. I'd scream for fear of impending danger that my rational side knew wasn't coming. I'd cry and tremble and scramble away while focusing on the blinding pain that erupted in my body, knowing there wasn't a magic pill that'd take it all away.

I was a mess.

"Is this fear detrimental to her health?" My mother whispered the question with a tremor in her voice.

"Think of it this way, when Sage was born, the doctor immediately put her on your chest. Why? Because humans need comfort in order to survive. The need for touch and human contact is innate, and the inability to be able to enjoy and accept that contact can place a staggering effect on her health. The good news is, haphephobia generally responds really well to a variety of therapeutic interventions. Sage has come a long way during our time. We still have miles and miles to go, but it's my belief Sage will not suffer forever."

I didn't believe it.

I didn't spend a lot of time considering my future, but when I did, it never included me leading any sort of normal life. I wasn't willing to open up to my brother or go to group therapy sessions like Julie suggested a million times each time I saw her. I wasn't willing to touch her, even if it was just my fingertip to hers. A slow and steady process wasn't going to help me. How could it when I'd wanted to barf at just the suggestion?

"Do you know how long it will take her to recover?" My mother asked, stroking my father's knee soothingly.

"Janice, you can't put a time frame on someone's healing process. Every person and every experience is different."

"Of course. I didn't mean to suggest she couldn't take her time. I just... I want to help her."

"Keep being her mother then." Julie suggested. "Do what you do every day, don't push unless she asks for it. I know it seems like Sage hasn't made any progress but she has."

"Sage." My mother started to say something then seemed to get flooded with apprehension.

I looked into her nervous eyes and tried to smile. "Mom, it's okay. You can ask something if you want to."

"I'd just like to know why you don't share anything with us."

"Because I don't want to."

The answer was that simple. I didn't want to tell my parents or Brett any details of what went down when I was away. I wasn't suggesting they pretend I was on a sixteen-month long vacation. I hated pretending. I just wanted them to accept that part of my life wasn't a story I wished to re-tell. It was hard enough telling Julie everything. Cracking open my thoughts and flooding myself with the moments I remembered was exhausting. Mentally, physically, and emotionally exhausting.

"I just thought that if she confided in us, we could help ease some burden." My mom spoke quietly.

"That's a lovely thought, Janice, but while you believe it'd ease Sage's burden, she believes it'd add to yours." Julie replied.

"I would carry the world for her."

That made me smile. "Thanks, mom. But I'd rather carry it alone."

Julie sighed. She did not approve of that plan. She begged me to bring someone along to counseling with me one day so I could confide in them too. She wished for me to share the load with a person I trusted. And it wasn't that I didn't trust the ones in the room with me, it's that I couldn't picture myself getting weak in front of them. I didn't want to subject them to the moment I broke down. It didn't happen often, but when it did, it was ugly and painful. If they couldn't handle the idea that I suffered from nightmares, how could they handle what's inside them?

Still, the anguish plastered on my mother's face was so evident. I was pulled in two directions, struggling to blurt out everything she wanted to hear so all this could be over, and keeping my lips locked forever.

Either situation was painful.

"Is there something specific you'd like Sage to share with you?" Julie asked. "Perhaps, it'd be easier for her to answer a question than simply sort through what's in her head. Would that be okay, Sage? If your mom asked you a question?"

"I don't have to answer if I don't want to, right?"

"Yes. Of course. That always applies."

"Okay." I nodded, facing my mother and squeezing my pillow tighter to my chest. As if it'd soften the blow of whatever question I was about to be asked.

She seemed to consider what she wanted to ask me. I appreciated the time she took. It gave me a moment to get it together too. "How come you don't like cookies anymore?"

My muscles went taut. I slammed my eyes shut and took two long breaths. Cookies used to be my favorite dessert. Now I despised them. Not the taste, but just... *them*. Cookies in general. I wanted absolutely nothing to do with any form of them. My mother learned that in the worst way possible when she tried to bring me cookies and milk the second week I was home. I screamed the house down and launched into an episode.

"Remember, Sage, you don't have to answer."

I appreciated Julie's reminder, but I wanted to answer anyway. I wanted to give my mother *something*.

"He called me cookie. It was a nickname."

"Who did?"

"Kade."

The room went eerily silent until a deep, drawn-out growl ripped out of my brother's throat just with the mention of Kade's name.

Kade was the anti-christ. Satan in human form. My brother wanted to kill him. My father wanted to hang him by his toes and light him on fire. My mother cursed his name at night. Julie cringed when I'd said his name. They all hated him with all pieces of them. And I hated myself because I didn't.

"He called you cookie?"

"It was a nickname. I don't like cookies anymore because I don't appreciate the reminder."

My mother nodded, working so hard to keep her face neutral. "Thank you for sharing that, Sage."

Julie looked at me and smiled. I knew what the look on her face meant. It said *"see? That wasn't so bad. Now she knows to never give you a cookie again."*

I didn't admit she was right. Sure, my mom knew to never buy a pack of Chips Ahoy again, but it didn't make me feel any lighter. In fact, it made me fidgety. And clammy.

I hated talking about Kade. The things he did to me, fine. I could maybe mumble a few thoughts to Julie, but him in general? No. I couldn't. The way I felt about Kade made me feel off balance.

I hated him, attempted to drive a knife in his throat twice and contemplated shooting myself with his gun so I could escape him.

But also, a piece of me was thankful for him. In his own fucked up way, Kade kept me safe during those sixteen months. All the suggestions he'd gotten to throw me out of the van, shoot me, sell me into prostitution, and he didn't do a single one. It's because of Kade that I'm not dead. And as many times as I'd wished he'd killed me when his asshole friend killed Trish, I'm still alive.

And that had to count for something, right?

"Sage? Why the tears?" Julie passed me a box of Kleenex.

I shook my head and sniffed aggressively. I was overwhelmed. "I want to go home."

Brett flew from his seat. "I'll take you. I drove separately."

"We still have half an hour left!" My father protested, but I was already out the door.

Brett was hot on my heels, holding open the front door and leading me to his car that was parked on the street. He used the remote to disengage the locks. I slid inside, pressing my head against the dashboard while tears poured out of me.

I shook violently, my body trying to rid itself of all the thoughts that included Kade Wilson.

"Oh God." Brett croaked. "Sage, I'm sorry. You never have to talk about him again, okay? I'm sorry. I'm sorry."

I knew without looking, Brett was crying too. Tears

were clogged in his throat. It was evident in every word he spoke.

I lifted my head and wiped at my face. "Why do you guys want to know?"

"I don't." He shook his head quickly, tears falling down his face and getting stuck in his beard. "Not if it hurts you this bad. I don't give a fuck. We don't have to talk about that monster ever again, okay?"

I nodded, dropping my head to the window. I breathed through the knot in my chest until the burn in my eyes disappeared. The two sets of rough sobs turned into low sniffles after a long stretch of time.

My mind was still racing, my stomach still churning with guilt and disgust towards myself. I knew I was on the verge of vomiting at any moment. But when I opened my mouth to gag, something entirely different came out.

A confession.

"I think I'm grateful for him." I blurted, looking straight ahead. "For Kade, I mean." I focused on the man riding a bicycle across the street rather than the sharp intake of breath that came from between Brett's teeth. "It's not..." I shook my head, trying to navigate my thoughts. "I hate him, okay? This isn't a case of Stockholm syndrome. I wasn't in love with him. I didn't beg to stay with him when the cops found me. But I also know that if it weren't for him, his friends would have killed me. Or worse, put me in a crate and sent me to a prostitution ring overseas."

Brett made a choking sound. More tears stained my cheeks but I trudged forward. I was sharing something, and it fucking sucked, but I was doing it.

"And it's so fucking hard for me to cope with despising him but also being thankful for not using me as target practice. I just... I don't understand, Brett! I don't like any part of what's happening in my fucked up brain. He did things to me, made me watch things that had me begging him to just shoot me and yet I can't say that I hate him because I'm alive. And what the fuck does that say about me? Huh?!"

"I think it says you're a better human than he was." Brett threw his fist in the dashboard. "I think you hate him, I think you hate what he did to you, what he did to Trish. I think you hate him for making you contemplate taking your own life. You hate him for being evil. But you, Sage, you're fucking good. You got me? You're a good person. Those sixteen months? It did not change that. You have no evil in you. You can't stand harboring hate. You never could. Our fights as kids lasted five minutes before you broke down crying because you hated being filled with anger." He took a few long breaths, and I knew how bad he wanted to wrap me in a hug.

And as much as I loved my brother, I was thankful he didn't.

"The good in you doesn't want to hate him, Sage. You don't want that extra weight pressing on your chest. Finding a reason to be thankful for him makes things easier for you."

I gasped, expelling long, wheeze like breaths. Tears of shame turned into tears of relief as I clutched my chest and an ocean poured from my eyes. "You don't think it makes me fucked up?"

"No, Sage. I do not, and would never, think of you as fucked up. I think you're looking for a reason to be better than him. And showing him gratitude after all he put you through is your reason. You're a good human, sis. And it's okay to want to hate him. It is."

I nodded rapidly, chanting his words over and over.

It's okay.

It's okay.

It's okay.

Did wanting to give Kade some thanks for not offing me actually make me a good person? I had no flipping clue, but I believed Brett when he said it didn't make me a bad one.

"What can I do to help, Sage?"

It was with that question I realized my breathing was still heavier and slower than it should've been. I was gulping for air as if I'd been underwater for a millennium and just breached the surface. I shook my head and closed my eyes, drawing in a breath for three seconds and letting it out for three more. I did that several times, attempting to find a happy place.

Julie encouraged me to find a place that calmed me. A place no one could touch or taint. A place that was just for me. One that brought me immeasurable amounts of peace.

I did not have a happy place. I knew that even as I'd searched hard for one. After all the times I'd done this, I knew this time would be no different.

But then something strange happened. The darkness I usually saw during these moments cracked open and made some room. I ran towards it, tilting my head in confusion when all I saw was orange. And then I saw freckles. Hundreds of them, complemented by a pair of blue glasses and a bright yellow shirt. I heard snort after snort as laughter rolled from his chest while he peered into a box of crayons.

My heartbeat found a steady rhythm. My tears began to dry as I stared, not at the darkness, but at the sun.

I peeled my eyes back open and looked at Brett, wiping my face. He was regarding me intently, worry marring all his features.

"You okay?"

"Yeah. I think so." I sniffed and pulled my seatbelt

across my body. "You're an amazing brother, Brett. You know that, right?"

The smile that erupted on his face made me feel like his baby sister again, taking the blame for breaking mom's vase so he could still go to the baseball game with Jesse. "I do now."

"Good."

He clicked his own seatbelt and turned on the ignition. "Ready to go home?"

"Actually, can we go to the store?"

"The store? Sure. Which one?"

"A craft store." I relaxed into his seat, letting more weight melt off my chest. It wasn't everything, but it was a small start. I told my mother the truth, confided in my brother. Most of all, I'd found my happy place. And I didn't intend on letting it forget how thankful I am it appeared when it did. "I feel like painting a picture."

MY LEAST FAVORITE nights were the ones I had nothing to do. I despised having the night off. I know, right? What an anomaly I was compared to the rest of the American population. I did not enjoy not having anything to do. The idea of spending an entire night relaxing made me itchy. If it were up to me, I would never have a night off, but Cruz forced everybody in Circuit to take at least two nights off a week. He claimed he didn't want the job to take over our lives. I understood where he came from, but it was ultimately bullshit. The job took over my life long before Circuit came along and two nights a week away from my underworld would not change that.

I could've easily taken a page out of August's book and went to some bar or a club. I could've even gone a tamer route and went to go see a movie and enjoyed dinner somewhere that wasn't my living room couch. But honestly? If I wasn't at Circuit, my favorite place to be was my home. It's where I was most comfortable. Where my thoughts and insecurities were the safest. I'd never been a people person.

Never been able to make a lot of small talk or feel confident enough to go somewhere I wasn't familiar with. I didn't like to think of myself as a boring person, considering the whole illegal hacker thing and all, but I was. Video games and my couch were basically what made up my life on a night I wasn't allowed to be seen inside Circuit. I tried showing up once, just because I had nothing better to do, and Cruz barked at me and kicked me out. Since then, I've dealt with it.

August and Zelda liked to joke that I had no life. It always annoyed me. But ever since Sage crept into my life, their little comments about me not having a life seemed to enrage me. I had a life, it just consisted of screens, junk food, and Diet Coke rather than getting drunk, meaningless sex, and getting lost at a party I didn't want to be at. I had a life, and I could live it however the hell I wanted to.

Complaining that I didn't have a life felt like an insult to Sage. It was her who spent sixteen months without a life. I mean, she was alive, yeah. But that felt like a technicality. Was she really living? Was she spending her days how she wanted to? Whether that meant playing video games in her underwear or going to dinner with a dozen friends, I doubted it. I knew nothing about what Sage went through but I knew she wasn't making a single choice for herself. Her life was taken entirely out of her hands, and while I could sit here with a bottle of Diet Coke and a long night of playing Fortnite, humoring my friends when they joked I didn't have a life, I knew it was Sage who spent so long without one.

I screwed the cap back on my 2 liter of Diet Coke and set it at my feet beside the couch. My sister wasn't home tonight so she couldn't give me shit for drinking straight out of the bottle. Truthfully, I had no idea why the hell she cared. She didn't drink the stuff. It was just for me. And why would I buy two twenty ounce bottles when I could buy a 2 liter for the same price? Seemed like a no-brainer.

I lifted my PS4 controller from my lap only to realize I hadn't actually turned on the TV yet. Considering Lilah lost the remote in one of the moments she tries to do a million things at once, turning on the television meant I had to actually get off the couch and press the button manually. That sounded like too much work. So I sat on the couch and drank my Diet Coke. It was laziness at its finest. And I was not mad. I was good at sitting in one place for a long period of time. The deep blue computer chair that perched at my desk in Circuit had my butt cheeks permanently molded into it. It was actually time I'd splurged for a new one. It was broken. A spring broke, and I hadn't realized how bad it was until I walked in one day and found the thing completely lopsided. I could still sit in it, but it would be any day now the damn thing would collapse and take me with it.

I lifted my phone and pulled up Amazon, deciding I was going to search for a brand-new chair. I had nothing better to do anyway. I would turn the television on when the pizza I ordered arrived. That way, I only had to get up once. Some called it laziness, I called it strategy. Before I could even type anything into the search bar, a low knock sounded at my door. I heaved myself off the couch and grabbed my wallet from the counter.

I pulled the door open, a polite smile etched on my face. The smile morphed into a grin my face wasn't used to when I caught sight of my visitor. It was not Dale, the pizza delivery guy whom I over tipped because he came here four nights a week. It was my phantom girl, standing on my welcome mat with her head dipped to the ground and white hair acting as a curtain. She had a wrapped gift clutched to her chest in an almost protective way. It was not in a box like the others she'd brought before. It was tall and flat. My first instinct was that it was some sort of photo or a poster.

Her feet were covered in a pair of pink shoes. They were fidgeting against the welcome mat. Her knees seemed to tremble underneath a pair of light washed jeans. The death grip she had on the gift had me wondering if she was worried someone was going to snatch it away from her. Her knuckles flexed and her grip tightened. She took a step back and barely lifted her head. Still, I could spot the apprehension and doubt that seemed to be plastered all over her face.

"Hi." Her voice was quiet. If there were anyone else in the hallway or any background noises, I wouldn't have heard her.

"Hi, Sage." I tried to keep my voice as light as hers, but it was virtually impossible. Sage didn't even seem to speak. Her words were wrapped up in the small breaths she took.

"I brought this for you." She held out the gift. It shook from the force of the tremble that seemed to control her hands.

I took it from her carefully, sliding it from her grip while being conscious our hands didn't touch and peered down at it. I was struck to find my name written across the top. Not Specter. But Wren. That combined with the realization she didn't just drop this off at the door and run, had me feeling like I'd just won a million dollars from a scratch-off ticket.

"Thank you, Sage."

"It's, uhm, just for you this time."

I smiled, hoping the freckles on my face masked any sort

of blush that might appear. The downside of being the same color as a Pringle was that not a single emotion could be hidden. "I really appreciate it, Sage. Thank you."

"You're welcome. I made it."

My eyeballs widened behind my lens. "You made this?"

"I'm not really an artist or anything. It's actually not even that cool. I just, uhm, yeah. I made it."

"Well, that makes it a million times cooler."

Her head was still dipped to the ground, and she hadn't even attempted to meet my eyes. I couldn't see her expression anymore, but I'd hoped she was smiling a little. She continued to fidget, her feet moving strangely as if she were fighting with them on whether they should take off or stay exactly as they were.

"Did you want to come in?" As soon as the question left my lips, I regretted it. It seemed like the polite thing to do after someone had hand-delivered a gift they made especially for you, but with Sage, I had to do things differently.

She stumbled backward, her hands wringing together quickly. "Uhm..."

"Or we could stay out here." I offered, trying my best to sound nonchalant. It was obvious she did not want to walk into a stranger's home. From all she'd suffered, it seemed perfectly reasonable to me. I did not want to make her apprehension seem irrational.

"Oh, no." She cleared her throat. "I didn't mean to interrupt your night or anything."

"You didn't. Trust me. I was literally doing nothing. Sitting on my couch, drinking Diet Coke."

"Oh. You don't have to go to..." She trailed off, looking around the hallway. I found it sweet she didn't say the name Circuit out loud. Even though we were the only ones in the hallway, it was obvious she wanted to protect that piece of me.

In that moment, I'd wished desperately I could protect whatever piece of her that seemed to be hanging on by a thread.

"No. I have two nights off a week. This is one. I was going to play a video game until I couldn't find the remote and was too lazy to turn on the television manually."

"Brett is like that. He'd rather sit and stare at the wall than stand off the couch and press a button."

"Brett understands me." I said, keeping my voice light. "It takes a strong man to sit and do nothing. Laziness is hard work."

There was a beat of silence before she lifted her head and finally gifted me with her gaze. I looked into her eyes, noting the way they reminded me of the crayons sitting back on my desk at Circuit. I searched her gaze, looking for any sign that I might be scaring her. There was a look on her face that told me she was scared, but she didn't seem to be filled with terror. Not like she was the day we met. She seemed apprehensive and jumpy. Like she was about to go to the doctors for a flu shot when she was afraid of needles. Or about to ride a rollercoaster when she was afraid of heights. She seemed to be trying to decide if conquering her fear was worth it or if she was just going to say "screw this" and take off running.

I wouldn't have blamed her if she went with the latter. But she didn't. She surprised me by taking a step forward. That small step seemed to be filled with determination. It took a lot of out her, and I repressed the urge to say I'm proud of her and give her a high five.

"I've changed my mind." She announced. "May I come in?"

"Of course." I stepped back and gestured with my arm. She angled her body strangely and slid inside my apartment, looking around and scanning all her surroundings. I knew from our first encounter her brain was working triple time, logging every detail of my home into her memory. As if she were an architect trying to memorize a blueprint.

I struggled with whether I should shut the door. Maybe I was overthinking the entire moment, but the last thing I wanted to do was shut the door and make her feel as though she couldn't leave whenever the hell she wanted to. Then again, I didn't want to leave it open and invite in whatever she was afraid of.

In the end, I chose to shut it partly, leaving it open just a crack. That seemed to give her what it was she needed. She walked tentatively into my living room and perched on the couch, still looking around. I thought about sitting next to her before warning lights flashed in my brain and told me that was a bad idea. I sat down in my chair with the gift in my lap.

I had never spent a ton of time looking around my own home. As Sage inspected it, I had to wonder what it looked like from her eyes. My sister made sure everything matched nicely, random wall decor hanging strategically around the television, coasters on the end table that matched the pillows she had on the couch. There was a massive rug with some swirls on it Lilah called paisley and a tall lamp that was crooked. It was supposed to be trendy, but looked like it was hit by a truck.

Whatever Sage was seeing, whatever thoughts were inside her head, didn't seem to be ones that frightened her.

I cleared my throat and nodded at the gift in my lap. "Can I open it?"

"Of course." She angled her body to face me, watching

as I slowly peeled the brown wrapping away from the gift. I let the wrapping hit the floor and lifted my gift so it was right in front of my face.

Staring right back at me was the color yellow. It was brushed on a canvas, a little bigger than the paintings my sister had on her wall. There were brush strokes going from the top to the bottom of the canvas. It became clear to me she didn't care much for smoothing it out. She wanted the uneven strokes and the globs of paint still on it. And it took me no time at all to uncover what this bright yellow canvas was supposed to represent.

Sunshine.

Sage gave me sunshine, and my God I wasn't sure if I could handle all the tightness that constricted my chest because of it.

"There was one like it in my counselor's office." I lowered the painting to my lap and pried my ears open so I could hear the words in her breaths. "I used to wonder why somebody would just paint it yellow. It seemed like they didn't know what else they wanted on it and just hung it up to deal with it later. Today I looked it at and I... thought of you."

"Me?" What is it about this girl that made a man feel so damn honored?

"Yeah. I thought of sunshine. And your yellow shirt."

"That's a good shirt."

"I guess I just wanted to give you that in case you ever forget how cool you are." She snorted and dipped her head. "Sounds super lame now that I'm saying it out loud."

"Not to me. I love when people call me cool. Please, go on."

I couldn't be sure, but I swore her lips quirked a little. "I spent a lot of time in the dark. And uhh, I hadn't thought I'd get to see the sun again. And then you and your computer made some magic. So, I just wanted to give you that as a reminder that you're a good guy."

"Sage." I named myself after a superhero, but it was her and this moment that truly made me feel like one. "Thank you. I'll hang this in my room."

Her lips parted as if she were about to say more. They slammed shut, trapping all her thoughts inside when the front door flew open. Sage went stiff as a board, her eyes slamming shut as if she were trying to pretend she was somewhere else. I jumped from my chair, throwing myself towards the front door.

"Hey, Wren!" Dale's loud, boisterous voice made Sage flinch roughly. "You know your door is open?"

"Yeah, man." I walked towards Dale, crowding his space so he was forced to move back into the hall. "How much do I owe ya?"

Dale rolled his eyes. "Same price as you always do, Wilder. Somebody needs to teach you how to cook."

I gave him some cash and took the pizza from him. "But then you wouldn't get to see me every week."

"Once a week is enough, my friend. Just because there's meat on that pie doesn't mean you're getting your daily protein count."

"What are you?" I scoffed. "My pizza man or my nutritionist?"

He smacked his gut. "Wife's been barking nutritional facts at me. I can't suffer alone."

"Here I thought you were looking out for me."

He flashed me a smile. "See ya tomorrow, Wren."

"Bye, Dale." I laughed, shutting the door behind him with a soft click. I turned around, eyes locking on my phantom girl. She was impossibly stiff. Like I could lift her up and crack her in half. The tremble that appeared to always control her body was gone. She was so still, and I had begun to worry she'd stopped breathing.

"Sage?"

I dropped the pizza carelessly on an end table and squatted in front of her, searching her chest for signs that her lungs hadn't seized up. I found it lifting and deflating slowly while she sat in front of me with her eyes closed. My first instinct was that her stillness was some sort of survival instinct. Ya know like when you go to the woods people always tell you to be very still if you come in contact with a bear. Or when a wasp lands on you and you have to make your muscles stop twitching until it goes away. Sage was waiting until the thing she thought would hurt her went away.

"Hey, Sage?" I wanted to tap her on the shoulder, but again, warning lights flashed in my head and told me what an awful idea that was. "It's just you and I again. Dale is gone."

She stayed still for a few long moments. I sat back, crossing my legs and letting my hands fall into my lap while I waited. I watched one of her eyes peel open, searching me tentatively. Slowly but surely, both her eyes opened fully. She looked around the room, taking in the door latched shut and then met my eyes again.

"Hey, you." I grinned. "Everything okay?"

She nodded slowly. And then, something that changed my world forever happened.

She smiled.

Her cheeks rose, her lips curling upward while she flashed me all of her teeth. I rocked backward, thanking the sweet Lord I was already on my ass. People smiled at me all the time. I was a nice dude. But when Sage did it? *Damn.* It affected me on such a profound level. That smile blinded me. Made me incapable of seeing anything but the way her cheeks pinked up and the dimples that lie within them.

I was shook. My whole equilibrium went off balance as I stared up at her like she was a unicorn falling from the sky. Her smile was rare, and here I was, staring directly into it.

I shook my head and cleared my throat, attempting to form words. "I'm sorry if Dale startled you. He's got a lot of energy."

She nodded again. "I was just caught off guard. I'm okay now."

I peeled myself off the ground and lifted the pizza, holding it out. "Do you wanna share?"

She shook her head quickly. "No, thank you. I already ate."

"Okay." I walked in to the kitchen and dropped it on the counter, grabbing a clean plate from the drying rack next to the sink and plopped a couple of pieces on top. I moved slow, knowing she was calculating my movements. After I'd snagged a paper towel, I walked back into the living room and dropped back down in my chair.

For just feeling like I was thrown into outer space a minute before, I thought I did a good job of acting natural. I took a bite, feeling all sorts of self-conscious she was watching me eat.

"Your friend seemed to think you eat too much pizza."

"My friend is correct." I wiped my mouth with my paper towel. "I don't cook."

"Me either. My mother is an excellent cook though."

"Yeah? What's your favorite thing she makes?"

She seemed to consider my question while I chewed. "My favorite meal or just anything?"

"Anything."

"Zucchini bread." Her answer rolled right off her tongue. "I could eat it for every meal."

"Zucchini bread? Like bread made of vegetables?"

"Sort of." She smiled again. It wasn't as large as the first one I'd seen, but it affected me all the same. "Have you ever had it?"

"No. The vegetables I eat are usually on a pizza."

Her smile stayed intact. "It's really good. Plus, it's kind of like the best of both worlds since you can say you're eating vegetables, but you're also consuming a mass amount of carbs."

"Now, you're speaking my language."

"What's your favorite thing?"

"Diet Coke." I pointed at the 2 liters resting next to her feet. "It's an obsession."

She looked down, inspecting the bottle that's half gone. Her eyebrow raised. "Diet Coke is your favorite food?"

"Yes. Without a doubt. Take away my pizza and give me a Diet Coke. I'll survive."

"You'll only survive for like three days. You'll need water."

"Ah." I set my empty plate aside. "Easy. Put ice in the Diet Coke. Then you just wait for it to melt and boom, ya got yourself some water."

Her grin exploded. "That's ridiculous! Why not just have water?"

"I would rather have flat Diet Coke than a bottled water."

"I guess it's good that it's diet. You'd have so many cavities."

I feigned hurt. "I'll have you know I have never had a cavity."

"I've had four."

I smirked. "Looks like I'm not the only one with an obsession."

Her cheeks turned a warm red color. "I have a thing for butterscotch candies."

"Like the old people candy everybody's grandma has in their purse?"

"More than just old people enjoy butterscotch candies." She argued.

"Really? I've never met another person who enjoys butterscotch candy. Do you have a club?"

She gasped. "You're kind of a giant butthead."

A burst of laughter rattled my chest. I had never been so happy to be called a butthead before. More so, I knew just by her demeanor I hadn't upset her. By the small smile still molded on her lips and the way her muscles had relaxed into the couch, I knew she wasn't mad.

"I tried to buy them at the candy store when I was there." She said. "But they no longer carry them."

"Have you tried Amazon? Amazon has everything."

She shook her head. "I don't spend a lot of time online anymore."

"I could order it for you." I threw the suggestion out there, hoping it sounded as genuine as I meant it. She'd bought me all these gifts, the least I could do was buy her some old lady purse candy. "I was on Amazon earlier looking for a new computer chair."

"Oh. You have a desk?" She looked around the room. "In your bedroom?"

"At Circuit." I explained. "My chair right now is two spins away from mass destruction."

"Did you find one you liked?"

"Not yet, but I'm really not that picky. As long as it has armrests and a lot of butt cushion, I'm good as gold."

"You should get a yellow one." She announced.

"Done." It was the easiest decision I ever made. Even if it turned out to be the least comfortable chair I ever owned, it would remind me of her. And that it would reside in the place I played a part in changing her life seemed perfect to me. "My phone is on the cushion next to you. Amazon is already loaded. Go ahead and pick one."

"Me?" She jerked backward. "You want me to choose it?"

"Why not?" I shrugged. "I'm not picky."

Her eyes narrowed and her voice dropped. "What comes next?"

"What do you mean?"

"Well." Her head dipped to the floor, and her muscles went back to mimicking a sheet of metal. "If I do this for you, what other things would you want me to do?"

The question tugged aggressively at my heart. I closed my eyes and took a long breath, repressing the urge to kick something across the room. I had no idea what she'd experienced, but that one question opened up a floodgate of possibilities my mind could not handle. What's more, my mind couldn't handle that she had no choice but to constantly re-live it.

"Sage." I cleared my throat, rolling my neck to loosen all the muscles that just went stiff. "I'm still a stranger to you. I know that. You have no reason to trust me yet, but I swear on your grandma's candies and the last bottle of Diet Coke in the world, I would never force you to do anything you don't want to do."

She took a long time and seemed to truly consider my words. Maybe she also considered my character, the person I've shown her I am up until this moment. I would never know what played out in her head, but I hoped with all there was inside me she liked what she found.

After a long moment, she reached across the couch and lifted my iPhone. She hit the home button and gasped. "Wren! You don't have a password on this thing? Don't you have important stuff on here? You're a... *hacker*."

I chuckled at the way she whispered hacker as if it were a dirty word. "Don't really have any incriminating evidence on my cell phone. It's all on my computer. And you need three passwords to open up that thing."

"One of them is probably Diet Coke."

I choked on my laughter. "Now who's being a butthead?"

She shrugged. "Your obsession seems to show no bounds."

This girl was a riot. I wondered when the last time was that she was able to just relax and make jokes. When I thought about it, I didn't like the answer I came up with. So I stopped thinking and just watched her. Her eyes scrolled with the screen as she took in all the possibilities. She pulled her bottom lip in between her teeth, a deep wrinkle forming on her forehead as if she were working every piece of her brain. I found it endearing she was putting so much effort into choosing me a chair. Then again, everything I've seen of Sage so far told me she didn't do anything without putting in all her effort. She could have easily mailed a package, or sent a simple thank you note. But not Sage. She wrapped them and hand delivered them all by herself. Sage didn't seem to do anything halfway.

"Any luck?" I quipped, resisting the urge to lean over and peer at the screen.

She nodded quickly and passed me the phone. "This one. It looks badass. Also, it's yellow."

I took the screen, grinning at the one she'd chosen. It was a gamer chair. The seat and backrest were covered in bright yellow fabric with small accents of black. There were sturdy silver armrests that looped into a cool design and had a high headrest. I clicked the purchase button without bothering to look at a price.

"It's perfect, Sage." I set my phone on my lap and flashed her the most genuine smile I was capable of. "Thank you."

"You're very welcome." She eyed the controller resting on the floor. "You like video games?"

"Uhh, yes." I laughed nervously. "It's like all I do."

"What games do you like?"

"I'll play just about anything. Before you knocked, I was gonna play some Fortnite."

"Brett loves that one. My favorite is Super Smash Bros."

"Yeah?" I grinned like the damn Cheshire Cat. She likes video games. "You wanna play? I have it."

She pulled a phone from her back pocket, frowning at the screen. She started to fidget again before standing up. "I can't. I should go before my parents find the American Girl Doll."

I stood up with her, frowning. "You aren't allowed out of the house?"

"Usually my brother comes with me." She shrugged. "They worry when I leave, and I don't like to make them worry."

I nodded with a small amount of understanding. I couldn't imagine how scary it'd be to open a door and find your daughter missing... for the second time. Then again, I had to recognize that if she had to hide it from her family, it was a big deal for Sage to leave on her own. And that's something that should be celebrated.

"Thank you for letting me hang out." She mumbled. "And for letting me choose you a chair."

"Thank you for my sunshine."

"Thank you for mine." She quipped, rocking on her feet.

The urge to lean forward and kiss her on the cheek hit me hard. I rocked backward like I'd just ran into a concrete wall. I felt like I was in sixth grade again, walking Jessica Scott to her front door after going to the movies in a group and holding hands the whole time. I thought she'd wanted me to kiss her. She didn't. She smacked me in the face and wiped at her cheek like I'd just given her a flesh-eating disease.

I made the wrong call then. I wouldn't do it again now.

I pulled the door open for her. "You can stop by any time you want and get schooled in Super Smash."

"Oh, he's full of himself, huh?" She'd flashed me her third smile of the night.

Yes. I was counting.

"It's just the truth, Sage." I shrugged. "I have Mondays and Wednesdays off if you ever want to come see for yourself."

She nodded. "I may do that. Thank you for the invite and for the company."

"Anytime." I stressed.

She lifted her hand in goodbye and scurried out the door, fast walking to the elevator. I watched her until she was inside and the doors slid shut. The second I pushed my own door closed, I'd cursed myself for not asking for a phone number. Not because I, ya know, *wanted her number*. But to make sure she'd gotten home okay.

Though I suppose she was sick of people asking if she was okay. It's clear that she wasn't, but I had my fingers crossed she would be. After all, she didn't just leave my sunshine at the doorstep.

She brought it inside with her.

And I can still feel the warmth it brought lingering everywhere.

I WOKE up every morning to darkness. I had one window in my bedroom, right beside my bed. I'd requested my father board it shut when I came back home.

He was more than happy to oblige.

I liked the darkness. I was not afraid of what lingered in it. The worst of the worst had already snatched me up, and when my mind was being rational, I knew they couldn't come back.

I was comforted by the darkness because it's what I knew. When you ask people what they're most afraid of, it's likely the answer they'll give you will be something they've had no experience in.

Trish was afraid of sharks.

Why? I had no idea. She'd never come in contact with a shark before. Ever.

People are afraid of what they aren't familiar with. Things or situations they don't know how to handle. Fear is powered by the unknown. It's only when we are completely oblivious to what's about to happen to us, or what is happening, does the panic cut off our air flow.

I wasn't *afraid* of the sun exactly. If anything, I was annoyed by it. Or simply what it did. The sun was a reminder to haul yourself out of bed and get on with living your life. But I had no life to live. And that's what scared me. There were days I was incapable of even opening my eyes. Days where my brain rendered memories of Trish, flashbacks of bruises, handcuffs, guns, and blood. Nightmares where I'd been the one that killed my best friend.

For months after I'd come home, my reasons to get out of bed were on a list that did not exist, and the sun only served as an ugly reminder. It felt like a slap in the face rather than the second chance it should've been. But how could I use the sun to remind myself to get up and keep living when I'd forgotten what living felt like? I didn't know where I was going. All the unknown that circled my life was pure terror. I had no idea if I'd even be able to make my body work let alone be able to go out and experience life.

I asked Julie all the time if I'd be like this forever. Not just scared of anything that walked, talked, or made a loud noise, but scared of myself and what I'd refused to do.

The more time I'd spent with Julie and her little yellow pillow, the more I'd believed I would stop despising the sun and all it stood for. Day after day, I'd stare into the sun, fighting tears and wondering why I'd been given a second chance when I was too afraid to do anything with it.

And then I'd realized I'd been counting on the wrong sun to wake me up. My sun was not in the sky.

It was inside apartment 905.

I peered up at the metal numbers that were screwed into the wooden door and lifted my hand to knock. I studied my fist and noted the way it seemed to be shaking less than it was a week ago when I was here. I knocked twice, making sure it was hard enough to be heard and waited. I hoped he wasn't out with his friends or his sister. I should've come last week. I was all ready to go. I tucked in my old American Girl Doll and was halfway here before I chickened out and went home. I wish I could've warned him I was coming or simply asked if the invitation was still open. But it's not like I have his phone number to give him a courtesy call.

The door flung open. I rocked backward, peering into a face that was not the freckled one I was hoping to see. "Hey! Phantom girl!"

"I'm sorry?"

Ace's grin went from ear to ear. He flipped his wild hair behind his shoulders and leaned against the doorframe. "Wren calls you his phantom girl. It's adorable."

"Uhm..." I ignored that bizarre nickname and tilted my body to peer around him. His stocky body was taking up the width of the entire doorway. Standing on my toes to peer over his shoulder was no use either. "Is Wren here?"

"Oh, yeah, girl. He's in the bathroom. You want to come in and wait for him?"

I opened my mouth to say yes before my instincts slammed it back shut. Ace didn't seem threatening. He didn't reek of violence or danger, but then again, neither did most killers. I liked to think my radar was good on spotting the people who'd found a sport in hurting others, but I couldn't rely on my mind not to malfunction.

I shook my head and took a step back. "No, thank you. I'll wait for him here."

"Okay." Ace shrugged and stayed where he was, looking relaxed as ever. He either was entirely oblivious to the fact I didn't want to be alone with him or he just didn't care. "Is it cool if I wait here too?"

"Sure." I took another step back, telling myself I was being rude but still giving in to the voice that said Wren wasn't inside and Ace could drag me in at any moment. I did my best to remind my brain that Ace helped save me too.

Wren was not superman, though when I was around him, it sure felt like he was.

I barely flinched when I heard a door slam. Ace tilted his head and shouted into the apartment. "Yo, my freckled friend, your phantom girl is here!"

There was the distinct sound of footsteps on hardwood floor before a flash of orange body checked Ace out of the doorway. Wren took over his spot with a wide grin on his face. "Sage! Hi."

His smile made the tremor in my hands loosen. "Hi."

The first time I saw Wren, I was terrified. He was a stranger, he was bigger than me, and he had the capabilities of knowing where I lived, where I slept, and probably how many times a day I used my electric toothbrush.

But the more time I spent in his presence, I began to feel as though Wren seemed to know exactly what I needed in exactly the right amount.

That sort of comfort was unfamiliar. Which is what made it terrifying. Was it possible to feel comforted by someone you're afraid of?

I wasn't sure, but I knew better than to believe something that brought me joy wouldn't turn into misery later on. But after an exhausting talk with Julie, I learned it was okay to clutch something that felt comforting. Exactly like I did with that little yellow pillow. I clutched the comfort I'd felt and basked in the sunshine that came with him being my happy place.

Because somewhere along dropping off gifts, a hallway talk, and a moment in my counselor's office, he'd become my sun.

And I wanted him to know it.

"Did you come to hang out?" The hope lingering in his voice made my heart speed up in a way it hadn't ever before. It wasn't fear or adrenaline. It was excitement. And though it was unfamiliar, it wasn't *too* scary.

"Yes, if that's still okay."

"Of course it is." He angled his body and let me into his home.

I kept a firm eye on Ace, watching his movements and growing confused at the smirk on his face. He padded to the living room and plopped down on the couch, distancing himself from Wren and I. I suspected that was for my benefit, and one day, I'd able to admit how much I appreciated it.

Wren shut the door behind me. "Are you still up for a night of Super Smash?"

I nodded and held out the dish I had a death grip on. "I brought you zucchini bread if you want to try it."

He took it from my grasp with a smile. "She leaves me presents and she feeds me."

"My mom and I made a whole bunch yesterday."

"What's zucchini bread?" Ace's head popped over the back of the couch.

"It's exactly what it sounds like, dude." Wren chuckled. "Zucchini inside bread."

That wasn't how I would've described it but the look on Ace's face was pretty funny. His lips pursed and he reared backward. "Vegetables in bread? Ew."

"Don't be a dick!" Wren flipped him off. "Sage made this! It's her favorite."

"It's okay." I thought the way Wren defended my vegetable bread was very sweet. "It does sound gross, Ace. But it's really good."

"I'll try anything once, phantom girl." Ace winked and fell back onto the couch.

I watched Wren's eyes roll as he led me across the room and into the kitchen. It was much smaller than the one I had at home, but it was beautiful all the same. Stainless steel appliances all around with granite countertops and a double-decker oven.

A girl could make a lot of bread in that oven.

"Have a seat if you want." Wren gestured to a wooden stool with a leather cushion and a high back. He came around the counter, grabbing three plates from a cabinet above the stove. I unwrapped the already sliced bread, placing a piece on each of the plates.

Bringing Wren gifts had started as something that gave me a purpose. A small thing I could add to my list of why the sun had to rise every morning. But now I seemed to care less about giving gifts and more about being around him.

And that realization was what made me smile for the first time in a long time. And by the look on his face last week, the painting wasn't the only gift I'd given him that day. Even now, his smile seemed permanently molded to his cheeks.

My own grew when he bit into his bread and groaned like he'd just tasted ice cream for the first time.

"Ace!" Crumbs went flying when he talked with his mouth full. "Get in here! This doesn't taste like crappy vegetables!"

There was a thud I assumed was Ace flopping off the couch. His hair flew behind him as he slid into the kitchen on his socks. He eyed a full slice on a plate and stuffed the whole thing in his mouth.

Wren smacked him on the back of the head. "You have no manners, bro."

"Me?" There were giant bulges of bread packed in Ace's cheeks as he tried to talk. "You just spit crumbs everywhere!"

"You two remind me of my brother. Brett once put two slices of pizza on top of each other and shoved the whole thing in his mouth. My mother was disgusted."

"Disgusting my mother is one of my many talents, phantom girl." Ace quipped.

I tilted my head, watching as they stuffed their faces. "How come you keep calling me phantom girl?"

They both went still. Ace began to chew really slowly while Wren seemed to choke on what was left of his slice. He flipped on his faucet and stuck his head directly under the stream. Once he was done sputtering, he faced me and wiped his mouth.

"When gifts started arriving at my doorstep, I referred to you as my phantom friend. Ya know, always around but never caught or seen? When I saw you on a security camera, you were upgraded from phantom friend to phantom girl."

"Yeah but you were extra phantomy." Ace blurted. "'Cause how did you even know where Wren lived?"

Wren's eyes shot up like he hadn't considered that.

"Because Lilah Wilder owns a million dollar company." I shrugged. "Once Wren said her first name, I peeked at the doctor's chart and got the last one on my way out the door. Google basically told me everything I needed to know."

"Google has my address?" Wren spat. "What the hell? I need to take that down immediately."

"Google doesn't have your address." I reassured quickly. "I called Lilah's office and made up a story about how I was trying to RSVP to an event and lost her address. Some guy named Hal told me what building you lived in and the name of the dude who works in the lobby. All I did was wait until I saw her walk in, and then I followed her and memorized the numbers on the door.

"Fucking Craig!" Wren scowled. "Who gives out people's addresses?"

"It was Hal."

"Same person." He grumped. "What a moron."

"He didn't give me the address. Just the building."

"Hold up!" Ace raised both hands in the air. "How did you know Wren lived here too?"

"I didn't. I just assumed based on him being the one that was around to escort her to the hospital they lived together or near each other." My smirk could not be contained. "I also hoped she would give the gift to you if you didn't actually live here."

"You put a lot of faith in a conversation that happened behind a curtain, phantom girl."

I shrugged. "The universe owed me one."

They both went silent, Wren smiling at me and Ace looking dumbstruck. After a beat, they went back to the food.

What a couple of goons they were. I hadn't watched anyone have as much unrestrained fun in such an extensive amount of time. I knew if I'd mentioned it, they'd say they weren't having fun.

It was just their daily life, and I'd almost forgotten what it looked like. The way they kept swatting each other's hands to get to the dish first and pointing at the way crumbs were all over their respective chins was foreign to me. But like all things involving Wren, the unknown did not scare me.

It intrigued me.

Neither of them held any reservations or insecurities. It appeared as though they felt free enough to act however they wanted. I wasn't sure when or if I'd ever get back to that. So I folded my hands on my lap and attempted to live vicariously through them.

"So did you guys have plans to hang out?" Ace mumbled. "'Cause I could leave."

"You weren't even invited in the first place, dude." Wren cracked.

"I don't need to be invited when I have a key."

"I did not give you that key. You made it."

"I made it for emergencies."

Wren looked around his apartment, eyebrows raising. "I don't see any emergencies."

"You should stay, Ace." The last thing I wanted to do was kick him out of a place that obviously felt like a second home to him.

I felt a twinge of jealousy inside me. I didn't even have one place that felt like home anymore.

"It's cool, phantom girl. I can finish my free food and scoot."

"No, really." I plastered a smile on my face. "Stay. You can watch me beat Wren at Super Smash."

Ace whistled. "Girl, Wren grew up with two friends. Me and his game console."

Wren looked horrified at that statement. Me? I smiled because I could relate. The gamer girl in me was reduced to my GameCube and various games by Nintendo, but give me a controller and I was one that could not be reckoned with.

I drove Trish nuts because I never let her win.

My obsession was made evident when I brought my GameCube for show and tell in the fourth grade and dressed as Princess Peach.

Something Brett has never let me live down. Back when he teased me anyway.

"I don't know." I shrugged. "I think I'm pretty good."

"Yeah, but you had two years without practicing, right?"

The second the words left Ace's mouth, he looked mortified. It would've been clear to anyone across the country he regretted the sentence the second it was out there.

Wren's gaze went to stone, flashing Ace a look I'd consider venomous if I didn't spend almost two years looking into the deadliest eyes of them all.

"I'm so sorry!" Ace blurted, his face paling to a shade lighter than mine. "Oh God, Sage. I'm sorry. That was so inappropriate. I'm a total dick."

"It was." I nod. "It was totally inappropriate."

I think they were both expecting me to take off running. Or break down like I did in the hallway that day. With my track record, I did not blame them.

I shocked both of them by lifting my lips in a small smile. "But I liked it."

"I'm sorry... what?" Wren blurted. "Because I will totally put a dead fish in his car and let that thing rot."

Something inside me grabbed hold of his words and held tightly to the way his threat did not involve violence.

"Man, come on!" Ace groaned. "I'm sorry, okay?"

There was no way one could look at Ace and not see how upset he was with himself. His energy plummeted to the lowest level possible while his normally wild eyes went sad.

"Ace, it's okay." I told him honestly. "It was a bit inappropriate, and my counselor would probably scold you, but I don't mind at all."

He lifted his head. "Why not?"

"Dude, really?" Wren growled. He was trying really hard to be a grizzly bear, but all I saw was a cuddly red panda bear. "Stop."

"It's fine, Wren. It's kind of nice. Since I've been home, my parents and Brett don't speak to me unless their words are calculated and perfected in their heads first. They tiptoe around me, and I get why they do it. They don't want to upset me, but sometimes it feels like I'm a wild animal at the zoo or something, ya know?"

"No." Ace blurted. "I do not know at all."

"I think I do." Wren leaned forward, elbows on the counter and gaze meeting mine. "Your house is your cage, yeah? And every time somebody goes inside a cage with a wild animal, they act a certain way. And you're looking through the glass, watching the way people interact in the wild and remember what it's like."

He got it in one.

I gazed into a pair of green eyes and wondered what's held behind them. What's in his brain? His mind? His soul? How is he capable of reading my mind and showing such empathy for a once in a lifetime situation?

"Exactly. My family turned their life upside down for me, and it's hard to know that even though I'm home it's not going back to how it was."

"Sage, you do understand that it isn't your fault, right?"

I nodded weakly and looked down at my lap, picking at my nails. From the moment I met Julie, she'd been working on getting through my stubborn head that it wasn't my fault my parents and brother struggled with my disappearance. But even though I didn't ask to spend sixteen months in hell, I still did. That was me, and I didn't like knowing my reluctance to fight back caused so much pain and fear.

"Yeah, but if I were stronger then they might not worry so much."

"Sunshine, why do you think you aren't strong?"

I pressed my palms to my eyes and used my hair as a shield. The guilt and the fear and the unfamiliar comfort was so much to process. I knew by the burning in my eyes and the tightness in my chest I was not equipped to handle any of it.

Memories flew to the surface in an instant. I whimpered at the sight of Trish's blood and held back a scream when fabric was pulled over my head so tightly, I could barely breathe as I thrashed my legs and flailed my body.

I squeezed my eyes shut even tighter, trying to mask darkness with darkness. It didn't work. I breathed roughly and tried to find my happy place. Why did I ever start talking about that in the first place? Why did I even come here? Why didn't I just stay in my bed all damn day? And why can't I find my God damn happy place?

"Sage! Hey, look at me. It's okay."

Oh. That was why. I dropped my hands to my lap, lifting my head and finding my happy place.

"Hey." He grinned like I didn't have tears stuck to my cheeks. "There you are."

A paper towel was thrust at my face. Ace looked mildly uncomfortable and massively helpless. "Are you okay, phantom girl?"

"Dude, really?" Wren gawked at him. "A paper towel? That is scratchy! Go get her a Kleenex!"

"You don't have Kleenex!"

"Lilah does in her room."

Ace shook his head. "No way, man. I can't go in there."

"We are grown ass men, Ace! She won't cut off your hair in your sleep if you go into her room."

"It's fine. This works great." I took the paper towel and wiped under my eyes. "I'm sorry."

"For what?"

"Whatever the hell that was." I shrugged. "That's what I meant about not being strong. I can't talk about anything with anyone other than Julie. She thinks it'll help my family to know some details but I don't. Telling them would only hurt me by remembering and hurt them by hearing it. So, why do it? It's just a fucked up cycle of pain and bullshit memories."

"You don't think telling them would ease your burden?"

"Hell no." I looked at Wren as if he just guzzled crazy juice. "I would be on edge the whole time, worried about their reaction and what they'll think of me. The thought of reliving any of my past for them makes me wanna hurl. But Julie thinks I need to confide in someone that isn't her. So whatever. I don't know how to help myself."

"Who is Julie, Sunshine? A friend?"

"My counselor."

"Like a therapist?" Ace blurted, earning another growl from Wren.

"Exactly like a therapist." I smiled. "I was pretty adamant I didn't need a therapist when I first went to her. She told me to think of herself as a counselor. Like we had in school when we got bullied. It sounds dumb now but it helped."

"Nothing that helped you is dumb, Sage." The intensity in Wren's voice could not be missed.

"And think of this, phantom girl. You just shared some stuff with us and now we can go play some Super Smash to make you feel better. That counts for something, right?"

The fact that I was even here, talking this much and conversing with people who were virtually strangers, didn't just count for something. It counted for a full list of things. I fully expected Julie to fall from her chair when I told her everything I'd revealed to Wren and Ace. It didn't seem like much, but telling them about my insecurities and worries about my family was like dropping a can of beans on the floor. Everything spilled out. My problem was, I had a lot of cans to drop before I was ever in a place where I could consider my past and not go into shut down mode.

This moment wasn't that moment. Julie would say this moment was a moment for me to be proud of what I've done and try for more another time.

I slid off my stool and ended the conversation by walking into the living room area. I was gonna celebrate my moment with my human sunshine, his best friend, and Princess Peach.

SHE WAS all sorts of giddy. She could do absolutely nothing to contain her smile, and I knew she was only seconds from squealing in delight. I wasn't sure how old Julie was. Older than me by at least ten years, but she often acted like a sixteen-year-old when it came to me and my so-called successes.

"So, you and Wren have been hanging out?" She did her best to act neutral but it was such a failed effort. She was losing so bad, I didn't even want to give her a participation ribbon.

"Yeah, every Monday and Wednesday for the last two weeks."

"And why am I just now hearing about it?"

I shrugged. "Didn't want to tell you."

"You didn't want to tell me or you hesitated because you thought something would go wrong and it would be taken from you?"

Damn.

"Why do you have to ask all the hard questions, huh?" I laid down on my back, gazing at the ceiling with my sunshine pillow on my chest. "Can't you just keep freaking out like a mom whose kid just made their first friend?"

"I'm not freaking out, Sage. I'm expressing excitement. I'm obscenely proud of you."

"You are?" I turned my head, shifting my gaze from the ceiling to her. She set her notepad on her lap and crossed her legs. She looked fabulous, as always, in a pair of navy blue high-waisted trousers that flared at her ankles and a tight white blouse. "Why?"

"Because you've been reluctant to get close to anyone since you've been home. And you've not only found a friend, you've found someone you've slowly been opening up to."

"I wouldn't say I'm opening up to him. We play video games and Monopoly. We don't braid each other's hair and tell secrets."

"Yet, you've told Wren more than you've ever told anybody."

I shrugged and refused to make my time with Wren a big deal. I wasn't ready to admit to her or even myself that the time I've spent with Wren *is* a big deal. Admitting it means analyzing it and asking all the questions that require all the hard answers. I was not ready to do that. What happens when a question led me to an answer I did not like?

"Do your parents know you've been visiting Wren?"

"Nope. The American Girl Doll method works wonders."

She sighed. "Sage, I do not agree with that."

"I do not care. It works for me right now. I don't want them to ask questions or worry them. I'll tell them eventually."

"And what will you tell them?"

I shrugged. "Don't know."

"You seem reluctant to talk about Wren."

"Gee. Good observation."

"And now you're being defensive."

"Julie, I just don't want to discuss him."

"Why?"

She was not going to let this go. No matter how much I avoided it. No matter how good I'd become at deflecting, she would keep pressing, going around in circles until I cracked.

It wasn't something she normally did. And that told me this was already a big deal.

"Because I enjoy spending time with Wren. And then you're gonna start in with "why this" and "why that" and then I'll overthink everything and come up with some scenarios where I'm crazy and can no longer be his friend."

She nodded, shifting in her seat. It angered me that she seemed to read me impeccably though I would never know what her current expression meant. "How about I just ask you one question that I believe is important?"

"Sure, I guess."

"What is it that made you keep going back?"

"What do you mean?"

"What is it about Wren that has you continuously going to visit him? And don't say to give him gifts because from what you told me, you haven't given him a gift since the painting you made for him. So why, Sage? Why keep going back?"

"I don't know."

"You do know."

I huffed and flopped to my side, my head angled funny while it rested on the armrest and I glared at her. "Why do you have to ruin things by making me think?"

She chuckled. "Sage, this is my job. And I'm not trying to diminish the importance of what Wren has become for you, I just think it's important you consider why you keep going back."

"I keep going back because I like to be around him. He's my friend."

"Yes, but why? Is it simply because Wren is part of an organization that saved you? Is it really Wren you like being around? Or is it the idea of him?"

I frowned. "What do you mean?"

"Do you actually enjoy being around Wren? Or is it Specter you enjoy being around? Do you like the qualities Wren has? Or are you obsessed with the hero that Specter is? Because here's a tough one to hear, Wren is a criminal. Whether he rescued you or not, he did it in an illegal manner. If Wren were to ever be caught, he's facing decades in prison. He could possibly go to the same prison Kade is being held in. Both criminals. I'm asking you, what makes Wren different?"

Anger surged into my body so fast, I sat up and hurled her pillow across the room. The distinct feeling of whiplash rattled my body as I glared at her, pointing a finger in her direction. "Do not ever compare Wren to Kade again. They are not even on the same wavelength!"

"What makes them different, Sage? You think Wren is the hero and Kade is the villain?"

"And what? I'm the damsel in distress? This isn't a fairytale, Julie! Wren isn't a knight in shining armor and Kade isn't an evil witch with an apple. This is real life and they are real people. They have qualities and personality traits. Kade woke up every morning and did coke for breakfast before rolling over and smacking me awake. He took whatever he wanted and used people as targets at a gun range. He sold humans on the internet, and you think he belongs in the same category as a man who wears Fred Flintstone pajamas and goes to Sunday brunch with his parents? Kade was a sociopath, and Wren stops people like him. Wren and his team risk themselves to expose monsters. They are not the same. I feel warm when I'm around Wren. I don't have to censor everything I say. My heart doesn't drop into the pits of my stomach when he walks into a room. I don't break out into a cold sweat and throw my hands over my head when he steps towards me. He doesn't pull my hair or force shit up my nose. I'm not afraid to walk by a staircase when he's around. He doesn't have a gun or bruises on his fists. And when he needs something from his friends, it's a recommendation for a new video game. It is not a hit on someone who supposedly screwed him over or ten tons of vodka. And if you ever even think about comparing my best friend to the monster that killed Trish and destroyed my life again, I will walk right out of here and never come back."

I gasped, heaving air into my lungs. I wiped at my face, confused by the moisture on my cheeks and yanked a Kleenex from the box on the table in front of me. I can't believe, after everything I've told her, she'd still have the audacity to put Wren on a list of criminals. Sure, what he did wasn't legal but a lot of good people stood on the border of right and wrong for the sake of the greater good. Wren walked a tightrope every night, falling far into the depths of what society considered wrong all because he wanted to eliminate evil. He had courage and heart and a big pair of balls to be able to put himself on the line, knowing he could get locked away and never come back. What Kade had was a lump of ice where his heart should be, and though my mind often malfunctioned, and there were moments I questioned my sanity, I knew Wren would never turn into the man Kade is.

"And there it is."

I looked up to find Julie's small smile. Her hands were resting in her lap. She regarded me with something in her face I thought was pride. But that couldn't be right. "I'm sorry?"

"Sage, I would never, under any circumstances, consider Wren and Kade to be the same. I know why they aren't the same. I wanted to know if *you* did."

"You bitch!" My eyes flew from my head the moment the term flew from my mouth. I contemplated shoving a ton of Kleenex in my mouth to censor whatever else might come out. "I mean... that was super uncool of you. Saying that to produce a reaction."

Julie chuckled at my outburst. "It was uncool of me, but it was necessary. Because it just gave away so much."

"Uhm, it did?"

"Sage, you called Wren your best friend."

"He is, I guess."

"And what is a best friend? If you looked up the term in a dictionary, what do you think you'd find?"

Julie's exercises got more bizarre every time I came to visit her. Each time I left, my mind was reeling more than the time before. Still, I couldn't deny their results. "Uhm, I guess it's a person you're closest to. Someone who knows all your favorite things. Someone who knows when to push you and when you've had enough. Someone who makes you smile when you thought you never would again. Someone who keeps your secrets and covers for you when you mess up. And maybe..." I paused and cleared my throat, stalling for time while I thought up the right words that described what hanging out with Wren was to me. "Maybe a best friend is someone who likes the pieces of yourself that you find to be broken."

"You think you're broken?"

Why she said it as if it were a question was beyond me. She knew that's what I thought of myself. It wasn't a new revelation. "Wren doesn't make me feel like a freak for refusing to eat anything that doesn't come from my mother. He goes out of his way to make sure our bodies don't brush because he just somehow figured out that I can't stand when people touch me. That isn't normal. That indicates something is wrong with me and Wren doesn't care."

"Your parents don't care." She pointed out, forcing my eyes to roll. "So why slowly open up to Wren and not them?"

"Because Wren doesn't make sad eyes at me when I dodge a hug or refuse to go to a restaurant. He didn't know the old Sage. He isn't comparing what I used to be to who I am now. I'm not constantly trying to mend the two together to spare his feelings. I can just... exist. In whatever way I please without the fear of something going bad or somebody breaking down into tears. There is no pressure when I'm around Wren."

"Exist?"

"Huh?"

"You said you were free to exist. Why use that word and not live?"

"Because who only lives on Monday and Wednesday evenings for a few hours?"

"You're saying you feel like you're living your life when Wren is around?"

"I'm saying it's easier to feel comfortable. To relax. And not just because he's Specter. That is what brought us together, but that's not why I stayed. I stayed because Wren gives me hope that I'm capable of being a fully functioning person who has fun and doesn't think about what happened to me. It may only be a few hours-"

"A few hours is a huge success, Sage. Do not undermine how far you've come with the rest of that sentence. You went from never leaving your room to being able to leave your home alone and spend time with a person you haven't known your whole life. Be proud."

"But, I-"

"Stop." She held up a hand and silenced me with a pointed gaze. "No talking for sixty seconds. Close your eyes and be proud. Right now."

I rolled my eyes before I closed them and attempted to remember what pride felt like. I guess if I was gonna be proud of myself, now was as good a time as any. I was able to knock on Wren's door without shaking now. And Ace's loud voice had stopped making me flinch. I didn't panic when Lilah tried to shake my hand the first time I met her. I simply stepped back and smiled politely. I wasn't gonna fool myself into thinking that Wren was some magic potion that would make the nightmares go away. I still had them, frequently, and I wanted to run away screaming at the thought of somebody touching me. I was still an absolute mess who had no idea what her future held and couldn't handle the thoughts of what her weakness had done to her family, but for two nights a week, there was a chance to forget. And somehow, I trained my brain to forget when Wren was around. Because somewhere along the line, it trusted Wren to watch over me.

I peeled open one of my eyes, finding her writing fiercely on her notepad. "I think that was sixty seconds."

"It was." She set down her pen. "One more question about Wren."

"You are relentless, Julie. Honestly. You should write a book filled with hard questions people don't want to answer. I feel like I'm on the world's shittiest first date. And my first ever date I was kidnapped, so that's saying something."

She chose to say nothing about the joke I'd made and simply closed her eyes. I pictured her counting to ten in her head and trying to figure out if I'd been a cynic forever or if that was a product of spending sixteen months sleeping next to a monster.

"How come you only see Wren two nights a week?"

Oh. We're back to asking questions now. "What?"

"You told me earlier that Wren has invited you to see where he works. He's invited you to come watch movies on a Sunday evening. You've declined those invites. You won't even accept his phone number. Why? If Wren makes you feel like you're living, if he's your best friend, why keep him contained to four hours a week?"

The crack in my heart that was there just for Trish had begun to ache immensely. The pieces that were dedicated to her were barely holding on as I lifted my head and pointed my watery gaze at Julie. "Because the last best friend I had was killed."

———

There was a place in this cemetery. It was an empty place between Trish and a man named Winston who was ninety-four when he passed away. I googled his name during one of the long afternoons I'd spent here and found out he was a war veteran who only had one leg when he died. He lost it after an infection had spread. According to his obituary, he wore a cowboy hat everywhere and spent decades after the war dressing up as a clown and making balloon animals at children's birthday parties. He had thirty-seven grandchildren and great-grandchildren and a wife named Erma. Those were all the facts I knew about Winston, but there was something about that five-hundred-word obituary that made me believe Winston was the same type of badass Trish was. It was a force that only came out when necessary. A force that was hidden beneath loads and loads of kindness.

I couldn't think of a better person for Trish to spend an eternity next to than a person who embodied everything she was. Except, she wasn't right next to him. There was a plot right between them. It was empty. There were no flowers, no gifts, no photos, or letters of goodbye. There was a long, rectangular spot in the grass that was lighter than the rest. It told me there was a tombstone there that had since been drug away.

It took one trip here and the look on Brett's face for me to realize that spot had been for me, and the tombstone that was drug away had my name engraved on it. I don't know where it is now. I don't know if an empty coffin is still lying beneath me or if they dug it up months ago. Those were questions I did not want to know the answer to. What I did want to know is why my parents chose to bury me between Trish and old man Winston. Don't get me wrong, I liked that my place was between two beautiful souls who had the strength of a warrior, but I often wondered why I wasn't somewhere they could all be buried with me. It was a morbid thought, really. Wondering why I would be in the dirt on the top of the hill while they would be in the dirt at the bottom. Maybe it's because where our bodies lay wasn't what mattered. It's where they went afterward.

I laid down on top of the place that was mine and peered over at Trish. "What's it like up there?" She didn't answer me, but I was so easily able to envision the smile that crept up her cheeks. "Did you meet Winston? He's a badass, isn't he? I should bring him a crayon."

I pictured her laughing, her eyes sparkling the way they did every time she laughed so hard she snorted. Trish always laughed at the things I'd said when I'd intended for them to be serious. After a while, I started to believe Trish had a hard time being serious. She was full of fun. No reservations. No hesitations. If she wanted something, then she would go and get it. I'd always loved that about her personality.

Until one day, I'd come to resent it.

"I was mad at you once." I told her, wiping the tears before they fell down my cheeks. "I spent so long being mad at you for you just being you. And then I started to get mad at myself for having the audacity to be mad at you. I was just this ball of anger. I was mad at you, me, Kade, the men who hurt you and took me. I was mad at the police for never finding me. I was mad at whoever the hell created drugs and weapons. I was such a terror, Trish. I was pissed twenty-four seven. And let me tell you, pissed off and broken is a toxic combination."

She regarded me with sympathy and reached out to stroke my cheek, wiping away the drops of moisture.

"I kept thinking that if you weren't in such a hurry to get a damn tattoo, we would have never gone inside that bank. We would have told our parents where we were going. They would have tried to stop us. But, no. You wanted it to be spontaneous. Keep it a secret from your parents and make sure you withdrew cash instead of using your card so they couldn't track down the transaction from your statement. You were smart, Trish. That's what I thought. I thought you were being smart, but then I had to watch you die and I just wanted to scream at you for being so damn stupid."

She opened her mouth to say something. I shook my head, cutting her off with a sniffle before she started to apologize. It wasn't fair of me to call her spontaneity stupid. Teenagers get random tattoos all the time. They sneak out. They lie to their parents. They go overboard trying to be secretive. They spent their time so it was worth their life, and that's all Trish wanted to do. It wasn't stupidity that got her killed. It was cruelty.

My mind went back and forth, reminding myself of the difference between the two when Kade had tried so hard to convince me it was the former.

"Kade was a mind bender, Trish. He twisted my thoughts, confused me, manipulated me, used me. It's taken months and months with Julie to undo some of what he has done. And I thought I'd gotten over it, ya know? I was able to believe it wasn't me that got you killed. And then today, I blew it. I made one comment and it opened such a mass of floodgates, I took off running out of her office." I rolled to my back and gazed at the sun that warmed everybody except me. "I know you've been watching me. So I don't have to tell you about Wren. But what I should tell you is to brace yourself for how disappointed you'll be in me when you hear about the way I insinuated I'd get Wren killed if I continued to be his friend."

I didn't realize the underlying message beneath my words until it was already out in the open. The look on Julie's face was one of heartbreak and I took off running, crying fierce tears of frustration and overpowering sadness. I knew it wasn't true. My mind worked itself to the point of smoke flowing out of my ears before I believed I was not the reason her blood filled that hallway. For the first little while

I was with Kade, I reminded him every chance I got that he was a monster. I spat nasty words at him. Hurled venomous looks and did what I could to get him to kill me.

He must've known living would be worse. That's the only logical reason I can come up with as to why he kept me alive after I repeatedly reminded him how much I'd wished for him to be torn apart. He listened to me with a smirk on his face, even going as far as to say he was sorry for her death and starting an event that changed the person I was forever.

The more time I spent with him, the more he began to convince me it was my actions and my lack of responsibility that had gotten her killed. I knew it wasn't true on some level, but if you put something on repeat in someone's brain, it'll start to reprogram. Between Kade and all of Julie's help, my brain had been picked apart and put back together time and time again.

I knew it wouldn't ever function normally again.

"There were so many what ifs, Trish. What if I did this, what if I did that, what if we stayed in the bathroom, what if I got killed and not you. My mind was swimming in them, and I thought I'd moved past that giant bump until that sentence came out of my mouth."

I may not have liked pretending, but I didn't enjoy over-analyzing either. I didn't second guess my reluctance to spent additional time with my new friend. I went with it and thought nothing of it until I vomited the painful truth all over myself.

I didn't get close to my parents because I didn't want to hurt them.

I kept my distance from Wren because I didn't want to kill him.

I was a walking bomb. Due to explode at any time and

anyone in my path would be part of the wreckage. Danger followed me everywhere and there was a gnawing feeling in my bones that told me I'd led it directly to Wren the same as I did to Trish.

"I'm sorry, Trish." I whispered. "It should've been me. My spot should not be empty." I rolled over to find her angry face. Her red lips were pursed and there was a wrinkle hidden behind her bangs. I knew she was pissed at me, trying to tell me it was not my fault and I had to make peace with it. I couldn't start the process of convincing myself otherwise all over again only to have a setback for the second time.

Julie called it Survivor's Guilt. I called it overwhelming.

I studied Trish's face, noting the way tears were streaming down her cheeks. Tears that were for me. In the time it took me to blink, she held out a cyan crayon and tried to get me to take it. I shook my head, refusing to accept that I was deserving. I had badass moments, sure. But I did not lead a badass life.

She surged forward, attempting to force the crayon into my hand before giving up and thrusting it at my chest. I watched as her hand went through me and she dropped the crayon into my chest, over my heart where the crack that lay for her was.

"Stop punishing yourself for something you did not do."

I sat up quickly, looking frantically around the cemetery. Her voice was loud. It was *right there*. So close I could almost feel her breath on my neck.

"Let yourself have a life, Sage. I'm happy with the one I had. Get to a place where you're happy with the one you have too."

I wasn't sure how to do that, or if it was even possible. I turned around to ask her how she'd been happy with the way she died and leaving so soon, but she was gone. And it was just me, sitting in a spot that was supposed to belong to me but didn't anymore. My mind raced to keep up with all the thoughts and doubts that were swarming it.

Was I using Trish's death as an excuse to stop myself from making another friend?

Yes, I was.

But I had no idea how to stop.

Staring into a man's crotch was not what was on my agenda for the day. But here I was, peering into Craig's trouser covered crotch as he hovered over me, blocking any light and ensuring I couldn't see a damn thing. A distinct feeling I recognized as discomfort swept over me.

"Find anything?" He shouted much louder than what was necessary. Sure, he was tall and I was lying on my back underneath his wide L-shaped desk, but we were still alone and it's not like there was any background noise.

"Actually, Craig." I started, clearing my throat. "It'd be helpful if you backed up. You're blocking the light."

"Oh!" He chuckled at himself, giving me the light back and removing his crotch from my line of sight.

I peered upward at the power strip that was stuck to the bottom of Craig's desk. When I spotted the problem, I repressed the urge to howl and yank out all my hair. I closed my eyes and took a calming breath before reaching upward and flipping the switch.

"Hey!" I couldn't see Craig, but I was fairly certain he

was bouncing around in glee. "You got it! Good work! You're a genius."

I was not a genius. I was a human who knew how to work a power strip.

I wiggled my way out from the under the desk and stood up, smoothing out my shirt. Today, my polo was bright orange and looked absolutely ridiculous with my hair color, but there was nothing in me that cared. I liked bright colors. Even more so after Sage compared me to a sunflower and left a bundle of them outside my door. Any other day, I wouldn't have been keen on getting listed under the same category as a sunflower. But ever since Sage said it weeks ago, I felt as if I was being compared to the King of England. I felt powerful. Noticed. Important.

Like the tallest God damn sunflower that ever grew.

"Did you find the problem?" Craig rubbed at the back of his neck. He appeared nervous, as if he thought he blew something up or pulled the pin on a grenade.

Not today, Craig.

"Yeah. The power strip got turned off."

"Oh, did you fix it?"

"Uhm, yeah. I just turned it back on."

"Cool." He bobbed his head a couple of times. "How'd you do it?"

I peered over my shoulder, checking to see if somebody else had entered the room while I was stuffed under the table. There's no way that question was directed at me.

Except it was

"I, uh, flipped the switch, Craig."

"Oh." He hit himself on the forehead with the heel of his hand. "Duh. That makes sense. Sorry. I'm not great with all this techy stuff."

I wouldn't consider flipping a switch "techy stuff" but I

kept my trap closed. To me, Craig came across like a slice of old, wheat bread. Bland. Dry. And constantly overcompensating for the fact that he was everybody's second choice. My big, nerd brain couldn't figure how he had become a third owner of a million-dollar company.

But there was obviously something cooking inside his brain. And somewhere, to someone, he was a big, fluffy slice of French bread right out of the oven.

I just wasn't that someone.

"It's not a problem, Craig. Easy fix."

"Great. Thanks a lot, Wren. I'm sure I sound like a moron not knowing how to work the gizmo that's under my desk."

"Nah. It's fine. It's my job to do this anyway." I let out a dry laugh. "Better than paying me to watch ice melt, ya know?"

It was supposed to be a joke. It was such an awful one. I laughed alone for a second until I realized he had no fucking clue what I was referring to. I snapped my mouth shut and gazed at his cocked head and polite smile.

"You're an interesting guy, Wren." He held out his hand, waiting for me to shake it. "You're a great person to have on our team. Lilah's lucky to have such a great brother."

And there it was. The reason why Craig had so many clients. The man may have been wheat bread, but he was the wheat bread everybody pulled off the shelf first. When people needed help finding a job, they came to him. Not because he had connections. Or a successful company. Or two kick-ass business partners.

It was because he was a people person. His ability to empathize and understand a person's situation no matter how tough or bizarre was uncanny. It was admirable.

Twenty minutes in a meeting with him and clients left feeling like they'd made a new best friend to bring home to their mother.

People trusted him because he anticipated how they thought or felt about a situation before they even processed it themselves.

Maybe that's why he couldn't handle the knowledge on how to turn on a power strip. His hairless head was stuffed full of other's emotions and thoughts. Not to mention the whole own a business thing. Craig was an odd duck, but I was certain it was all part of his charm.

"Thanks, Craig. I keep trying to tell Lilah that, but she won't listen. Maybe you could slip her a post-it or something."

This time, he laughed. "You don't give your sister enough credit. She's sweet like a kitten."

If there was a gulp of Diet Coke in my mouth, I would've spat it all over him in complete astonishment. "A kitten?! Man, your interns about piss their pants when she comes within five feet of them."

"Oh, it's all for show. Like a good cop bad cop thing. She's the bad cop who comes in with a steel fist and heart of ice, making sure everybody's doing what they're supposed to in the quickest and most efficient way possible. And then Kate and I go around, ensuring everybody feels like a million bucks after they just accomplished what felt like the hardest six hours of their life. There's nothing like making somebody feel good after busting their chops."

That sentence had my brain spinning wildly and wondering what Ace would have thought of it if he were here. Lilah and Craig's plan seemed well thought out, really. The best way to make somebody feel appreciated was to reward them for a job they were already getting paid to do. I'd always thought the random cupcakes, company lunches, and doughnut days were overkill. Why give someone a treat when you've already given them a paycheck?

But with how successful SevTeck has become in less than two years, I'd say there's a method to their madness.

"Well, have a good one, Craig." I lifted my hand in a small wave and shuffled to the door. "Let me know if you need anything else."

"Thanks a lot, Wren. And call me Hal."

"Why?" It was the first time in two years I'd actually asked the question. After all this time wondering and making up my own scenarios, I could have just used my words like an adult and asked. That wasn't normally me. I kept to myself, especially when I was in this building, but hanging out with Sage had me feeling more powerful and confident than ever.

So, I asked without the worry I'll offend him or get decked in the face. "Is Hal your middle name?"

"No." He chuckled. "Hal is my father's name." He sat down in his desk chair and crossed his legs. "My father was twenty-one when he opened up his own business. It wasn't much. Just a small printing company whose only job was printing the local newspaper, but the small little shop on the fourth floor of a run-down building was his pride and joy. I used to go to work with him when I was a kid and swore up and down I'd take over the company one day. I told him I'd have a big, brown leather chair. Just like he did."

It was hard not to smile at the pride projecting off Craig's face or the way he rubbed the arms of the big, brown leather chair he was perched in. "What happened? Why didn't you take it over?"

"The business went under when I was seventeen. The

town I grew up in was small and a lot of the neighborhood just stopped buying newspapers. When the paper shut down, so did we. My dad got sick a few years afterward, died a few years after that, and attempting to reopen just never felt like the right move."

"I'm sorry, Craig." I was the worst type of human. Literal trash. Here I was, making fun of Craig's weird tendency to ask people to call him by a random name when the name wasn't random at all. It belonged to his father. His dead father.

Trash. That's what I was.

"It's okay, Wren." He fiddled with the watch on his wrist. "My father was a big inspiration to me. He's the sole reason I agreed to join in when Lilah approached me with the idea for this company. Truth is, I had no interest in recruiting. I just wanted to make my dad proud. I thought I was gonna fuck it up, so I started asking people to call me Hal as a reminder of why I was doing this. And to take it seriously."

Wow.

"Well, if it's any consolation, I think you're doing a fantastic job. Your employees love you. I don't see how your father couldn't be proud of all this."

"Thank you, Wren. I appreciate your kindness." He flashed me a smile that was nothing but genuine, and I wondered if that came from his father as well. "And thank you for fixing my mess up."

"It was nothing, Hal. Enjoy the rest of your afternoon."

I was barely out of his office when he turned back to his desk and started flipping through packets of paper. I shuffled back to my own office, mulling over Craig's past and what I'd just learned. I was exactly like him.

Wasn't I?

I spent the better part of a year judging him for living a life with two names when I'd been doing exactly the same thing. Nobody outside the internet world referred to me as Specter, but I'd still created an alias based on a dream I'd had for myself. I chose a name based on a hero I longed to be. Craig found his own hero, and after that story, I'd say his hero was way cooler than mine.

SAGE

I wasn't sure what was so fascinating about the inside of a paper cup, but Wren's gaze was focused so intently on what was floating inside the dark liquid, my curiosity heightened as I took a tentative step inside his office.

I knocked lightly on the doorframe, announcing my presence. His head rolled upward, eyes null and face blank behind his glasses. He looked more bored and vacant than I'd ever seen before.

And then he scanned me standing in the doorway and seemed to jolt alive. A surge of energy overtook him as if somebody had just flipped the power switch.

"Sage, hi!" His eyes started to sparkle as he flew from a massive computer chair that was nothing like the yellow one I knew was perched in front of his desk at Circuit. His lips curled into a smile, making his freckles dance as he approached me.

"Hi, Wren."

"How are you?"

He looked stunned that I was standing here but was too polite to say so. After more than a month of dodging any invitation to go anywhere or do anything outside video games and his apartment, here I was. I'd be shocked too.

"I'm doing good."

"Great. I'm happy to hear that."

He rocked on his feet, grinning up at me.

Why are you here?

The question was on the tip of his tongue but I knew he'd never ask because he just didn't care. The details didn't matter to Wren. If I offered them up, he'd take them and tuck them some place special, knowing how hard it was for me to spare them. But he never asked. Because Wren knew getting me to talk was like pulling teeth sometimes. It was easier when he was around, but I still did not enjoy it.

"So this is your office, huh?" I took a step inside, peering around the small space. It was basically made up of just a large, basic wooden desk with a monitor on top and a paper cup next to a keyboard. There was a vast window on the wall behind his desk, but other than that, it was pretty sparse. There were no colors or paintings or pictures like there were in Julie's office. There was nothing that said it was Wren's. It could have been anybody's. Actually, it could've been vacant. Aside from the cup and the messenger bag beneath his desk, there were no signs of life.

"Yep. This is where I spend my days before heading off to fight crime with my cyan crayon and yellow chair."

"Well, even Clark Kent had a day job."

He went silent for a long moment, gazing at me like I was sweating glitter. It was after I'd cleared my throat that he came out of whatever state he was in. "True, but his is cooler."

"I don't know." I shrugged and walked across his office, peering down at the city below us. There were people everywhere, likely oblivious to all the darkness our world held, while the man behind me worked to remove it. "I think you're a million times cooler than him. I mean, Superman isn't real. But you are, ya know? You actually use your day job to help cover up what you do at night. You may not possess super strength or spend your nights flying around in a unitard, but you're fighting crime all the same."

"Sometimes it's easy to forget why we do what we do." He admitted, his gaze mirroring mine. "But ever since you came along, I've never forgotten."

"So, I'm like your living, breathing success story, huh?" I teased. "Do you have posters of me all over Circuit?"

"Something like that." His smile crept up his lips. "Cruz reminds us all the time that what we do is admirable and good and brave and all that. But it wasn't until you and your gifts that we were punched in the face with the undeniable truth that we are literally saving people's lives."

His smile deflated as he kept his gaze focused on the cars speeding below us. I was sure he wasn't actually seeing them, and just stuck in his own head. "Wren? Are you okay?"

He bobbed his head and spun around, leaning against the window. He crossed his arms over his chest and propped one foot against the wall. "I'm just having a strange day."

"Oh. Do you want to talk about it?" It was an odd change, being the listener instead of the talker, but I liked the reversal. I was afraid Wren felt like a trashcan. I kept dumping all my problems on top of him like piles and piles of garbage, and I often wondered who he dumped his problems on. I was more than willing to be his human trashcan. I wanted to be someone he unloaded on. I wanted to be something for him other than the phantom girl he'd saved.

"Do you know that guy Craig?"

"The one who also calls himself Hal?"

"That's him." He looked down at the floor. "I learned today he calls himself Hal because it's his dead father's name, and he's been working his ass off to be half the businessman his father was. I mean, how fucking incredible is that? There I was, walking around like a giant orange dick, judging him like some nutso when all he'd been doing was trying to remind himself why he was doing what he was."

I couldn't see his face, but I knew by the way his voice cracked he was struggling majorly with the way he'd judged Hal Craig. "Wren, everybody judges people. Even people who claim they don't judge people, judge people. It's human nature. The fact you're able to admit you judged Hal Craig wrongfully says enough about you."

"Does it though? I mean, I'm exactly like him. Except, Craig doesn't hide the second part of him. He doesn't hide who he is or who he wants to be. I hide who I am all the time to protect myself."

"Craig asking people to call him Hal and you being Specter is not the same."

"Isn't it?"

"No. Not at all. To me, it sounds like Craig is doing it to better himself. Which is why he had no problem admitting it and embracing it. You're hiding Specter because you don't necessarily do it to better yourself. You do it to help others. And if you got caught, you wouldn't be able to do that anymore."

He nodded his head, seeming to absorb my words. I wasn't sure if I was saying anything that was actually helpful or just putting words together to form a sentence. But when he lifted his head to look at me, his smile told me at least a few of those words had been right.

"Ya know, I used to think that saving you was the

greatest thing that could ever happen." He cleared his throat and wrung his hands together but did not drop his steady gaze. "But then I got to know you, and I've decided that whatever friendship that formed between us is the greatest thing that has ever happened. I guess I just... I guess I wish Wren was as cool as Specter, ya know? That it's the cool hacker man everybody sees and spends time with. Craig flashes both parts of him proudly, and the part I flash is the one that wears briefs with cartoons on them, eats Lucky Charms for dinner, and watches ice melt."

I broke.

I broke watching him deflate like an old balloon. He went slack against the wall, his shoulders hunched forward and head angled downward. It was a miracle his glasses didn't slide down his nose. I longed to give him some sort of comfort. Form the right words to tell him that Specter was only a piece of Wren. That the man who spends hours changing the world for the better could have never existed without the dorky one who wears polos every day and works for his sister.

They were one and in the same. They worked together to make all he is. A beautiful man with a soul that shines bright, overpowering a cloud of darkness. My mind spun, letters flying in circles around my head as the right words formed.

"I told Julie you're my best friend." I blurted, keeping my eyes locked on him so I didn't get lost in all the truths that are eager to flow out of me. "I told her you're my best friend, and she started asking these hard, annoying questions about why I'd refused to hang out with you unless it was during a specific time frame. I'd blurted out I was afraid you were gonna die. Because, ya know, the last best friend I had died right in front of me. And how fucking ridiculous would it be if I got the man who saved my life killed?" The look on his face reminded me of worn out concrete. There were cracks forming everywhere, but it still longed to be sturdy. "That was almost two weeks ago, and I've been mulling over it in my head, trying to tell myself it wasn't my fault somebody shot Trish, and that if I ever wanted to walk down the street with you, it was super unlikely you'd get shot. But I just... I couldn't do it, Wren. I do not want to be the reason you get hurt. But then today, I was with Julie and she'd mentioned if I didn't go into that bank with Trish that day, and everything would've worked out like it was supposed to, I would've regretted it. I would've regretted not being there." It was a miracle I was still on my feet by the way my body started shaking. "And I think, with the bad shit I've had to see in life, I forget how much good there is too. Actually, I think there's more good than there is bad because there are people like you putting a stop to it. The darkness blinded me. It still does. And when the light cracks through, I just turn around and pretend I don't see it. It's easier that way." I forced a rough breath out of my chest. "I probably sound like I'm rambling, going off on a tangent, but I guess what I'm trying to say is... when my mind gets all heavy, you're my favorite place to go when I need to feel light again."

His breathing hitched. The world took a timeout and things started moving really slow. I focused on his low breaths and his steady eyes. "And I think it's unfair of me to restrict myself to feeling that way because I'm scared for you. Especially since you don't seem scared for yourself."

"I'm not scared, Sage. But I do understand why you are."

"I don't want to be scared anymore, Wren. And I think that's why I came here. Because I'm sick of being so damn scared all the time. And also maybe because counseling made me feel like I weigh ten tons."

"And I make you feel lighter?"

"Yeah. It's like... when my mind needs an escape, it always chooses to visit you. Not Specter. Wren."

He blew out a long breath, looking absolutely shook by all I'd revealed. "I've never been anything so important before." A lesser person would've run for the hills. But Wren? He took on that responsibility like he was born to be the person that made my life a bit easier to live.

"I think your day job and all your quirks are pretty fucking cool. I'm even really obsessed with this orange shirt you're wearing even though it looks ridiculous with your hair color."

A laugh wafted out of him. "Doesn't it? I wore it because I like feeling bright. Brings me closer to you, I guess." He frowned. "Oh, God. That sounded massively corny."

"And everything I just revealed didn't? I just admitted to you that you're my happy place."

"You really know how to make a man humble, Sunshine."

"There are a lot of different types of men, Wren. You were good before I came along."

"Can I tell you something?"

"Of course."

"Sometimes I worry you'll remember I'm a criminal and never school me in Super Smash again."

There are only so many things a girl can take. I thought I'd hit my max long ago, but when he said sentences like that, my chest just couldn't take the weight.

"I've never thought of you as a criminal. And like I told

Julie, I spent a long time around criminals. You are not one, okay?"

"I am though, Sage." He argued, frowning deeply. "You left one criminal only to get wrapped up in another. *God.* Sometimes it makes me feel sick. Like I'm prancing around, spending time with you, and acting like I won't end up in a federal prison. And I know what I do makes a difference. Hell, the difference is standing right in front of me, but technicalities say I'm a criminal."

"Fuck technicalities, Wren. You aren't a criminal. And I know that because I'm standing less than a foot away from you, and I'm not scared at all."

"But-"

Before I could even process the action, I surged forward. He jolted when I threw my arms around his neck and put my head on his shoulder. I struggled with the way my arms felt like they were breaking against his neck and held on tight.

He needs this.

My body started to crack, and I thought for sure I was going to disintegrate. My eyes started to burn, and I contemplated every life decision up until this moment. I suddenly couldn't remember why I was there, why I admitted all that stuff to him, or why I'd just broken a very important rule.

But all thought fled my mind when two arms wrapped around my back and held me against an unfamiliar chest. A hand fell gently to the back of my head and held me in a way that seemed to shield me from any danger that was happening around us. The cracks in my bones healed over as I melted into a touch I've never known.

He was the first person I let touch me in eight months.

And it didn't hurt at all.

I FLEW ACROSS THE APARTMENT, my socks sliding on the hardwood as I launched myself at the front door. My equilibrium started to shift as my balance went out of whack. My arms flailed like a wild bird, my heart going crazy beneath my ribs. I reached for the couch to steady myself and defeat the clumsiness that was attempting to ruin my night.

Not today, Satan. Not today.

I barely righted myself before I stumbled to the door and yanked it open.

"Hi, Sunshine!"

"Hi!" She bounced on her toes, her cheeks warming as she smiled up at me. "How are you?"

"He's clumsy!" Ace shouted behind me, body checking me out of the doorway. My grip tightened on my doorknob as I struggled not to fall over. "Hey, phantom girl. This smooth mother fucker over here about broke his legs rushing to open the door for you."

"My socks are slippery!" I defended, peering down at

them. I wiggled my toes, making Sage giggle. They were fuzzy ones with the real Specter on them.

"You could've been wearing non-slip boots and still taken a tumble. That run to the door was wild. Lucky Sage didn't see it or you would've embarrassed yourself."

"Actually, Ace, you seem to be taking care of that for me."

He flipped his hair behind his shoulder and flashed me a grin I knew very well. The grin that earned himself the name Mischief. "What are friends for, huh?"

"You guys are funny." Sage announced, politely waiting for Ace to move so she could get inside. "And I think your socks are cool, Wren. I love fuzzy socks. There's something about them that makes me feel all cozy."

"That's why he wears them." Ace quipped. "That and he likes living dangerously. Ya know, the entire apartment is hardwood flooring. Who knows what would happen?"

She grinned when Ace winked at her. "If that's all the danger Wren lives with, I fully approve. In fact, I feel like we should buy a pair and join in."

"I'm liking the way you think, phantom girl. I'm gonna get online and purchase you a pink pair with Princess Peach on them. Then we can move the couch and have races."

"Okay!" She bounced on her toes again, reminding me of a little firecracker. "I weigh the lightest. So, I'll win. Ha! Losers!"

Ace howled in laughter and turned to let her inside while she practically floated behind him toward the living room.

I'd never had the privilege of witnessing her so at ease. I could never be sure, but I thought maybe it had to do with the hug she'd gifted me with a few days ago. That hug tilted my world on its axis. Everything I thought I knew was challenged by that one moment. I'd thought a hug was just a hug. And then Sage put her arms around me, and I knew then how intimate two humans wrapped around one another could be. Studies say if a hug lasts longer than twenty seconds, it can act as a stress reliever. A prolonged hug apparently releases oxytocin, making a human feel all light and dopey and safe. And I was struck with alllll sorts of feels I wasn't familiar with. Our moment lasted so much longer than twenty seconds. We stood there for what felt like hours, holding onto each other until our breaths began to syncopate and I wondered if she'd fallen asleep.

That one hug.

A small act that people gave to someone they'd just met was a monumental step for Sage and I. The effect it left on me was profound. Sage didn't just refuse to touch anyone. She physically couldn't bear it. And the moment she chose to conquer that fear, she chose me. And it wasn't a simple brush. Or a fingertip to a fingertip. It was chest to chest. Cheek to cheek. We were so close, I could count her slow heartbeats as she breathed lightly in my ear.

I no longer felt like the low-grade criminal or loser computer nerd.

I was the one she'd felt was worthy, and I was the one that helped her put some of her pain to rest.

"So, what are we watching?" I shut the door and made my way over to Sage, plopping next to her on the couch while Ace settled in my ugly recliner.

"Why ask me?" Sage shrugged. "I'm the guest."

"Exactly why you pick." I said. "If you don't, Ace and I will pick The Fast and The Furious again."

"It seems very fitting you two would be obsessed with those movies."

"Why do you say that?"

"Well, because they fight crime by breaking laws. It's not exactly the same thing as Circuit, but the concept is similar. They destroy fancy cars and entire cities to stop bad guys."

I blinked.

"Woah." Ace blurted. "I think phantom girl just analyzed us. Girl, that therapy is working your brain."

"Counseling." I corrected, knowing there wasn't much of a difference, but it mattered to Sage.

"Counseling, right." He cleared his throat. "Anyway, that explains why I'm in love with Vin Diesel."

"Dude, get real." I snorted. "You're in love with Vin Diesel because he's got major muscles and can kick ass."

"Truth." He winked at me and settled in the chair. "Take your pick, phantom girl. If we don't have it, Wren will hack something and get it for you."

"How chivalrous of him." She chuckled. "I don't mind what we watch, but I'd prefer something light. No violence or horror."

Ace flew from the chair and hit the floor, pulling open the drawer in the entertainment stand that housed all the DVDs. "I got the perfect one. Standby for greatness."

"Do you guys always do movie nights on Sunday?" Sage asked. "How come you aren't at Circuit?"

"Cruz said Sunday is for Jesus!" Ace cracked, pushing the button that opens the DVD player.

"Oh." Sage blinked.

"He's kidding, Sunshine. Nobody is at Circuit on Sundays. It's Cruz's day off, and he doesn't like anyone there unless he is too."

"And let it be known, Lilah isn't here either." Ace grabbed the remote to the DVD player and plopped back in his chair. "Sunday is sex day."

I flipped him off. "My sister, man!! Gross!"

"Are Lilah and Cruz dating?" Sage wondered.

"I have no idea." It was the honest truth. "They dated officially for almost two years before breaking up. Nobody really knows any details about the relationship. Neither of them talk about it."

Sage frowned. "Oh. That's sad. I know what it's like not to be able to talk about things."

"I think it's more than that. Cruz is a bit of a mystery. Nobody really knows anything about him."

"Hell!" Ace shouted. "I don't even know his first name."

Sage gaped. "It's not Cruz? How can you work for a man when you don't know his whole name?!"

"Cruz is his last name, and I don't work for him. I work *with* him."

I rolled my eyes. No matter what Ace wanted to believe, we worked for Cruz. We may not get a weekly paycheck, but it was his organization and he reserved the right to kick us out at any time.

"Cruz is just Cruz." I shrugged. I made my peace with his lack of openness years ago. "What he does for others is enough to know the kind of person he is. Cruz'll put his ass on the line for all of us. I think his anonymity has a lot to do with that. Circuit is his whole life. He doesn't have a day job like the rest of us."

"Then where does he make his money?"

"Another mystery." Ace answered, fast forwarding through the previews. "Maybe we should analyze his tattoos. We might find a map to a hidden treasure."

Sage went still beside me. "He has tattoos?"

"Oh, yeah." Ace nodded, eyes glued to the TV, not at all conscious of Sage's mood change. "He's covered in them. Neck to his toes is all ink. Looks pretty hot if you ask me."

Sage swallowed so thickly, I heard her throat click. "Does he, uhm, have any under his eyes?"

Ace dropped the remote on his lap and flipped his gaze toward her. The enormity of the question she asked swallowed the whole room.

"No, Sage." I answered softly. "He doesn't. Despite being a mystery, Cruz is a really good guy. Lilah told me he's a total softie."

She nodded. "I guess it counts for something he's the leader of the badasses that saved me." She managed a smile. "And also if you trust him, I think I can too."

"Yo." Ace cleared his throat. "That was adorable as fuck."

"Man! Why did I even invite you?" I laughed, chucking a throw pillow at him. "Your chill level is below zero."

"I invited myself because you have zero hospitality skills."

"It baffles me you don't live together." Sage chuckled.

"We used to." I tell her. "When I was in college, we had a really shitty apartment in a complex full of partiers."

"Truth." Ace smacked his chest. "A brother could not hack into NASA with all that bass bumping. Zero respect in that place."

Sage looked between us with amusement all over her pretty face. "Is that when you guys got into hacking? College?"

"Oh no, darlin'." Ace chuckled. "Like a decade before that."

"I can't believe I've never thought to ask you about this before." She shook her head, looking entirely dumbstruck. She said nothing for a while as she seemed to sift through all her thoughts. I had never given much thought as to why she'd never asked. I had always assumed it didn't matter to her. What mattered is that we did it at all. "Wow. Okay. I need to hear this story! When did you start hacking and when did you meet mystery man Cruz?"

Ace smirked and pressed pause on the movie that hadn't even started.

I relaxed backward and propped my feet on the coffee table in front of me. "I got my first computer when I was twelve. It was a pretty nice desktop my parents gave me for Christmas. I wanted it to play video games, and it ended up being the computer Specter and Mischief were born on. Ace didn't get a computer until two years after me, but he basically lived at my house. So we shared mine."

"When did you decide you were going to hack into something? I mean, that's kind of an odd thought to have randomly. There had to have been a reason."

"Oh, there was." I looked to Ace, hoping he'd take over. It was his story to tell.

He sat up straighter and cleared his throat. "We wanted to find my dad."

Sage looked at him with sweet confusion on her face. "Your dad?"

"He left when I was seven, and my mother made an awful judgment call by telling me he went to jail. She refused to let me go visit him, so when Wren got a computer, we got it in our heads that we could hack into some sort of police database and find where he was at."

"Did you find him?"

"Negative, phantom girl. Turns out, my father is a real asshole and just left. He wasn't actually in jail. Learned that the hard way."

Wringing her hands together, Sage met Ace's gaze. "I'm really sorry you never found him, Ace. He missed out."

Ace looked away for a long moment, working hard to

school his gaze. I don't remember a lot of Ace's father. My tiny child brain couldn't summon up many memories from that time. Poor Ace remembers even the smallest of details. He spent almost a year going over details and moments of his life, trying to find some sort of clue as to why his dad left. He came up with nothing, and eventually, he was forced to stop looking out the window for his car and dropping letters with a name and no address in the post office drop off box.

And then I got a computer and the cycle began all over again.

"Thank you, Sage." When he turned back to meet her eyes, his haunted look was gone. He was Mischief again. "Anyway, it turned Wren and I into the badasses we are today."

"Well, I for one am thankful for that." She smiled a smile that was nothing but genuine. "I have to say it was pretty ballsy of you to start off by hacking into a police database."

"It was stupid." I corrected with a chuckle. "Ace and I thought of our master plan over bowls of superman ice cream and then asked my mom to take us to a bookstore. We spent one night reading Hacking For Dummies and thought we were pros."

"You didn't get caught though, right?"

"Of course we got caught!" Ace shouted. "We did everything wrong. We did nothing to attempt to protect ourselves. The damn police showed up on Wren's doorstep like two hours later."

Sage's eye went wide. "No."

"Oh, yes." I grinned at her stunned face. Of course, she could never picture us getting caught. "But we were young so we didn't get in any kind of trouble. Especially when Ace told them he was looking for his dad. My mom did take away my computer though."

Ace rubbed his hands together deviously. "But she didn't take away the book."

"So it was a book, huh?" She chuckled. "One book was the catalyst to Specter and Mischief?"

"Sort of." I nodded. "One of the book sections was all about ethical hacking. Using hacking for good, and that's something we both really resonated with. We basically just kept buying more and more books, researched what we could, and learned everything as we went. I think hacking can be an acquired skill if someone has the patience and passion for it, but I also think Ace and I just have talent."

"I'll say." She grinned. "Look at you now. Saving girls and what not."

I resisted the urge to bop her on the nose. "The more we did it, the faster we became at it. It pretty much took over our entire life. When I was in college, there was a group of people hacking into the school's network for petty shit like changing grades, canceling class, and setting off fire alarms. Stopping them was exactly the kind of thing Ace and I liked to do. We spent a whole night drinking Diet Coke and eating Red Vines beating them at their own game."

"And then Cruz showed up, banging on our door in the middle of the night." Ace popped his neck and propped his hands behind his neck. "That sweet, sweet man changed me forever."

The look Sage gave Ace was the same one he'd often get from people who didn't know him since birth. "I'm confused. Was Cruz part of the group that was changing grades?"

"No, Sunshine. Circuit was in the process of taking down that group when Ace and I got involved. Cruz tracked us down, because he's the best, and long story short, he offered us a place in Circuit."

It wasn't really that simple, but the details were boring. Ace and I underwent a background check that could've given the one the FBI runs on new candidates a run for its money. It was almost two months after meeting Cruz before he'd let us inside the underworld and offered us an official spot. It was two months of him hacking into our shit and vetting us before he decided he could trust us. During the entire process, I was equal parts terrified and excited. I thought I'd never feel that odd combination again.

And then I met Sage Maddison.

"You guys are so cool." Sage blurted. "Honestly, I wish I had something like that. Something to put all my energy into. A hobby to feel passionate about."

Her grin disappeared, her lips drooping downward and cheeks paling. Her hands started to wring together as her feet began to tap restlessly against the floor.

"Sage." I caught her attention, holding her gaze. "You okay?"

She nodded her head and swayed, her hands squeezing each other so tightly, her knuckles whitened. I heard her breathing hitch and sat up quickly. Desperate to provide her with the comfort it took to rid her mind of whatever just attacked it, I wrapped my arm around her shoulders. She flinched slightly, and I almost pulled back. She stopped me by relaxing into me. She wrapped one arm around my stomach and grabbed a fist full of my T-shirt as if she were begging me not to move a muscle while she decided how to proceed.

She nuzzled her head under my chin and rested her cheek on my chest. A low shudder rocked her body before she fully relaxed. Very slowly, I eased backward so I was propped against the cushions and she was propped against me. I put my nose to the top of her head and inhaled the scent I've come to long for. There wasn't anything super random about the way she smelled. She didn't smell like tangerines or coconuts or strawberries. No overpowering body spray or eye-watering body odor. Sage smelled *clean*. Her scent reminded me of the laundry detergent my mom used when I was a kid. It was a smell that comforted me and put me in a position to feel safe and vulnerable. Everything about Sage reminded me of home.

A loud, completely unnecessary and very fake, cough interrupted my moment. I lifted my head and glared at Ace. "Yeah?"

"Oh, I'm sorry!" He threw his hands in the air and flailed. "Was I just supposed to pretend that you and phantom girl aren't over there snuggling? Good God, the heat level in the place just went off the charts. Since when did this start happening? Are you using protection? Please, tell me you showered first. Sage, do the curtains match the drapes? Oh, wait, I already know that they do."

I was swallowed by a giant hole of humiliation. I attempted to use my eyes, my glasses, and the light from the TV to light Ace's hair on fire. I glared at him like I never have before and lifted both my middle fingers. Sage jerked against my chest, and I hoped to hell she was gawking at him and not planning her escape.

She sat up straighter, and something remarkable happened.

She threw her head back in laughter.

Not a chuckle. Or a small fit of giggles I've heard before.

It was a full-blown howl. She clutched her stomach and cackled unrestrained.

Her laugh was miraculous. And fucking adorable. It

was a bit strangulated, like the beginnings of her giggle fit got caught in the back of her throat and turned into her gulping for air in a natural and contagious way.

It was the first time I'd witnessed her be so expressive. I grabbed at the moment with two fists and held on tight.

"You are so extra!" She shouted at Ace, wiping at her eyes. "The stuff you say is so inappropriate. You would've loved Trish. She was exactly the same."

My grip on her tightened at the crack in her voice.

Ace gave her a wobbly smile. "If she was anything like you, I have no doubt she was amazing."

"Oh, she was nothing like me." Sage settled back on my chest, sniffling. "Trish was a lot like you, Ace. She said whatever came to mind and did things with no hesitations. I was more of an overthinker. I said what if *a lot*, and Trish had no room in her vocabulary for that saying. My mom would say we were like yin and yang, completely different but fit together like two pieces of a puzzle. I think our differences are what made us such close friends. Trish used to say I grounded her, kept her feet level with the earth while she made me feel brave. And spontaneous. She was my Mischief." She swiped at her face. "I miss her so much."

The room went silent. It wasn't a deafening silence that caved in on a person and thickened the air, making it hard to breathe. It was a comfortable silence. A relaxed pause in time when we all shared a moment of peace for my girl's best friend.

It was Sage who broke the silence. "I used to tell her I wanted to be just like her. She would get so mad every time, spewing about how I was perfect the way I was and yadda yadda. Mostly, I just meant that I wanted to be able to do something with confidence. Or, at the very least, make a damn decision. Ugh. I was so bad at making decisions."

I ran my fingers through her snow-white hair. "What kind of decisions?"

"Important ones." She shifted, her grip on me tightening. "I spent all of senior year trying to figure out what to do with my life and didn't come up with a single answer. Trish practically knew the moment she was born she was going to go into elementary education. She loved kids. She'd be able to have a conversation with a toddler for hours. It was her *thing*. I didn't have a thing. I was just gonna go to college and hope it came to me."

"Ya know, college isn't always for everybody." Ace said casually. "It was never an option for me. I hated school and could have never afforded it. You ever think about just getting certified in something?"

"I didn't at the time." Sage snorted. "My dad never really made it seem like not going to college was an option. I applied to four and enrolled in the one my brother and Trish were going to. Trish made it her mission to spend all summer helping me figure out a program to study. And then I was kidnapped by a drug dealer and a murderer. So, there's that."

Ace's jaw dropped at the way she so casually threw out those words. I gave him a look that told him to school his expression and didn't say anything for a while. I knew Sage well enough now to know that those sentences are just words she says so she doesn't have to actually feel anything. If she pretends it was just a regular day, she can stop her mind from remembering it was one that changed her forever.

"So..." Ace began. "Do you want to go to college now?"

"Honestly? I never wanted to go to college, and it's not like I was thinking about what degree I wanted to earn when I was being tossed around. Until you guys, I didn't even have a desire to leave my bedroom. But then a little bit ago, my father started asking questions about my plan for the rest of my life." She huffed, her voice cracking as she spoke. "Which is totally unfair considering eight months ago I didn't even know I'd have the rest of my life."

"Sunshine..." I kissed the top of her head and held her close, fighting emotion. Something in my chest seized painfully at the way she spoke about not knowing her fate. It fucking gutted me. I felt like my insides got tossed into a blender and were trying to replace themselves where they belonged.

"It's just upsetting because my brain can only handle a few things at once, and the last thing on my mind right now is getting a job or going to college. Like, I won't let people touch me or eat anything from a public place, but let's go to college." She sighed, swiping at her face again. "I don't want to let down my family, but I can't do it right now."

"You don't have to do anything you don't want to, phantom girl!" Ace declared. "Live off the land."

She chuckled, sniffling. "You are such a weird-o."

"And damn proud." He smacked his chest and held up a Vulcan V. "Weird-o for life."

She snorted. "I'll figure something out one day. Or I keep saying that to my father, at least."

"You will, Sunshine. One day, you'll just know."

She shrugged against me, nuzzling her cheek against my chest. I hoped it was because my chest was my chest and the shirt I was wearing wasn't just super soft. I did a lot of research on haphephobia and was well aware of how psychically painful it can be for someone who suffers from the disorder to touch anyone. To see her so relaxed with my arms wound loosely around her was not something my mind or my heart would ever take for granted.

"Can we watch the movie now?" Sage's voice was almost a whisper, reminding me that no matter how many jokes she made, or how comfortable she seemed with her past, it was taxing for her to speak about it.

"Sure thing, girl." Ace flashed her a friendly smile and raised the remote.

Before he had even a second to press play, our apartment door flew open. Sounds of wood splitting filled the small space.

Crack!

The remote in Ace's hand went flying from his grip, smacking the wall behind him with a loud thud as he catapulted himself off the chair. I spun my upper body, wild eyes locking on two police officers, guns raised high. Sage's scream ripped out of her and bounced off the walls. Her small body scrambled from my lap and curled into a ball on the floor.

Ace held his hands up quickly and stepped over Sage, blocking her from seeing the guns. The urge to protect her from whatever the hell was happening overcame every single molecule inside my body. I threw myself on top of Sage, caging her in and pushing my face in her neck.

"Whoa!" Ace shouted. I heard the tremor in his voice. I knew he was losing his shit, but I could not bring myself to move away from Sage. She was shaking like she'd been outside in a negative wind chill all day. I wanted to hurl and beat the shit out of those police officers all the same. I had an eerie feeling why they pounded in my door. I engaged in illegal activity on a daily basis. It was a consequence I knew was there, and I always told myself I'd go willingly if, god forbid, the time came. Now? After hearing Sage's soft cries while her bones go stiff as steel beneath me, I sure as shit will not be going willingly.

"Guns." I heard her whimper. "Please, no more guns."

"Put the God damn guns down!" I had to force myself not to shout in her ear. "Please, put down the guns! You're scaring her!"

"Come on, man!" Ace growled. "We will do whatever you want. One of those things killed her best friend! Put it down!"

"Where is Sage Maddison?" An unfamiliar voice boomed.

Sage flinched. "I don't want to go." Her muffled sob tore a crack down my heart. "Don't let them take me. Not again. Please, I don't want to go."

Moisture burned my eyes. "I won't let anyone take you, Sage." Wherever she was, she wasn't here. Not in my apartment or in my arms. She was transported back to a place that had brought her nothing but darkness. I tightened my grip, wanting so desperately to show her the light was still here and would never leave her again.

"Where is Sage Maddison?" The man demanded again. I craned my head to attempt to see him but was met only with Ace's back as he widened his stance to keep Sage from seeing whatever was happening.

I had never loved my brother more than I did at that moment.

"Sage Maddison is right behind me, terrified because you burst into her best friend's apartment and shoved a God damn gun in her face!" I didn't need to see his face to know it was bright red. His blood was likely boiling over just as mine was. "Do you have a reason for why you just destroyed my friend's property and are aiming two loaded guns at my chest?"

Heavy footsteps shook the ground, causing Sage's sobs to worsen. "Where the hell is my daughter?"

My eyes went wide.

Her body stiffened beneath me. A shaky hand lifted as she gripped my forearm, squeezing with a force I didn't know she was capable of.

"Dad?" She choked.

SAGE

I WAS NEVER A GREAT STUDENT. I wasn't a bad one either. Just... average. I got As and Bs, scored pretty well on my state tests but I wasn't in the top ten or a winner of any scholarships at graduation. I paid attention in school and never cheated, always passing the tests and turning in my homework. But I'd never once asked a question when I didn't understand something. I was too shy. Raising my hand in a room full of teens, watching them rub their hands together deviously and just waiting for their shot to judge me, made me dizzy.

I kept my hands in my lap and mouth zipped shut, choosing to guess rather than ask a question. That method worked fine for me for so long. I'd never once regretted it.

And then my brain stopped functioning normally, and I found myself wishing I would've asked questions junior year when we were learning about the brain and the importance of neurons. If I'd asked a question or two, I might've been able to explain why my neurons didn't seem to work properly anymore.

I spent four days in my bed, asking myself that question over and over.

Why did my brain make my eyes see things that weren't actually happening?

Why did my mind jump to conclusions?

Why does my mind hate the rest of me, and will it ever stop?

I was sure there were no real answers to any of those questions, but I came up with a few that made sense to me.

I was broken.

There was a glitch in me.

Something was failing to work right.

They were the only logical explanations as to why I was relaxed one minute, conversing with friends like a normal human being, and on the floor the next, my eyes only seeing the barrel of a gun, Trish's blood, and darkness when that bag was forced over my head.

I could hear nothing, see nothing, feel nothing that didn't take me back to the moment that broke me. It was my dad's voice that ultimately cleared some of the fog. My mind was barely functioning when people started shouting, talking a mile a minute about tracking my cell phone and accusing Wren and Ace of taking me.

My American Girl Doll Method had failed me. What's more, I failed Wren and Ace. The first real friends I had and I'd managed to get a gun pointed at them, forced Wren's property to be destroyed, and had a panic attack on his living room floor.

I was barely functioning when I told the cops Wren was my friend and I drove my mother's car to his place willingly. My mind registered more policemen, Brett, and my father's stoic face as he scanned the way my limbs refused to detach from Wren.

I couldn't explain it then.

Four days later, there was still no explanation.

My bedroom door creaked open. "Sage?"

I peeled my comforter from my head slowly, long strands of hair sticking to the sweaty surfaces of my face. I blinked at the fluorescent light coming from above me. My groggy gaze found Brett in the doorway, looking like hell. "Hmm?"

"Can I come in?" He stepped inside and shut the door behind him before giving me a chance to answer. "You remember that time in my car we had that really nice, honest talk?"

I wouldn't have called it nice, but I nodded against my pillow anyway.

"Could we have another one of those?"

"To be honest, Brett." I swallowed roughly in an attempt to rid my dry throat. "I'm not sure I have it in me."

"Okay. I respect that. Would you try though?"

He was desperate to help me. That was something that'd always hold true. "Sure."

"How come you won't see Julie?"

"Because she'll ask questions I don't have answers to yet."

"What do you mean?" He walked slowly to the side of my bed and sat carefully on the edge of my nightstand.

"I just mean she'll ask why I did what I did, and I don't know."

He nodded, scratching the scruff on his chin I'd never seen so long. "Why you did what you did. You mean, like, touching a human who's also a stranger?"

Understanding dawned on me, and I thanked my brain it could at least recognize when I was being played. "She put you up to this, huh? Julie? She, mom, and dad are conspiring about me."

His hands tightened on the edge of my dresser, his knuckles turning white with the force of his grip. He peered up at me with a miserable expression. "Yes."

I sighed and rolled the other way, blinking back tears that seemed to sneak up on me. I wasn't sure what they were derived from, but they were there.

They were always there.

"Sage, I'm sorry." His voice was thick and wobbly. "They said it would help. I didn't know what to do. I just wanna help."

I took a slow, drawn-out breath and stared at the wall as I told him the truth. "It would help very much if I could just be your little sister again. I hate being a patient and a victim around you. I just want you to be my brother." I rolled back over, watching the way he picked at his nails nervously. "I'm thankful you respect these boundaries I have now, but I don't want you to hold back when you talk to me. Be honest, don't beat around the bush."

"You want me to be honest?" He whispered.

"Yes." I pleaded. It was what I was longing for. A conversation with my brother that didn't tread lightly. A moment with him that didn't involve calculated responses, fake smiles, or nervous laughs.

"I was honestly pissed off and terrified when I found a doll in your bed!" He said, voice cracking. "I was honestly losing my mind when dad tracked your cell phone and found you halfway across the God damn town in an apartment building! I was honestly livid when I saw that guy on top of you, and I was *honestly* gutted when I saw that a fucking stranger could touch you and I couldn't!!"

A sound I'll never forget ripped from somewhere inside

him. He clutched his chest and bent at the waist, sobbing roughly. My own tears filled my pillow as I laid there and watched my brother come unglued.

My body trembled with the need to comfort him and the fear of actually doing it. "Brett." I choked his name and yanked back my comforter. "Brett, come on."

He wiped his face and let out a gasp. His whole body rocked before he dove into my bed. Even a mess, he was conscious not to touch me.

He squeezed his eyes shut, attempting to stop more tears, yet they found their way out anyway. I cracked into a million pieces watching him. I was a porcelain doll someone took a hammer to and watched as the cracks spider-webbed until there was nothing left but dust.

I didn't want either of us to become dust, so I inhaled deeply and held the air in my body as my hand slid across the sheet and fell over the top of his.

All my breath rushed out of me when the pain hit. A whimper escaped my lips. I didn't move my hand. I shook as I laid there, hoping my pain would erase some of what my brother held.

His eyes flew open, shock filling them. They focused on where we were linked. "Does that... does that hurt you? Physically?"

"Yes." I whispered. "I don't know why."

He slid his hand away from mine. I blew out a shallow breath of relief, counting in my head as I kept breathing. I pulled my hands into my chest, rubbing them together to rid the ache he probably thought was pretend.

"It doesn't... it doesn't hurt to touch him? That guy from the other night?"

"No." I met his eyes. "And I don't know why that is either."

"Who is he, Sage?"

"Wren Wilder." I answered, wiping at the snot and tears coating my face. "He's my very best friend."

He looked away. "Since when?" He asked the wall.

"I met him a couple months ago on accident. I basically had a panic attack in his apartment building and he... made it suck less." It was the best way I could explain it without giving up Wren's secret. I wanted nothing more than to tell my brother all about how wonderful Wren really is, but that wasn't my secret to tell. And I would never break Wren's trust.

"On accident? You were accidentally in his apartment building?"

"I'm not telling you the whole truth as to how we met." I confessed. "But I can't because that is his story not mine. What I'll promise you is that Wren is a really good person."

"Then why did you hide him?"

"I don't know that either, Brett!" I sighed. "I just didn't want to answer all these questions I'm getting now! I don't know why I'm not scared around him. I don't know why it doesn't hurt to touch him. I don't know why I'm comforted by his presence! Okay? He just makes things brighter! Less scary!"

"Sage, don't cry." He looked horrified at my tears. "Please, sis. It's okay."

I sobbed, aggressively swiping at my face. "They keep coming and coming! The worst part is, what the hell am I even crying for? I don't know! I've been laying here, trying to figure out all my thoughts. It's so hard sometimes, Brett! I just cry, not knowing if it's because I can't open up to my parents, I'm scared I'll be stagnant forever, my brother lost his life because of me, and that my best friend hates me now because I got his home destroyed."

"Sage, breathe." He commanded. "Come on, breathe. It's okay."

"It's not okay!" I shouted at the ceiling, fisting my sheets in rage. "None of this is okay! It's not okay Trish was killed! It's not okay I was taken! It's not okay you quit college to mourn me. It's not okay I'm scared of public food and slight touches. It's not okay dad is so heartbroken he can't express anything! It's not okay mom is in denial. It's not okay I was the catalyst to Wren getting a gun pointed at him! None of it is okay, but ya know what? He is! Wren is okay, Brett! Out of all the things that aren't okay, Wren is not one of them." I slapped my hands over my face, muffling my cries. "Wren is okay."

"Honest big brother truth?"

"Yes, please."

"I want to kick Wren is okay's ass."

"What?" I gasped, meeting his gaze. "No! Why?"

"I don't know." He mused. "You seem real sweet on him. You've never been sweet on anyone before. Aren't I supposed to kick his ass?"

"Absolutely not!" I gaped. "And I'm not sweet on him! I just like to be around him! And anyhow, he'll probably never talk to me again. So, there's that."

"Sage, he jumped on top of you when he saw a gun." Brett drawled. "He ain't just forgetting you."

I peered at him with remorse and hope all wrapped in one look.

"I'm so sorry for letting him in and shutting you out." I held his gaze and talked for what felt like hours, telling him all about the times I'd hung out with Wren. I told him about Ace and Lilah. I talked to him about SevTeck and Wren's Diet Coke addiction. I even told him, while tears ran down a face that looked similar to mine, why I felt like it was easier to open up to someone who didn't know me before my life flipped.

"He knows the questions to ask and when not to ask anything." I explained quietly. "And also, I don't want to hurt you with the details. I hurt you enough."

He reared back. "You did not! What are you talking about?"

"I didn't fight him, Brett." I finally broke our gaze, unable to face him while guilt lit me on fire. "I didn't fight or attempt a plan. I could've been stronger! Tried harder! Instead, you quit college and moved back home when you were supposed to be curing people!"

"Sage, look at me!" He pleaded. "Look at me!"

I couldn't look at him.

"God damn it, Sage! Listen, okay? You are the strongest person I have ever known! Do you understand me?"

"Do not say that to me!" I shouted. "That's so wrong!"

"It's right!" He growled. "You survived, Sage!"

I rolled my head, feeling dejected and miserable and so damn tired while I looked at him. "People survive every day."

"They do not survive what you did." He said, holding my gaze so intensely I was afraid to break it. "You survived hell and are clawing your way to a life that screams heaven. I'm proud of you. And I do not blame you for the reason I stopped going to school. I was broken, okay? I'll be honest. It destroyed me and I would've flunked out if I continued going. But I do not blame you."

"Do you want to go back? Move out again?"

"Maybe one day." He shrugged. "I care more about spending time with you than studying twelve hours a day."

I went still. "Spending time with me?"

He looked confused. "Of course. It was almost two years. I missed you."

"I thought..." More tears. I pinched the bridge of my nose. Christ, you'd think I would've run dry. "I thought you didn't go because you thought you had to watch my every move."

"I think you have enough people watching your every move, though they seem to be doing a shit job at it." I let out a watery laugh. "I wanna watch your back, Sage. Be your brother."

"I want that too."

"I can't do that if you don't give me a little bit of how you're doing. Open up when you can and tell me the lines you don't want me to cross. I'll respect them, and try to stop acting like a freak if you try to do something for me."

"What's that?"

"Try to stop blaming yourself for my dropping out. It was not you."

"Okay."

"Okay? You'll try?"

"Yes." An effort was all I could promise. Because sometimes, even that was difficult for me.

"Thank you."

I nodded, wiping my face for the millionth time. "Hey, Brett?"

"Yeah?"

"I missed you too."

He smiled and the cracks inside me that were all for him started to fill.

"Do you wanna play-"

THUD

I flew upward at the sound of our front door slamming and my dad's hoarse shout. Brett was already off my bed and flying down the stairs. I sucked in long, even breaths, my legs shaking as I placed them on the floor and rose from my bed. I shuffled to the doorway and craned my neck, peering into the hall.

I saw nothing and heard nothing but loud whispers and the shuffle of shoes on hardwood flooring.

My bare-feet flopped against the ground as I carefully made my way to the staircase, gripping the railing so hard, I thought my knuckles might burst from the skin. I peered over the railing and down into the living room, my knee caps bobbing and my mind racing with the possibilities of what I might find.

I found no broken doors.

Or guns.

Or people screaming.

I found sun.

I blinked a few times, resisting the urge to pinch myself. My brain liked to malfunction, and I wanted to be sure that wasn't what was happening.

I gazed at him, watching as he had some sort of show-down with my father while wearing that ridiculous yellow polo and a pair of jeans. Even with a red face, his freckles stood out. His eyes were on fire behind his glasses, his lips moving at a rapid pace. I couldn't be sure what he said to my father, but I thought it may have had something to do with the stuffed sunflower in his hand. It had a long stem that spanned the length of his arm and large petals I wanted to rub my face on.

Brett was standing between them, his arms crossed over his chest as his head whipped back and forth, taking in their expressions.

I must've made a noise because all three of them stopped and turned to look at me.

I looked only at Wren.

The minute his eyes met mine, they softened and he smiled wide.

"Hi, Sunshine." He called. His voice was light. Casual. Like he wasn't just having a staring contest with my father while holding a plushy flower.

I lifted my hand and gave him a small wave. A smile curled up my lips just seeing him. After I basically ran full speed out of his home and neglected to return his phone calls over the last four days, I had no idea why he still wanted to be my friend. But I was sick of trying to answer questions. So I just thanked the universe and started down the staircase. "I see you wore your best shirt to come visit me."

"What? This old thing?" He chuckled, stepping around my father.

When he was close enough, I held his gaze. "I'm sorry."

"What for?"

"Getting your house destroyed, a gun in your face, and ghosting you."

"Well." He smirked. "We call you phantom girl for a reason. And I forgive you."

I jolted. "Why?"

He cocked his head. "Why do I forgive you?"

"That, and why do you still want to be my friend? I have so much baggage. I'm like the heaviest suitcase ever. You can't zip me up, Wren. You think you can and all the shit will come pouring out through a tear in the fabric or at the seam."

"Sunshine." He moved so we were toe to toe. I didn't flinch when he pressed his palm to my cheek. I nuzzled into the touch. "You are not what happened to you, Sage. That's part of you, yes. But it's not *all* of you."

"Sometimes it feels like it is, Wren. Sometimes it just consumes me."

"I know." He whispered. "I know that's why you didn't call back."

Of course he knew.

"And if you need more time to breathe, Sage, take it. I just came here to bring you a present." He lifted the flower between us. "I wanted you to have a little sun."

I threw myself at him. He stumbled awkwardly before righting himself and squeezing me. The flower was wedged between us while we held each other. I pushed my face in his neck, reveling in his comfort. I even leaned into his touch when his lips hit the top of my head.

"Thank you." I whispered. "Thank you for bringing me sun."

HOLDING someone else's hand was a normal gesture for most people. To them, it was relaxed and comfortable and comforting. To me, it was an absolute victory. I felt like I'd won a medal when I slid my hand in his and linked our fingers together without an ounce of hesitation. When he lifted our linked hands upward and his lips brushed the back of my hand repeatedly, I thought, screw the medal. Where is my trophy?

"You sure about this, Sunshine?"

I nodded, my knee caps bobbing as we moved up in line. "I'm sure."

He looked very skeptical but said nothing. I knew he could feel me shaking and my palm sweating. I had to force my brain to think about other things so I wouldn't back out of what I was about to do. The line moved upward. I glanced nervously at the large man in a white apron, making sandwiches quickly as people stood behind a plastic case and pointed at what they wanted.

I cleared my throat, doing weird things with my tongue to bring the moisture back into my mouth. I'd lost my appetite the moment I stepped foot inside Gervasio Bros. I knew that even if I was able to take a bite of the sandwich I'd had yet to order, there was a chance I'd barf it up.

But that wasn't the point.

The point was that I was making an effort. Crossing a bridge I'd thought was broken.

"Sage, are you sure?" He didn't ask to be condescending or because he thought I couldn't do it. He asked to give me an out. Normally, I'd appreciate that, but I didn't want an out.

Not this time.

"Stop asking me if I'm sure, Wren." I clipped. "It's making me cranky."

"Yes, ma'am." He chuckled, kissing the back of my hand again.

An elderly woman in front of us peered over her shoulder. She smiled politely at our clasped hands and the way I was leaned into Wren so nobody else would touch me.

She speared me with a look that said she wanted to pinch my cheeks and give me a good shake. "You two make such a lovely couple."

Couple.

That word surrounded Wren and I since the moment he brought me that sunflower two weeks ago. My dad wasn't even going to let him inside the house that day until Wren passed a background check, a lie detector test, and a tough round of twenty questions. He'd managed to get himself through the door long enough to have a showdown with my dad, arguing about why he should be allowed to see me. My dad's refusal came to a halt when I spent a good five minutes relaxed against Wren while he hugged me.

That started the slew of questions.

Are you together?

Is this your boyfriend?
How did you meet?
Why didn't you say anything?
Are you sure you're ready for this?
What are your intentions with my daughter?

That last one made me giggle. Mostly because Wren didn't have any intentions when it came to me. He took whatever I gave him and was genuinely happy. He was patient and kind. Respectful and knew when to back off. Being around him was easier than breathing sometimes. I didn't have to count or force my chest to move. I just had to exist and things clicked into place.

Did that make him my boyfriend?

Hell if I knew. I wasn't rushing to answer that question. When my parents demanded an answer, I told them Wren was my sun.

Wren seemed perfectly satisfied with that.

The line kept inching forward. My saving grace was the lunch rush. The horrendously long line was practically out the door when we got here. It gave me loads and loads of time to back out and take off running. I didn't back out but I started to think I should. When it was almost our turn, I went a little dizzy. My legs became comparable to a jar of jelly. I clutched Wren's hip with my free hand and tried not to pass out. I looked around the small restaurant, watching as people ate and kept their gazes on their cell phones or the person across from them. Not one person was passed out or stumbling around unaware. I mumbled to myself repeatedly that there weren't drugs hidden in the salami. I wasn't gonna go weak the second I took a bite and wake up hand-cuffed to a pipe in an unfamiliar bathroom.

But my positive sentences weren't convincing enough. There was still a piece of my brain asking me what the fuck

I was doing here allowing myself to be vulnerable. When it was the little old lady's turn, I shuffled forward and repressed the urge to vomit in her oversized handbag.

Wren shifted so he was standing behind me and wrapped an arm around my middle, molding his front to my back. I shook as he pressed his nose to my cheek. "Let's just order, yeah?" He suggested. "We don't have to eat it. Just order. One step at a time."

I nodded. I could do that. Order something and pay for it like everybody else did. Just ordering it didn't sound so bad.

When I'd decided in Julie's office this morning I was gonna do this, I called Wren and asked him to come. He met me outside the sandwich shop on his lunch hour, smiling at me and telling me how much he loves this place. I'd never been here. I chose it because it was close to his work.

"So, you eat here a lot?" I mumbled, trying to keep a conversation going. Being alone with my thoughts for too long was never a good thing.

"All the time." He answered. "Pizza for dinner and sandwiches for lunch."

"That sounds terribly unhealthy."

"Oh, it is." He chuckled. "But don't tell Pepperoni Pauly I said so."

"Pepperoni who?"

He let go of my hand to point at the large man with the round face that was making the old lady's sandwich. "Pepperoni Pauly is one of the owners. See that guy cashing people out?" I shifted my gaze to the left and found a shorter version of Pauly giving out napkins and taking money. "That's his younger brother. Salami Sal. They own the place together."

I chuckled. "Do their birth certificates have those names on them? Or is that a Wren thing?"

"I don't know about their birth certificates, but their name tags say so. And that's pretty much the same thing, right?"

I smiled when he kissed my cheek. It wasn't the first time he did it. The first time was after he'd given me the sunflower. I thought I was gonna collapse at the tingles that erupted in my bloodstream.

When I giggled and leaned into the touch, he kissed my cheek again, forcing butterflies to erupt not just in my stomach, but anywhere inside my body they'd fit. I knew my face was red when I stepped up to order.

Pepperoni Pauly smiled politely at me and then looked over my head to find Wren attached to me. "What's up, Wren?" I rolled my eyes with a smirk. Does every restaurant worker know him by name? "You want the usual?"

"You got it." Wren answered. "My girl wants to order too. Sage?" Wren prompted. "You know what you want?"

I shook my head, gazing up at the large menus hanging on the wall above Pauly and Sal's heads. All this time in line and I didn't glance at it once. There were a lot of choices. Holy shit, how many things can one person put on a sandwich? It wasn't that hard. People liked what they liked, and I had my favorites, but it'd been a long time since I ordered a damn sandwich. Hell, this shop didn't even exist two years ago.

"Sage?"

"I didn't look at the menu." I confessed. "There are a lot of choices."

"You can build your own." Wren said. "Like Subway."

Pauly let out a rude noise. "Compare us to Subway again and you'll get kicked out."

Wren chuckled, and I mumbled off the name of the first sandwich I saw on the menu. I wasn't a picky eater, and judging by the way my stomach was rolling, I wasn't going to eat it anyway.

I widened my eyes and watched Pauly like a hawk. He didn't turn around or move his hands out of my view once. I watched him carefully lay out slices of meat and cheese on a piece of bread. When he asked if I wanted it toasted and gestured to the oven behind him, I practically shouted at him not to move my sandwich. He slapped some veggies on top of the cheese while trying not to look at me like I was a lunatic.

Except, I was a total lunatic.

That was made even more evident when I scrambled out of Wren's hold and took off down the line so I could watch the salami brother roll it up in wax paper and smack a sticker with the business's logo on it. He pushed it across the counter and punched some things into the computer. My hands shook as I reached into the small purse slung around my body and produced some cash. I dropped the change he tried to give me twice before cursing at myself and chucking it into the tip jar. I grabbed the sandwich I knew for sure I wasn't going to eat and just about smashed the thing between my nervous fists.

"Good job, Sunshine." Wren appeared beside me and grabbed his own sandwich, swiping a credit card. "I would've bought yours, ya know."

I nodded and watched him sign a receipt. "I wanted to do it by myself."

He grabbed my hand, trying hard not to be affected by my words. It'd been a really long time since I'd done something for myself and by myself. He knew that as well as I did. Buying a sandwich wasn't a huge victory, but it was a step I couldn't take yesterday. "Proud of you." He mumbled, pulling me from the counter.

He put his arm around me and dodged the groups of people, leading me to a small table in the corner and away from the chaos. It was bright red and made of hard plastic. The chairs were made exactly the same with the logo stuck to the back. I took a seat across from Wren and hoped the small chair wouldn't tip over from the force of my bouncing legs.

"How do you feel?" He asked.

"Like I'm gonna barf up the waffles I ate for breakfast."

He reached for my hand across the table. I gave it willingly, not caring at all my arm hair was now stuck to a sticky substance that hadn't been wiped down before we claimed the table. "I'm really happy you called me to be here."

"Wouldn't have made it to the counter without you here."

His lips quirked. He felt the weight of my words but didn't make a big deal over them. "I guess I'm pretty cool then."

"Julie is gonna lose her shit."

"I like Julie." He said, taking his hand back and unrolling the wax paper that contained his food. "She's really nice."

"You're saying that because she loves you." I watched him take a bite and wink at me. He didn't glance at the half smushed sandwich sitting in front of me. But I knew he'd ask eventually.

"What's not to love?"

"Careful." I chuckled. "You're starting to sound like Ace."

Wren met Julie the day he showed up at my house to surprise me with an oversized sunflower. The second my mom witnessed me hanging off Wren, she'd called Julie. Jules showed up in a bright blue jumpsuit, bouncing around in glee at the thought of meeting the man who'd become my exception. And Wren, bless his heart, stood there with his hand in mine while my dad glared at him and Julie fawned all over him.

I sat in the living room with Wren and my parents and allowed Julie to be the mediator of the discussion I knew had to happen. I told my parents the truth and smiled sheepishly when I explained the American Girl Doll Method. After I told them how many nights I spent hanging out with Wren in his apartment, my dad went from glaring at Wren to looking as though he wanted to strangle him. It took Julie, and a lot of frustrated tears from me, for my parents not to see Wren as a threat or a man with danger stamped across his forehead. My parents agreed to accept my visits with Wren as long as I agreed to stop lying about them. I'm not sure I would've agreed so quickly if I knew that agreement was also me signing an invisible contract that said my mom was going to text me every ten minutes, and my dad was gonna drop me off and wait in the parking lot the entire time I spent with Wren. I tried hard not to let it annoy me. My parents went through hell when I went missing and were prepared to take every action possible to ensure that would never happen again. I was grateful and frustrated all the same. Then again, they didn't know who Wren was or why he'd become so important to me. If they knew what he did for me, they'd kiss his feet.

"Thank you for staying that day." I said, watching him eat. "I'm sure it was weird."

He glanced up at me, licking Italian dressing off his bottom lip. "What was?"

"Being in attendance for an impromptu counseling

session in my living room."

"Why do you think that was weird for me?"

"Uh, because I even need counseling in the first place?"

His lips flattened. "You need counseling because you went through something painful and traumatic. Don't start apologizing for healing, Sage."

"I'm not." I argued. "I'm just saying I recognize that it was probably really awkward for you, and I'm grateful you were there."

"It wasn't that awkward." He said, and I knew he wasn't just saying that to placate me or get me to shut up. If he said it, he meant it. And that's what I loved about being around Wren. He never lied to me or held back his thoughts. "Babe, I honestly didn't mind being there. I'll go anytime you think you need me."

"So every time I go then?" I teased.

"You don't need me every time." He shook his head with a smirk. "You're tough, Sage Maddison." He gestured at my sandwich. "Look how far you've come in just the few months I've known you."

I snorted. "Because of you."

"I don't believe that. I didn't make you do anything, Sunshine. You made the choice, I just held your hand."

I gave him a smile and nodded my head as if I agreed with him. Honestly? I wasn't so sure. I was a hermit before Wren came along and entirely happy with being one. I dealt with the pain and the darkness, not putting in half as much effort to heal until I met him. I don't know what that said about me. Every self-help book in the history of America probably said I shouldn't be doing it for a person I'd only known for a few months. But for some odd reason, the idea that Wren spent hours on end saving me was like a slap to the face to recognize I was worth saving.

"Thank you."

"What are you thanking me for this time?" He gave me a knowing look.

I rolled my eyes with a chuckle. "I suppose for sitting here watching me stare at a mangled sandwich."

"It's not mangled." He protested. "Just a little... dented."

"Dented?" I snorted, looking at the way I'd practically folded my sandwich in half while I twisted it nervously in my grip. The wax paper was torn down the middle and pieces of lettuce were poking out of the tear. A pool of mayo was getting all over the table. "This sandwich is more than dented."

"I'm sure it tastes fine though." He shrugged. "If you wanna give it a shot."

"Nope. I don't."

"Alright." He reached across the table and drug my sad excuse for a sandwich toward him. "I'll eat it then."

"You hate mayo."

"What?" He feigned confusion, pretending he doesn't remember the night we spent two hours talking about the foods that made us groan and the foods that made us hurl. "I hate mayo? Since when?"

"Since forever." I watched, my brow wrinkling when he unrolled the wax paper and tore the sandwich down the middle. Lettuce and some pickles plopped onto the wax paper. He scooped them up with a pinch of his fingers, dropping them into his mouth. There wasn't a single moment of hesitation when he lifted one of the halves and took a heaping bite.

"This is good." He talked with a mouthful, and my oh my that sweet man didn't even gag when the mayo hit his tongue and slid down his throat. He even licked it off his top lip without making a face of disgust. I was so damn confused as to why he was torturing himself with a sand-wich dressing over my seven-dollar lunch.

Then it dawned on me.

He was showing me it was safe.

I sat there across from him, my jaw resting on top of the table while he ate that thing like it was his last meal. He mumbled many times, telling me how good it tasted. That it was the best sandwich he'd ever eaten. He scooped up all the veggies that fell out of the bottom and ate those too. His stomach was probably rolling. No doubt his taste buds were screaming at him.

He didn't complain once.

He finished the half and leaned back in his chair, grinning and patting his stomach. "Yum."

"You hate mayo." I said it again because I wasn't ready to address what he had done. He was clearly fine. His eyes weren't drooping behind his glasses. He was still sitting upright in his chair. His chest wasn't pumping at an acceler-ated rate.

Wren was fine, and he was trying to show me I would be too.

I cracked my knuckles to stall for time before stretching a few shaking fingers towards the wax paper. I pinched the corner and drug the other half of the catastrophe sandwich directly in front of me. I took a long, drawn-out breath, trying to get rid of the whatever was inside my body that made me want to pass out.

It didn't work. It never did, but I trudged forward anyway.

I squeezed my eyes shut and lifted the sandwich, trying to pretend it was something my mother made in the safety of our home with groceries she'd bought herself and closely examined. I took a small bite, keeping my eyes closed as I chewed and swallowed. Before I even considered taking another bite, I sat there and studied the way my body was reacting. I waited to start floating. I waited for the moment that I'd longed for back in that run-down house but came to hate once I'd realized how much my brain had missed when it was rolling.

It did not come.

Not a damn thing happened. I wanted to cry right in the middle of that busy sandwich shop with two chubby brothers named after sandwich meat. Instead, I took another bite. A bigger one. I kept taking bites until the thing was gone and I was not high as a kite with a bag over my head.

I lifted my chin and opened my eyes, finding Wren beaming at me. All the sun that was inside him had made its way to his eyeballs and was shooting directly into my chest. He looked absolutely enamored. "I am so damn proud of you, Sunshine." He whispered. "I knew you could do it."

I gave him a weak smile. "I'm sorry you suffered through mayo for me."

"Psh." He batted his hand at me. "For you? I'd do anything."

There was no missing the blush that crept up my cheeks. I could feel it. My face ignited like someone put a torch to it, and his freckles danced with his chuckle. "You are so damn cute."

"Are you flirting with me?"

"I'm trying to. Do I suck at it? Should I pop the collar on my polo? Would that help?"

"Oh, please do." My cheeks rose watching him lift the collar on his polo of the day. Today, it was bright blue. The exact color of his badass crayon. I barked a laugh when he winked at me. "Looking good."

"Well if you think so, then it's good enough for me." He stood from his seat and gathered our trash, depositing it into the trashcan beside the front door before grabbing my hand and leading me out the glass door.

We walked down the sidewalk, hand in hand. I'd parked right on the street, as close to the restaurant front as I could get. By the way Wren was walking, I knew he'd spotted the car and had intentions to make sure I got inside safely.

Knowing him, he'd probably buckle the seatbelt and start the car.

"So, are you gonna tell Brett about your deli victory?"

"Yep." I was still reluctant to share a lot of things with Brett, but victories did not fall under that category. "But I think Julie will be more excited. Add one more thing to list of reasons why she loves Wren."

"I have no idea why she loves me. Is she a fellow Diet Coke addict?"

I nudged him with my hip. "No, you goon. I don't think she'd ever say so, but she loves you because you saved me."

His hand jerked in mine. Both his feet stumbled on the concrete before coming to a complete halt. My arm twisted strangely when I tried to keep walking. "Wren?"

He dropped my hand and stepped close to me. All the hair on my body stuck up at once as I peered anxiously around the town, looking for the reason why Wren had stopped so abruptly.

"Wren, what's wrong?"

He moved so we were toe to toe and dropped his voice to barely a whisper. "Did you just say Julie loves me because I saved you?"

"Yeah, I-"

"Julie knows who I am?"

My mouth went dry at his even tone. "Yeah, she... encouraged me to keep giving you gifts."

"You told a stranger I work for an illegal organization?"

Sweat pooled in my hairline and ran down the back of my neck. "She isn't a stranger. She's my counselor. She knew everything from the beginning. Before I ever met you."

He pinched the bridge of his nose, his chest pumping.

"She can't say anything, Wren. I'm her patient. There are confidentiality laws."

"It doesn't matter, Sage. How well do you even know her? How do you know she doesn't have friends in the FBI?"

"Wren, I... that's crazy. Julie doesn't have drinks with federal agents on the weekends."

"How. Do you. Know?" He clipped. "Sage... that..." He took a long breath and a big step back.

When he lifted his eyes, the sun in them was gone and replaced with a look I wasn't familiar with. I hated it right away. His eyes wouldn't meet mine, his shoulders were slumped. He looked... disappointed.

There was a sharp twinge in my chest.

"I'm sorry." I choked. "I didn't know you then, Wren. I just... I was telling her about the gifts and the way we met. I didn't have anyone else to talk to. And then you were kind to me and for the first time in counseling, I found something that wasn't painful to talk about." I blinked fiercely to rid the burn in my eyes. "I'm so sorry."

"Aw, Sunshine. Don't cry. None of that."

"I didn't realize how serious this was back then, Wren. I don't want to let you down."

"You didn't, Sage." He sighed again and rubbed the

back of his neck. "It's just... I have to head to Circuit, okay? Let Cruz know somebody else knows."

"I fucked up really bad, huh?"

"No, babe. I don't mean to make you feel bad. We just keep tabs on anybody who knows. It's a precaution, yeah?"

I wiped at the corner of my eye. Why the hell was I even crying? Again, I had no idea. I thought it may have had something to do with the shame and embarrassment sitting on my chest. "She's a good person. She won't tell anyone."

"I believe you. It's just something we have to do. Can you tell me her last name?"

"Clemmons." That was easy. Everybody called her Dr. or Mrs. Clemmons. I was the only one in her office who referred to her informally. "Julie Clemmons."

"Do you know anything else about her?"

"Not really. She's married. Has a cat. Likes bright colors. I think she said something about living in Florida once. She just... she seems pretty normal, Wren."

"I'm sure she is, Sunshine. I'm sorry for making you feel bad."

"I'm sorry for breaking your trust before I even had it."

"Come on now." He came close again, palming my hip and kissing my cheek. "No trust is broken. You caught me off guard. I just gotta run down to the old lair and do some investigating. It's all part of the job."

"You make it sound like you're gonna go sell fudge pops from an ice cream truck."

"That job sounds just as cool."

"It's not."

He kissed my cheek again and led me to my mom's car. I pulled the keys from my purse and clicked the lock button, folding my body inside. Unsurprisingly, he watched me buckle my seatbelt. I peered up at him. "I'm sorry."

"No more apologizing. Don't forget how awesome this day was. We are gonna celebrate on Wednesday, yeah?"

"Sure."

He kissed my cheek one last time. "Proud of you, Sunshine."

The door clicked shut. He waved at me before disappearing down the sidewalk in the opposite direction of SevTeck. He no longer seemed disappointed and his smile before he left was nothing but genuine. Maybe I had caught him off guard or maybe he'd done a good job at hiding his anger. Shame overtook me. I felt like I'd jumped into a pool and forgotten to plug my nose. My insides burned, the air in my lungs got pushed out, and tears pricked my eyes.

I felt like I had betrayed Wren, though at the same time, I felt like I hadn't. I confided in my counselor about the person who saved me from my kidnapper. How the hell was I supposed to know how much he'd come to mean to me? I flexed my hands against the steering wheel and took deep breaths, reminding myself there were laws in place. Repeating how sweet Julie is and always has been.

Wren and all he is will be safe.

I told myself that simple fact enough times but still didn't believe it. Something was gnawing at me. Guilt. Shame. I had no idea. But it was there, and it fucking hurt. It yanked at my chest over and over, as if someone tied a rubber band around my lungs and were snapping it repeatedly. It was overwhelming and made no sense.

Wren wasn't mad at me, and Julie was still as awesome as ever.

Right?

I rested my head against the back of the headrest and did something I hated doing.

I started to truly think.

I DID NOT TRUST my own instincts. The natural impulse had failed me many times before, and I didn't trust it in any sort of way. Thinking back, there was nothing happening inside me that told me not to go inside the bank that day. There wasn't an eerie feeling crawling up my neck. Nothing inside my bones that made me feel heavy. My mind wasn't racing. My palms weren't sweaty. I didn't feel anxious or scared or on edge. I felt normal. I walked right into that bank, my arm linked with my best friend's without a cloud of doubt hovering over me.

Since then, I cursed my instincts and damned them straight to hell. They couldn't be trusted. I'd argue I had no instincts at all. Some people were born without certain limbs. I was born without instincts. And I knew it might not be fair of me, but I wished I could give one of my limbs for some instincts that actually worked.

Maybe my best friend would still be alive.

Maybe I would've felt someone behind me and ran before that bag was secured over my face.

And maybe I would've thought twice before driving to Julie's house after dark and knocking on her front door.

As it turns out, I wasn't the best thinker. There wasn't a right or a wrong way to think, was there? If you asked me two years ago, I would've said there wasn't. A person's mind is supposed to be their safe place. A place to think and analyze and pick apart people and situations in any way they choose. I did not believe in mind readers so every thought inside my brain should've been safe. As long as I didn't voice them aloud, my horrifying thoughts and painful memories were safe from truly hurting anybody. That's what I'd always thought. But then as I sat inside my car, on the side of the road beside a sandwich shop, it dawned on me my thoughts weren't safe from hurting everybody. They hurt one person especially terribly.

Me.

And if there was one person in the world who knew how to navigate my thoughts into a territory that didn't totally suck, it was Julie. But by the time I'd come to the conclusion I needed to talk to her, the sun had already set and her office hours were over. Luckily for me, I had her address. She put it in my phone during our second appointment and told me she'd make herself available at any time.

I pulled into her driveway and walked up the cobblestone pathway to her front porch. I hesitated to knock on the bright red door and just stood there, deciding if I should interrupt her night. What would I even say?

Hey, Julie. I think I upset Wren but I suck at thinking so I was wondering if you could do it for me?

I fidgeted subconsciously and rocked on my feet, wanting to leave and not wanting to leave at the same time. I wanted just to go home and accept the genuine smile Wren gave me. But I knew I couldn't. I knew the idea that he hated me would still be there, chomping at me while I tried to sleep. I knew the only way I'd be okay was when Julie told me she didn't have mimosas with the FBI on Sunday mornings. It was that thought that prompted my fist to raise and drop light knocks against her door.

Julie's home matched her personality effortlessly. If I had to describe Julie in one word, it would be colorful. The colors she saw in the world matched her outfits, her office, the handbags she carried, the flowers that lined her front porch. Julie did not see the world in black and white. She saw it for what it was meant to be. That was made so evident by her canary yellow windowpanes and electric blue Toyota sitting in her driveway. The day I met Julie, I was reluctant to speak to her, not because telling somebody the truths that soaked my brain made me vomit, but because there wasn't an ounce of darkness in her life.

I did not want to be that darkness. But then she told me something that changed me forever.

I harbor darkness, Sage. I use the colors to mask it.

At the time, that sentence excited me. I didn't question what her darkness was or what she was trying to mask with the paintings on her wall. All I wanted from her at that moment was a lesson on how to mask my own darkness so it'd stop hurting my family.

After the fourth knock, I started wondering if I should've at least enquired about her so-called darkness. That's what a sane person would've done, right? After spending two years in darkness, the last thing I should've wanted was to confide in a woman who claimed to harbor it. But again, there was nothing inside me that made me reluctant to sit down in her office and answer her questions.

Even now, as I perched on her front porch and kept knocking, there was nothing that told me to go away.

Nothing that told me my sixth knock was a bad idea. I raised my fist to knock a seventh time when the front door flew open. I cried out when a hard hand locked around my outstretched wrist and yanked me inside so forcefully, the joint in my shoulder began to flare up. A scream barreled out of me when the door slammed behind me. The sound of a deadbolt locking into place penetrated my ears as I pulled free of the grip on my wrist. My body scrambled as far away from the assailant as possible. It wasn't until I was separating our bodies did I look up.

"Sage, I'm so sorry. I didn't mean to touch you like that. Did I hurt you? I'm sorry. I wasn't thinking."

"Julie?" I pulled my wrist to my chest and wiped a tear that escaped my eye. Yes, she did hurt me. It felt like the dozens of bones in my wrist were taking turns exploding but I was unable to express that. I tried to, but the words fled my brain when I got a good look at her. "Oh my God."

The long locks Julie always had curled or twisted nicely into a braid were unrestrained and matted. There was mascara smeared down her cheeks and a tear in the loose dress she was wearing. She shook as if she were a feather that had gotten picked up by a gust of wind and stared at me like I often stared at her. I peered into her wild eyes and saw something familiar.

Fear.

"Sage, go home right now."

I ignored her words and the rasp in her voice that made it seem like she'd been screaming for hours. I stepped forward and examined her closely. Bile rose in my throat when she tilted her head and a chunk of hair that was masking her face fell behind her shoulder. It revealed a handprint across her cheek. Bright red and so defined, I could see each finger of the person who'd put it there.

"Sage, please go home."

I should've. I should've run home right then and there, but of course, that's not what I did. And it wasn't even about instincts this time. It was about her. And our strange friendship.

"Julie, who did this to you? Your husband?" I didn't admit it, not to her and rarely to myself, but I knew what an abusive relationship looked like. The signs were on the fingernail marks down her arms and the crack in her bottom lip. "Is he still home?"

"I don't have a husband."

She breathed the words so quietly, I stepped closer and tucked my hair behind my ear to hear her better. "What?"

"I don't have a husband, Sage. I lied to you."

"Oh." I wasn't sure what that had to do with whatever had happened to her but I stood still and listened anyway. "What about the man in your photos?"

"He's dead." There was a void in her eyes as she stared at a spot above my head. It's like she was talking to me, but not really. She was just talking to talk. Talking because she needed to say the words. I knew what that need felt like, so I rooted my feet into her carpet and tried to give her what she needed. "My husband was in a car accident almost five years ago." Tears dripped down her face. Her shaky and bruised arms drew into her chest as if she were trying to hug herself. "There was nerve damage in his leg after the accident. Damage that prevented him from being able to walk without howling in pain or falling over. Damage doctors couldn't fix and refused to try to fix with surgery. So, we found some people who could help. I knew they weren't good people, but they helped him walk. He stopped crying in pain and frustration, so I just let it keep happening." A sob tore out of her frail body. "I should've stopped it."

Her eyes pulled away from the spot on the wall and found mine. Tears filled them and poured down her cheeks like a fountain that kept overflowing. "I'm so sorry, Sage." I had no idea why she was apologizing to me. Nothing about her physical and emotional state were making any sense. "They told me it was the FBI. They lied, and I'm so sorry."

My mouth went dry at the acronym. "Julie, you know the FBI?"

She shook her head. "I wish."

I was confused. So confused, and I didn't know if my mind was spinning because I was me or if Julie was truly taking me on a mental ride. "Julie, do you want me to drive you to a hospital?"

"No!" She practically shouted the word, stumbling towards me and waving her hands at the front door. "Go home, Sage. Go home right now and know how sorry I am."

There were a lot of people in the world who owed me a giant fucking apology. She was not one of them. "You have nothing to be sorry for."

"I do, Sage." She rubbed at her arms. "Those men who helped my husband.... they gave him drugs, Sage. Drugs that helped him walk but weren't legal."

"I'm not a cop, Julie. I-"

"It was Kade, Sage. The men who gave my husband drugs worked for Kade."

My stomach rolled, and I threw up. Right there. On her carpet, my shoes, down my skinny jeans. I vomited so aggressively, I stopped breathing. Tears fell down my face and mixed with the sandwich I ate.

She knew Kade. She was in cahoots with the man who made a sport out of abusing me. The woman I'd poured my worries to. The woman who taught me how to numb my pain was friends with the biggest source of it.

"I never even met Kade. I swear. I didn't meet any of them. My husband went every month, got what he needed and came home. I had no idea who any of them were or what they did to others until after my husband had already died."

"They killed him, didn't they?" My words sounded like somebody had put my vulva in a blender.

"They told me it was the FBI. They told me the FBI killed him during a drug raid, and I believed them."

I shook my head violently. She shouldn't have done that. They're all a bunch of liars. And Kade was the worst. I knew that better than anyone.

She choked on a bucket of tears. "They said they were going to give the FBI payback for what they did to my husband."

I shook my head again. Kade and his friends never did anything for anyone but themselves.

"They said the FBI killed their friends and took more into custody. They said the FBI had to pay for taking away their leader."

My head snapped up so fast, I swayed on my feet. "What did you just say?"

She nodded miserably, tears coursing down her face at a rate that had me wondering if she was ridding her body of all its natural water. "The FBI raid that got my husband killed was the same one that saved you."

My head spun. I found myself on the floor, next to a pile of my own vomit. I should've been disgusted but it wasn't the first time. Or even the second. I laid there, my chest heaving and head throbbing while it tried to wrap around all she was telling me.

Julie's husband got drugs from Kade's cronies.

Julie's husband died when the FBI came to save me.

Kade's cronies told Julie it was all their fault.

"Sage, I'm sorry. I'm so so so sorry."

I couldn't move. I laid there, my mind going over and over all the moments I'd met with Julie. There was nothing that could have given me a hint. Nothing that could've told me the darkness she claimed to harbor was her relationship with a gang led by the man who destroyed my being.

"Sage, please go home. Please, leave."

I sat up. I knew better than to lay flat on my back when I was vomiting. I made that mistake once, and I wouldn't make it again. "Did they do this to you?"

"Yes."

I knew the look in her eyes so well. The look felt like home. "They are coming back, aren't they?"

"I think so."

"What do they want?"

"Information." Her throat bobbed aggressively with the force of her swallow. "About you. About Circuit."

"What?" Sweat poured from every surface that covered my body. It wasn't even me I was worried about. I lived through hell before and as fucked up as it sounded, I grew used to it. But Circuit? Wren, Ace, Cruz, Marshall, and all those who saved me? Not them. Never them. "They want Circuit?"

"I made a deal with them."

If she signed a deal with them, she basically signed her death certificate.

"They asked me to move to Arlington and take a job as a therapist to a girl they considered a liability. I was supposed to keep tabs on her. Make sure she didn't try to get the press involved or convince the FBI to keep searching for the men who'd gotten away."

"Oh, God."

"I'm sorry, Sage. They told me I just had to do it until they could get justice for my husband. But then they started asking questions about Circuit and I realized that's who they were truly after."

I threw up again, clutching my heaving stomach. "No. No. No. No. No."

In the time it took to click his keyboard, Wren became everything I needed to survive. In one therapy session, I became everything that would get him killed.

"I didn't tell them anything." She sobbed. "I swear to God, Sage. That's why they were here. The minute I met Wren, I stopped communicating with them! They don't know anything about Wren or Circuit. I promise I won't tell them."

I stood on shaky legs and looked her dead in the eye, hoping to convey the truth behind my words. "They will kill you if you don't."

The look on her face told me she knew that already. "I'm gonna run."

"They will find you."

She knew that too. "My sister lives overseas. I called a car. I'm going to the airport."

"Won't matter."

"I fucked up, Sage. I will not let you or Wren or the wonderful people at Circuit pay for it."

I shook my head, wiping at my face and my mouth. "Jules..."

"Get out of here, Sage. Go find Wren and tell him he'll be safe."

I stood there, my legs refusing to move. I was caught between taking off towards Wren and my happy place and refusing to leave her all alone. I knew the chances they'd find her wherever she went were greater than the opposite.

"Sage, please." She begged, tears running down her face. "Please."

I was stubborn. I knew that, but it didn't hit me how much until I planted my feet into soggy carpet and shook my head. "No."

She approached me and lifted her head. "Go." She demanded with a force so strong, I knew she wouldn't back down. "The worst that can happen is I'll see my husband again."

I choked at the image that flashed in my brain. "Go, Sage. Please. It wouldn't just be your family that'd miss you this time. What about Wren?"

I wanted to smack her for what she did. Bringing Wren into it was like dropping a bomb on an already destroyed town. The mention of him was all it took. I loved my mother. My father. My older brother, and all my new friends. But it was him I was afraid to leave. It was Wren I refused to shatter.

It was the mention of my sun that had me fleeing her darkness. Her bright colors were nothing but lies that plastered her walls. Her paintings, the cushions, her outfits, her handbags.

All lies.

Wren's brightness was not a lie.

My feet took off through her small house. I thrust my shaky hand at the deadbolt and flipped it. My feet stumbled backward at the force of my own strength when I wrenched the door back open.

"Hello, Sage. It's been a while."

The blood pumping in my body turned to ice in a nanosecond. My heart stopped, my lungs seized, and I quit functioning. I couldn't breathe, couldn't think, couldn't move.

I was paralyzed.

Rooted in place.

My eyes roamed the familiar build of the man standing on Julie's front porch. My muscles shook taking in that familiar half snarl, half smirk. I went light headed at the sight of the gun clipped to his belt. He winked at me with the eye that wasn't behind his eyepatch and took a step closer.

I didn't step backward.

I didn't scream.

Nothing seemed to work properly anymore.

I stood there and stared at Kade's right-hand man.

I blinked, the tears running down my face an afterthought while I made eye contact with the man who killed my best friend.

THERE ARE moments in life that make you question all the ones that came before it. Moments that force you to take a step back and reevaluate your life. Reevaluate how you got to where you are, and how the hell you can get yourself back to where you were before. As I walked through a metal detector and stood with my arms stretched outward while a prison guard used a wand to double check I wasn't hiding any metal objects in the crevices of my body, I began to severely question each moment that played out in the last twelve hours of my life.

In one of those moments, I was standing in a doorway that was not mine, vomit drying on my shoes while attempting to remind my lungs how to breathe. In the moment after that, I was on the ground, hands over my head while I sobbed into Julie's carpet. I became useless in a nanosecond. It took the familiar clicking noise of him cocking his gun and the barrel between my eyes to take me from functioning human being to sack of sobs. I don't remember anything that came after those moments. I stayed on the ground, shaking and wailing and waiting for the bag to be tossed over my head.

It never came.

And I truly don't know how long I stayed on the ground, but when my mind decided to give me a break and the memories of Trish's lifeless body fled me, Julie was gone. I sat back on my heels and peered around her home. The front door was still wide open. There was a bullet hole in the wall next to a framed photo of a daisy, and glass from a broken lightbulb a few feet away from me. The place reeked of sweat and vomit and fear. I stood on shaking legs and grasped the nearest wall for support while I drug myself towards the front door.

It was quiet outside. I didn't hear any animals or cars driving by. The wind wasn't blowing, horns weren't honking. Everything was still. I could've closed Julie's front door and nobody would've known of the catastrophe that had happened inside of it.

Everything was calm.

Quiet.

Still.

Everything, except for me.

I was not still. Not in that moment. In that moment, I was a grenade whose pin was just pulled. I'd reached the end. The last button had been pushed. The last string had snapped. Any sense of reason or sanity I had left, fled my body. I collapsed on my knees right on Julie's porch and threw my head back, screaming loud enough to wake the town that hadn't paid any attention when it mattered. Nobody heard Julie screaming for help. Nobody heard the gunshot that turned me to stone. Nobody heard the struggles or the cries of desperation.

But they heard the crazy girl covered in vomit screaming on their neighbor's porch.

And if I hadn't already lost it, I would've right then.

Because there are moments. Moments that define you. Moments that make you or break you. And up until that moment, there were too many moments that broke me and not enough that made me. In the twenty years I had lived, there was suffering after suffering. Trauma after trauma. Pain after pain. Heartbreak after heartbreak. Self-loathing after self-loathing, and the end of my rope had been reached. I'd spent years feeling sorry for myself, asking the universe why it chose me and what the hell I did to deserve the shit hand I got dealt.

But then I sat there, on a porch in the middle of the night, screaming until my throat went raw and decided I needed a wakeup call. I was alive, and that was so much more than what I could say for Trish or Julie's husband or possibly Julie herself. I was alive and it was high time to stop punishing myself for my lack of fighting back then and start fighting now.

I contemplated many things in that moment on the porch. I could've called the police. Actually, I probably *should've* called the police. But I didn't. I didn't call my parents. I didn't call Brett. I didn't even call Wren. Because he'd saved me once and that ended up with him in a situation so horrendous, he had a target on his back. Out of all the scenarios I'd contemplated when I came to, there was one that made the most sense.

I should've done something to save Trish that day.

I should've done something to save myself.

I should've done something to save Julie instead of having a panic attack on vomit infested carpet.

It was too late for Trish. But it wasn't too late for Julie.

Or Wren. Or even me. And after relying on people to save me for so long, I stepped off that porch with legs that were struggling to work properly and came to my conclusion. With sanity no longer an issue, I decided it was time for me not only to save Wren, but it was time for me to save myself.

So that's how I ended up in this moment, halfway across the country getting clearance from a maximum security prison in a new pair of jeans and some clean sneakers I'd bought at a supermarket. After presenting my ID and forcing down bile after hearing I was listed as "fiancée" on an approved list of visitors, I was flanked by two officers and led down a hallway that appeared to be made of concrete and steel. There were no windows, and I started to contemplate the moment on the porch that led me here.

My skin felt patchy. My shirt felt too tight. I was sweating something fierce, and air was hard to come by.

The officers stopped outside a steel door. I avoided glancing at the guns secured to their hips and waited for one of them to scan their keycard. With a click, the steel door opened. I slipped through them as soon as there was enough space for my body.

"Take a seat, miss. The inmate will be led in shortly."

I followed a finger to a row of chairs. It was exactly like I'd seen in the movies. Exactly the way I'd pictured it. There were six chairs lined up, privacy barriers on either side. A single phone was secured on the right side of the barrier, hanging there while it waited for a visitor to pick it up. I swayed on my feet, a waft of dizziness falling over me. I fought with my body, begging for it to cooperate just once. My feet began to move as I sat down in a seat in the center of the row. The dizziness hit me again. I fought it, resting my arms on the small table in front of me. There was a sheen of tears in my eyes as I opened them fully and gazed at the empty chair behind a wall of glass I knew would be occupied shortly.

My knees bounced as I waited. I chewed on my finger and ate the ends of my hair. I gripped the edges of the desk to keep from collapsing three times and was seconds away from running full speed out the door when a buzzer sounded and a flash of orange caught my eye. My lungs seized, my heart went wild in my chest before it stopped completely and the orange blob sat directly in front of me. My hand shook with fear and adrenaline as it reached towards the phone.

Again, my instincts had failed me. There was not a single warning sign sounding loud and telling me to put down the damn phone. No flashing lights that told me to get up and walk out while I still could.

All I felt was hard pressed determination behind a thick layer of fear. I wrapped my bony fingers around the phone and pressed it to my ear, keeping my head down.

The first thing I heard was deep breathing. It went on for a few breaths before I heard words that sent a chill down my spine. I shivered in my seat, tears racing down my face when the voice that haunted my dreams became a reality once again.

"Hi, Cookie. I missed you."

Just the sound of his voice sent me into a downward spiral. It was enough to get me to crawl right back into the hole I'd spent months and months clawing my way out of. It was too much. Too overwhelming. It brought back a flood of memories and nightmares I wasn't sure I was strong enough to relive.

I'd barely made it out alive the first time.

"Aren't you gonna say you missed me too?"

I choked, refusing to meet his gaze. My hand slid across the back of the phone, coating the hard plastic in sweat. My teeth ground together as I fought with myself on whether to run back to my safe place or get what I came here for. I thought about Julie and what that crazy fucker was doing to her and lifted my gaze.

The moment I met his eyes, he grinned. That smug grin had such an effect on me. I wanted to hide under the table and throw my fist through the glass that separated us all at the same time. Seeing the handcuffs snapped around his wrists, and the security guards keeping post at the door stopped me from doing the former. It was the idea of my hand staying intact that stopped me from doing the latter.

He looked disgusting.

Kade never looked good, but now he just looked gross. The horrific storm that normally brewed in his eyes had gone calm. There were deep rings of red around his pupils and purple bags under his eyes. The gold tooth that was normally on full display was gone. In its place was nothing. It was just a hole in his mouth. Maybe some people thought it made him look tougher. More intimidating. Me? I just saw it as weakness. Somebody took that tooth from him, and though it was just a small victory, I felt a little better knowing after all he took from me something was finally taken from him.

"I did not miss you, you psychotic bastard."

His lips quirked. He used the edge of the phone to scratch the side of his scruffy face. He didn't always have facial hair, but now it was grown out and scraggly looking. Just like the hair on his head was. The dark locks were tied in a knot at the base of his neck. It looked as though he slicked his hair back with a glob of grease. I wondered what would happen if he ever wanted a haircut and prayed nobody would give this man a pair of scissors. I'd seen what he could do with sharp objects. There was a scar on the top of my right thigh to prove it.

"The first time you come and visit me I get sass? You know how I feel about sass."

"I don't give a shit how you feel." His lips quirked again. My "sass" was no surprise to him. It came a lot in the early days when I was hoping he'd just kill me. And then I found out he made a sport out of not doing it.

"That's one, Cookie."

One strike, he meant. One slap. Kick. Punch. Pinch. Tumble down the stairs. It didn't matter, really. Just one strike of his choosing to come in no certain form, at no certain time. It's what happened every time I "acted up." It was his fucked up way of finding validation for the abuse. Back then, I cursed myself. I'd considered walking up the wooden staircase and throwing my body down it all on my own accord for being so stupid even after I'd learned his triggers and came to the conclusion he wouldn't kill me.

But in this moment, I knew better. And maybe it was my time with Julie. Or all the sun I've gotten from Wren. Or maybe my brain just decided to stop being a jackass. No matter the reason, I knew what happened to Trish wasn't my fault. I knew all the bruises that marred my body weren't deserved. What's more, I knew he couldn't follow through with the strike he so easily threatened.

He kept scratching at his face and it dawned on me he wasn't scratching his skin off simply because he was itchy. He was scratching as a side effect of the drugs he took daily being yanked away. The days I was locked up and going through withdrawals, I'd practically scratched a hole in the back of my neck.

After spending over a year forced to be at his side, I still didn't know what his drug of choice was. Kade didn't discriminate. He took whatever was hot that day. Kade was a million times more abusive when he was doped up on whatever the hell the drug of the hour was. And though he didn't have that shit running through his blood anymore, I knew he didn't need drugs to be in cahoots with the devil. It was whatever he was made of that made him pure evil.

"Stop calling me cookie. I'm not your cookie. I'm not your anything."

"Oh but you are, baby." He leaned toward me, propping his elbows on the desk in front of him. There was glass separating us, but I didn't necessarily trust its strength, so I scooted my chair back as far as it would go without yanking the phone out of the wall. "You're whatever the hell I want you to be."

I looked down at my left hand and wiggled the fingers. Not a single one wore the monstrosity ring he'd forced on me the night he told me we were getting married. He told me if I ever took it off, he'd sew it into my skin. I'd spent every day with Kade living in fear, but that night, I thought fear might be what finally killed me.

"Ya know what I am, Kade? I'm your victim. I am not your girlfriend, your fiancée, your cookie, your baby, your sweet thang, your bitch, your hot piece of ass or whatever hell else term you used to degrade me. I am your victim and I'm so sick and tired of even being that."

He chuckled. The sound sent shivers throughout my nervous system. "Sick of being my victim? You aren't my victim. I didn't kill you. I kept you alive! Ya know what your issue was, Cookie? Your issue was that you didn't know how to show gratitude. I got you off drugs and what did I get in return? God damn sass mouth!"

"You were the reason I was on drugs in the first place,

you monster!" It was a dead end arguing with him. His brain didn't work like a normal brain did. In his mind, nothing he did was wrong. And he was the king. It should've been my absolute honor to bow down to the king and take his drugs without complaint.

He jolted in his seat and pressed his fingertip against the glass so hard, the tip of his finger went stark white. "Where the fuck is your ring?"

"Don't know. Probably somewhere in evidence. I'd love to find it and shove it up your ass. I'm not your fiancée, Kade. I'm the girl you kidnapped."

He'd never understand. I knew that. But I was saying it for me. Julie spent months trying to get me to say my thoughts out loud.

If you say it out loud, it's easier to believe.

"That's two." He snarled.

"Two what? Kade, look at you! You're in handcuffs inside a federal prison! This is done! You can't get to me anymore."

He shook his head, pressing the cheek that didn't hold the phone to the glass. "That's the thing, baby doll. I'll spend my life in here but you still won't get rid of me." He lifted a finger and tapped the side of his head repeatedly. "This is where I'll be, Cookie. In your head, your dreams, your thoughts. You hired a therapist to erase me and look at you. Look where you're at. Sitting across from me thousands of miles away from your family. Why is that, Cookie? Why come all this way without telling a soul? Because you didn't, did you? Nobody knows you're here." My limbs shook violently as he sat back and popped his neck. His eyes held me and no matter how badly I wanted to look away, I couldn't. Once again, I'd been trapped by Kade Wilson. "You think I don't know you, Sage. But I know you. I know you don't have the balls to erase me from your brain because you don't have the balls to do anything that requires an ounce of strength. Do you want a trophy, Sage? A medal? You aren't a victim. You aren't a survivor. People survive every God damn day. You. Are not. Special."

People survive every day.

My body went limp as the words filled my ears. My bones dissolved into sand. Each breath in my lungs grabbed hold to something inside my chest, and I struggled not to spiral.

People survive every day. You are not special.

Those words had been playing inside my head over and over again, taking up any extra space and refusing to give me a moment to think about anything else. I'd beaten myself worse than Kade had ever beaten me with those few words.

You are not special.

Except, I was. It was true, people did survive every day. But there were so many people who didn't. Especially not when they were faced with what I was. Here I sat, in front of the man who kidnapped me, abused me, manipulated me, and gaslighted me. In front of a man who'd spend his life behind steel bars and he was still trying to get inside my head. Still believing I was going to allow him to chip away all the best pieces of me.

I had a long way to go in the recovery department, but I was done letting Kade Wilson take any more pieces of me.

Tears ripped down my face. What felt like bricks of concrete fell off my chest. I stood from my chair and walked back towards him. The phone bit into the side of my face and I slapped one hand down on the desk in front of me. I pressed my forehead against the glass and pierced him with my eyes.

I held his gaze and made sure he heard my words. "I do

not belong to you, Kade Wilson. Not a single part of me is yours. Not my mind, not my body, and sure as hell not my heart."

Not my heart. Hell no. That piece of me belonged to the man who taught it how to work again.

"I came here because you have something I want."

He slumped in his seat and ran his tongue along his yellow teeth. "What could I possibly have, Cookie? I've been locked up for months."

My hand hit the glass with the thud. The security guard stepped forward and gave me a look that told me to stand down or get out.

I did neither.

"Information." I snarled.

"Information?" He said the word like he'd never heard it before. "I'm not sure what you mean, baby. What information?"

He smirked, which told me he had exactly the words I wanted to hear on the tip of his tongue. I could tell by the way his eyebrows rose he was also surprised I had the balls to ask. Truthfully, I was shaken down to my very core when Julie revealed the truth. I'd never felt so betrayed. Never been so positively livid, but the more I thought about it, the less angry I became. Julie was nothing but a victim. She was used and manipulated exactly like I was. The difference? Julie knew when to stop. Julie did not harbor darkness. She harbored the strength it took to say no.

Now she was God knows where with God knows what happening to her and there was one person who could tell me where to find her. Kade Wilson was a man who liked control. That gang belonged to him. It didn't matter where he was and that he wasn't ever going back. It was his, and I wasn't dumb enough to believe somebody wasn't feeding him information on the daily.

It wasn't that I had no faith in our legal system, it's that I knew the resources Kade had, and I knew he was crazy enough to risk everything and use them.

"Where did they take Julie, Kade?"

"Julie?" He tapped his chin like he was trying to conjure up the name. "Oh. Julie Clemmons? So sad what happened to her husband, don't you think so, Cookie?"

"You smug son of a bitch!" I pounded the glass, ignoring the security guard stomping toward me. "Tell me where Julie is! What the hell do you want from her?"

"You see, Cookie. Somebody went against me. And you know how much I hate it when people go against me." He shoved the tip of his thumb in his mouth and started chewing. "I thought maybe it was the man who came to get drugs from my crew every once in a while. So, he had to go."

I went still. "You ordered a hit on Julie's husband?"

He reared back and spat a chunk of dead skin into the air. "Well, what was I supposed to do, Cookie? The FBI pounded into my home and he was a stranger. It was only logical of me to believe it was the stranger that had betrayed me. Thankfully, I didn't have to order the hit. One of my men took care of it before things went south."

"The moment you were born into this world was when things went south." Tears filled my eyes for Julie's husband. That poor man just wanted to walk again. He didn't go about it in an ethical way, but he didn't deserve to die either. "You are a monster."

"I'm not a monster, baby." He shoved his thumb back in his mouth and tucked the phone between his shoulder and head as if we were discussing where to meet for lunch tomorrow. "I was trying to protect my crew. Imagine my surprise when I hear the real reason my home was raided and you were taken from me was because a group of computer nerds stuck their noses where they didn't belong."

I used all I had in me not to react. "That has nothing to do with Julie."

"Ah, but Cookie, that has everything to do with Julie. We don't care about your therapist friend or her husband. What we care about are the names inside her head. And now she's resting nicely in a hospital with no severe injuries because she was smart and she gave us what we wanted."

I faltered. "What?"

He spat out another hunk of skin. "I gotta tell ya, Cookie. It was real brave of you coming all this way in secret to try and save your friend." He chuckled. "And that's with the assumption I'd actually tell you where we held her. Rest assured, baby, your friend is safe and sound. But let me ask you this."

He sat forward and met my gaze. My body wobbled at the storm that broke out into the eyes I thought would be void for the rest of time. "While you were racing here to save your friend, who was saving your boyfriend?"

I HEARD once that in the time of a crisis, it'd be your adrenaline that'd save you. Fight or flight would kick in and you'd somehow know exactly what to do. Either that or you'd acquire sudden superhuman strength and destroy the ground your enemy walked on. I didn't need superhuman strength to destroy anything. All I needed was a computer. I helped dozens and dozens of people every damn day. I saved my phantom girl's life.

My computer was enough.

Until it wasn't.

"Do you think they will let me see him?" Brett's knees bounced uncontrollably next to mine. He had a death grip on the flimsy armrest. There was a fire burning deep in his soul fueled by nothing but pain for his sister. "I'm going to kill him."

"Whoa, big guy. Pump the brakes." Ace laid his hand over Brett's. "He's locked up, man. No way can that mother fucker touch her."

"What the fuck was she thinking?" A sound tore out of

Brett. He pushed his face into the crook of his elbow and shuddered.

I sat next to him, eyes glued to the screen in front of me. It was somehow stuck inside the back of the seat. There was a map on the screen, a plane flying across that map with an estimate on when we'd touch down in Indiana.

I hadn't taken my eyes off that little plane since the moment it appeared on my screen.

One hour and forty-six minutes left.

That was too long.

I cleared my throat. It was clogged with panic so thick, I had a paper bag in my lap for the moment I'd start hyper-ventilating. A flight attendant gave it to me after I lost my shit when she told me how long the flight would be.

"There's something between them, right?" It was the first I'd spoken since we sat down. "Glass or metal or a ten-ton door?"

A tear fell from the corner of my eye. I let it. Fuck all the stereotypes that said I wasn't allowed to be scared. Fuck everyone and everything that said I had to toughen up and beat the hell out of Kade Wilson.

That was not me.

I didn't want to punch him. I didn't want to press a gun between his eyes. I didn't want to torture him and cut off his manhood like Brett wanted to do, though I would if it meant protecting her. I didn't even want to kill him.

I wanted to sweep my girl off the ground and take her far, far away from the man who abused her.

I was drowning in my worry for her. I was wearing my fear like a second skin and didn't give a shit who saw me crying for my girl. I used to be a firm believer in everything happens for a reason. But I couldn't, for the life of me, think of one fucking reason why all this had happened to Sage.

"It's a federal prison. They won't let him close to her." Ace's words were meant as a comfort, but I knew even he was struggling to believe them.

Less than a day ago, I spent hours sitting in my desk chair at Circuit, watching ice melt instead of contributing to the dozens of missions my fellow hacktivists were on. My eyes took turns flicking between my ice cube friends and my cell phone screen. When it'd been four hours since her victory lunch and I still hadn't heard from her, I bit the bullet and called her brother to make sure she got home okay.

I knew it'd upset her on some level that I thought she couldn't take care of herself, but I simply could not focus without knowing she was okay. It was a major day for her. She climbed a massive mountain when she ate that sandwich. For all I knew, she was having a panic attack on the side of the road, and I didn't want that for her. So, I checked to make sure there wasn't an American Girl Doll tucked into her bed.

What I wasn't expecting was Brett to tell me Sage hadn't been home yet. When I heard that, I shook the panic out of my body, cracked my knuckles, and did what any hacker would do. I hacked the GPS system in her mother's car and found her last location.

What I thought I'd find was a nice conversation happening between counselor and patient.

What I found instead buried me.

So much fear fell on top of me I forget how to reason. I just stood there, taking in the blood, vomit in the carpet, broken glass, bullet hole in the wall, and one of Sage's shoes. All while the rest of her was nowhere to be found.

My chest collapsed. It was as though someone took a

sledge hammer and started wailing on my lungs while I stood there and fought for air.

That was almost an entire day ago, and I still hadn't found any air.

"Mrs. Clemmons is gonna be okay." Ace spoke quietly. "August texted me before we boarded. He's been camped out at the hospital."

I nodded my head. Knowing Julie was going to be okay did not make it any easier to breathe, but I knew how desperately Sage wanted her friend safe. I didn't want to bring her any bad news when I brought her back home.

"What about them fuckers who took her?" Brett ground out, his knees still bouncing.

"In custody." Ace answered. He put his hand on Brett's thigh and the bouncing stopped. "One of them..." He cleared his throat and dipped his head. "One of them was the man who killed Sage's best friend."

"Trish." I rasped. "Her name was Trish."

I pinched the bridge of my nose as if it would hold me together. Really, I was being torn in two. I couldn't celebrate the victory of taking down the scum bag that killed Trish and kidnapped Julie when Sage was miles and miles away from me inside a prison while her abuser looked her in the eye.

My stomach rolled.

I threw my fist at that dumb fucking screen. A roar escaped my throat. "Does this plane move any fucking faster?!"

"Come on, Wilder." Ace shot daggers into me. "If you make a scene, they will take you to security the minute you get off this plane."

"Fuck security, bro! My girl needs me!"

"I still don't know what she thought she was gonna do." Brett sighed. "What is she gaining?"

I knew my phantom girl. Probably better than she knew herself sometimes. I knew the way her heart operated even though she's claimed it didn't function. I knew how smart she was despite how often she said her brain didn't work properly. And I knew she wished she was stronger because she didn't know she was the strongest woman I'd ever met.

"She was trying to save Julie." I answered. "She thought she could get Kade to tell her where Julie is."

"Well, that was dumb." Brett spat. "Circuit saved her."

I wasn't sure how long I'd stood inside Julie's home before I smacked myself in the face and got a grip. I about broke my phone when I yanked it out of my jeans. I called a dozen people in what felt like sixty seconds.

The FBI showed up before the county police did and that's when shit hit the fan. It was clear as day someone had taken Julie and by the car in the driveway, we'd all thought Sage was taken too.

Her parents were an utter wreck. I couldn't look at them without fighting the urge to burst into tears. Brett was screaming at the Feds and risking being detained.

Me?

I snuck away, got my ass back to Circuit, and hacked like the tips of my God damn fingers were on fire. I'd never worked so fast in my life. The entire team was going after different leads, going down every road that may end with the location of Sage and Julie.

In the end, it was Cruz who found Julie's medical records and discovered she had a pacemaker. As fucked up as it sounded, we used Julie's pacemaker to find her location. The FBI busted in there, guns blazing.

It was the first time I was able to take a breath. And

then I found out Sage wasn't with them and the sledge hammer started pounding again.

"She is such a stubborn brat." Brett wiped at his face. "She really thought we wouldn't find her?"

"I think she knew Circuit would find her." Ace massaged the shoulder he could reach. He'd only met Brett once before, but I knew it was his way of providing comfort. Brett didn't seem to mind. Or maybe he didn't notice.

"So she ditched the cell phone and the car so she couldn't be tracked?" Brett snorted. "But she didn't think about how easy it is to track credit card transactions? That's nothing. You don't need fancy hackers for that shit. I could've logged into my parent's account and found out she purchased a plane ticket to Indiana. Whoop de doo."

"I think Circuit is pretty sweet." Ace shrugged.

I rolled my eyes.

"They're fucking awesome." Brett nodded. "I'll bow down to them if I ever meet them. I'm just saying, why take one extreme and not the other?"

"I think she was buying herself some time." I sighed.

She knew I'd find her. What's more, she knew I wouldn't stop until I did. Still, she'd bought herself so much time, I didn't actually find her until she used her father's card to pay for an Uber that took her from the airport to Terre Haute Federal Prison.

I put my face in my hands and begged the universe to keep her from any more pain.

Give it to me. I'll carry it for her.

▭

The ride from the airport to the prison was the longest of my entire life. Sage's mother was sobbing. Brett screamed at every red light. Ace was trying to give everyone a massage, and I was a total basket case. The closer we got, the more terrified I became something had happened to her.

I wished I'd brought that paper bag with me.

Marshall turned around in the passenger seat of the Cadillac Escalade we were in courtesy of the FBI members in Indiana. He scanned us all behind a pair of aviators, his gaze landing on Brett.

"When we get inside, we're all gonna have to go through security. If you make a scene, you will not get through."

Brett grunted but said nothing.

Marshall turned back in his seat. This wasn't normally in his job description, but I'd asked him to come. He talked to his supervisor and bought a plane ticket with no questions asked. I didn't know what it took to get inside to see an inmate in a federal prison, but I wanted someone I could trust with me.

I was playing every card I had to make sure I could get to Sage.

The moment the vehicle rolled up to the prison, I flipped the lock and fled the car before it even came to a complete stop. I didn't stop to take in any surroundings or memorize what the place looked like. I ran full speed at the doors with one mission and one mission only.

Get my girl.

To my horror, it wasn't as easy as I hoped it would be. After going through security, I thought maybe she would magically appear. That's not what happened at all. I demanded to be taken to Kade Wilson and got laughed at.

I was not a violent person, but my hands shook with the urge to strangle anyone who kept her from me.

"Each inmate has a list of pre-approved visitors." Marshall explained to all of us. Once everyone got through security and he stopped me from strangling a prison guard, he hauled us off into a corner. "Only people on that list are permitted to see Kade."

That made no sense. "How did Sage get in then?"

Marshall did not meet my eyes. "Kade has her listed as his fiancée."

I choked on vomit.

Her mother about collapsed. "How can he do that?" She demanded. "Don't these people know what he did to her?"

"I don't have all the answers, ma'am." Something in the wrinkle that formed above Marshall's eyes told me a few things weren't quite adding up. But when he didn't elaborate anymore, I let it go.

"Sage has been here for six hours." Marshall told us. "I was just informed she was with Kade for an hour and then she was detained."

"Detained?!" I spat. "What the hell for?"

"Uhm." Marshall rubbed his face. "It seems Sage tried to break through the barrier and attack him."

My body jerked. I cocked my head and stepped closer. "What?"

"She was described as ruthless, vengeful, and dangerous."

"Sage? My Sage?"

He nodded and gripped my arm, pulling me from the group. His voice dropped to a whisper. "They said she kept screaming for Wren over and over. They assumed she was talking about a bird."

My hands flew out and gripped the sides of his shirt. I twisted and yanked him so hard, the bottom of his shirt popped free of his trousers. "Take me to her. Now!"

"Wren." He clamped a hand on my wrists and pried me

off him. "I have clearance to get her. They aren't charging her. You have to stay here though."

"Why didn't they call her parents?"

"Apparently, she hasn't spoken. Wait here, Wren. And don't do anything stupid."

He pushed me aside and explained the situation to her family and Ace before he disappeared with another agent behind a steel door.

I collapsed against a wall, struggling to breathe and sweating through my shirt. She was asking for me back there. Screaming my name while she stood in front of the man who beat her. It cut me so fucking deep I wasn't there the first time she sobbed my name. I was an absolute mess thinking of how fast I went from the guy who saved her to the guy who didn't come when she called.

Tears were dripping down my cheeks when I heard it.

"WREN!"

I flew off the floor and swiped aggressively at my cheeks, almost knocking my glasses off my face. I gravitated towards the steel door and everyone went quiet.

"WREN!"

Her unrestrained sob hit me so hard, I gasped for breath and rocked backward.

"SAGE!" I screamed, launching myself at the door that separated us. I became desperate. I kicked and punched the ever loving shit out of that door while she sobbed my name over and over. My knuckles split from the force of the hits but I didn't stop.

Blood was smeared across my knuckles and there would be a hefty bruise on the side of my foot but I could not stop.

She was screaming for me and I was still too far away.

"SAGE! SAGE!"

There was a loud clank before the doors began to open.

I shoved my body through the crack the minute I saw an opening. I heard my shirt tear and took off running down a hallway I wasn't supposed to be in. My chest burned with the loss of oxygen and the need to get to her.

My lungs were spasming. My heart was erratic.

My eyes found Marshall, and then I saw her.

She was barreling down the hallway, a monsoon pouring down her face. She was sobbing so hard she could barely keep herself upright.

And then she was mine.

"I got you!" I pressed my face into her neck the moment she collided with me. "Sunshine, I got you. I got you."

"Wren!" She was hysterical, wailing into my chest. Her knees buckled. She started to melt towards the ground. I tightened my grip on her and lifted her off the ground, coaxing her legs around my middle so I could carry her from the hallway.

"Sunshine, it's okay. I'm right here."

The steel doors clanked shut behind us and not a single person approached her. We all stood there, listening to her sob while she fisted the back of my shirt like I was about to take off.

"Sage, I'm not going to leave you, okay?"

She nodded aggressively, shaking so violently, I slid down the wall and sat down with her in my lap. "Look at me, Sage. I'm right here."

Her head came off my shoulder and she pressed her forehead against mine. Her face was blotchy, her eyes were bright red, hair was stuck to her cheeks with snot, but she was still so fucking beautiful. I palmed her cheeks and held her to me while she cried. "He told me he took you!" She sobbed. "He told me he didn't need Julie because he took you instead."

My grip on her tightened. "What?"

"Kade!" She cried. "He told me his men took you. He told me he was going to cut you into pieces and mail them to me! I tried to get him to take me instead. I wanted to make a trade, but he wouldn't listen and-"

"What the hell did you just say?"

A bomb went off somewhere inside me. My bones cracked, the world around me went up in flames, and my ears popped. I could not hear anything but that one sentence.

I wanted to make a trade.

"Did you just say you tried to trade yourself for me?"

"Of course I did! Wren, you didn't hear what he said they were going to do! I couldn't let that happen to you! I'm so sorry. I drug you into so much darkness and now they are gonna be after you! He wouldn't take me, Wren! I'm so sorry! You have to run!" She tried to scramble off my lap.

I moved my hands to her hips and held her against me. "Listen to me, Sage. Nobody is going to take me anywhere, you hear me? Circuit found Julie. She's safe, and the men who took her are in custody."

She sniffed. "What?"

"Kade was lying to you, Sunshine. Nobody is going to hurt me. It's over."

"Did you say they caught the man who took Julie?"

"Yes."

Her chest heaved. "That man was... that was the man who..."

"I know, babe. I know who he was."

She collapsed against me, shoving her face in my neck. "Thank you." She whispered. "Thank you."

"It was all of us."

She let out a small sob. "Trish would want you to have so many crayons."

"It'd be my honor to place them on my desk."

The room went silent for a while. I could feel several sets of eyes on me but didn't lift my head from the crook of her neck. I held her until her sobs slowed and she sat up.

"I never want to see him again."

"You won't." I cupped her cheeks and brushed away leftover tears. "And, Sage? If you ever try to trade my safety for yours again, we will have so many problems. Do you hear me?"

She looked taken back. "If I had to choose between me or you, Wren, I would choose you. Every time. Besides, it was me who drug you into this life. I should've left you alone."

Now that was a sentence that ripped out my insides. "Please, don't." I begged. "Don't ever leave me alone, Sage."

"You don't know what they'd do to you. You didn't hear it."

"You're right." I conceded. "I didn't hear it, and you know what? I'm so fucking sorry you had to. But here's the thing, I am not scared of Kade Wilson. I am scared of losing you."

She pushed a lock of hair from her wet face. "Why?"

My lips quirked. "You have no idea, do you?"

"Know what?"

I pulled her face close to mine and brushed my lips over her ear. "I love you, phantom girl. I love you so much."

There was a hitch in her breath. She yanked away from me and grabbed my face, staring me in the eyes as if she were looking for a sign that told her I was lying. Her big blue eyes were popping from her head. Before she could say anything, I pressed my lips to hers.

Her body flailed in surprise. For a moment, nothing happened. We sat there, our lips pressed together and neither of us moved. My chest was going wild against hers. I could feel her trembling in my lap as I waited for the moment that came next.

That moment was spectacular.

A soft sigh went from her lips to mine a second before she deepened the kiss. Her hands went from fisting my shirt to gripping the hairs at the nape of my neck. She sunk into me like she trusted me to shield her from all the darkness the world had.

"Sun." She whispered against my lips. "You're my sun."

Something inside me happened after that. It was as if my whole world had tilted just a smidge. Like loving her made the world feel different. The air felt lighter. Everything appeared brighter. And things didn't seem so scary anymore.

I pushed my fingers into her snow-white hair and kissed her until we were forced to come up for air. She rested her cheek against my shoulder and kept peppering kisses along my neck and cheek until her body went slack.

"That was my first kiss." She whispered. "Well... the first one that mattered anyway."

Not a damn thing could stop the grin from forming on my face. "That was my first kiss too."

She flew upward. "Really?"

"The first one that mattered anyway."

She shook her head, a slow smile forming on her lips. "Wren?"

"Sage."

"I love you too."

SAGE

SEVERAL MONTHS LATER...

IF SOMEONE HAD TOLD me a year ago I'd be standing in a private elevator in an abandoned building descending into a top-secret underworld that housed a dozen criminals, I would've insisted they get tested for every drug known. Yet here I was, typing in a password created especially for me and taking the short ride into Circuit.

The first time I'd stepped off the elevator, I was awestruck. Ya know those moments when a teenage girl meets her celebrity crush and she geeks out so bad there's nothing more than flailing hands and loud squeals? My first time in Circuit was similar to that. I guess I was sort of picturing a run-down building with newspapers covering the windows and beer bottles everywhere. I should've known better than to compare Circuit to any one of Kade's hideouts. When I'd asked Wren to take me to Circuit I wasn't expecting to walk into a place that looked like it was funded by a tech nerd with millions and millions of dollars to spend. I didn't even know what half of the technology in the place was called but I had a feeling the enormous blinking thingy on the back wall rivaled the cost of a small house.

"Phantom girl is here!" Ace shouted my arrival before I had both feet off the elevator.

"Hi, Sunshine!" Wren bellowed, not bothering to look up from his screen. There was a foam cup on the corner of his desk I knew was filled with warm Diet Coke. I grimaced when he lifted it and took a sip.

"What treats did you bring us?" August hollered.

"It's not my girl's job to feed you." Wren barked. "She ain't your mama."

"His mama doesn't feed him." Zelda cracked. "And his girlfriends keep dumping him."

"Why do I need a girlfriend to feed me when Wren's girl feeds me all the time?"

"You act like you're special, man." Ace leaned back in his chair and placed his right foot on his left knee. "But she feeds all of us."

It was true. I did feed them. It started the first time I came to Circuit. After Wren had gotten prior permission from Cruz, he introduced me to the wonderful people who made up the circuit board. I'd made cupcakes as another token of my gratitude and personally thanked each one of them for what they did for me, Julie, and everybody else whose lives they made significantly better. Since that day, I'd been bringing them treats at least once a week. It stemmed from my boredom at home. What's more, baking meant I got to spend more time with my mom, and since the hard questions became easier to answer, I reveled in making up for the time I'd missed with her.

"I come with zucchini bread." I announced, holding up a tray everybody seemed to miss.

Ace let out a dramatic groan and thrust his hands outward. I rolled my eyes and plopped the tray of pre-sliced bread on the corner of his desk.

"What the hell is zucchini bread?" August blurted.

"Bread with vegetables in it!" Ace shouted, rubbing his hands together and licking his lips. "It's the shit!"

"Come get it!" I hollered. "Before Ace devours it."

The clicking sound of a hundred fingers hard at work stopped abruptly. The silence was accompanied by desk chairs rolling across the cement floor. I smiled watching August shove his sister's chair and send her flying. Ace had two slices down his throat before anybody had even gotten to his desk. Zelda was smacking Marshall's hand to stop him from taking the big piece and there were cackles all around.

These people are not criminals, I thought. These people were one big family. And how lucky was I that I got to be a part of the family?

I grabbed a slice of bread before it was gone and carried it towards the man who kept this family together. My feet halted at the bottom of the small staircase and knocked on the railing as if I were about to enter a teenage boy's bedroom.

"Hi, Cruz."

"Hi, Sage."

Cruz drug his eyes from his screen. I knew from experience I'd only be able to hold his attention for a moment. The first time I laid eyes on Cruz, I was massively intimidated. I squeezed the shit out of Wren's hand and my legs shook as I approached him, taking in his tattoos, the gauges in his ears, and the scowl on his face. And then he started to talk, and I learned that Cruz with no first name is the second kindest man I'd ever met. He lives and breathes this organization. Ace likes to joke if we cut Cruz open we'd find a giant circuit board rather than bones and muscles.

"Do you want some zucchini bread?" I held my hand out, wincing over the fact I didn't have a napkin or a plate to put it on. "My hands are clean."

He chuckled and jerked his chin. "Sure, mama. That'd be awesome."

I climbed up the stairs and transferred the still warm bread from my hands to his. He took a huge bite.

"Thanks for this, by the way." He mumbled, crumbs flying. "You don't have to keep feeding us."

"August says otherwise."

"I'd say August should learn how to feed himself but last time he tried to cook here, he blew up the fucking microwave in the loft."

A laugh burst out of me. "I think I'll keep bringing snacks."

He nodded and shoved the rest of the slice in his mouth. "Good idea." He turned back to his screen. I took that as my cue to leave. My conversations with Cruz didn't last much longer than that but I'd made it my personal mission to get to know every member at Circuit a little better.

Despite the remain anonymous rule, they'd accepted me with open arms.

Figuratively. Not literally. I still couldn't handle when people touched me. I was getting better. But I was not ready for a full-on hug from somebody who wasn't named Wren Wilder.

Speaking of Wren Wilder...

"Hi, babe." I scampered across the building and plopped my bottom on the corner of his desk that didn't hold the day-old soda.

"Hey, you." He finally lifted his gaze and gave me his attention. "Please tell me you saved me some of that bread."

I grinned and pulled a pre-wrapped slice out of the purse that was slung across my body. I held it outward. He clasped his hands and looked toward the sky, mumbling a thank you.

"She loves me." He told the sky.

I nudged his shoulder. "You goob."

"Sunshine, you know I get excited when you bake."

"You get excited by a two-dollar bottle of Diet Coke from a vending machine."

"That's different." He barely had the foil off the bread before he shoved half the slice in his mouth. "Diet Coke is its own category."

"What category is that? My strange addiction category?"

He shook his head and adjusted his glasses. "The things I can't live without category. Diet Coke used to be in the top spot."

"What took its place? Lucky Charms?"

He chuckled and gripped my chin, pressing a light kiss to my lips. "You, Sage. You're the number one thing I can't live without."

"Oh God!" Zelda gagged. "Can you two stop with this lovey dovey shit on the daily? Josie and I are engaged and we ain't even that bad."

"Specter and Phantom sitting in tree! K-I-S-"

"How old are you, bro?" Wren chuckled at Ace's song and finished the rest of his snack.

I grinned at the use of my honorary code name.

Phantom.

Ace, August, and the rest of the crew decided I needed a code name. Cruz agreed for safety precautions.

The day I got my code name was also the day I was given my own secret lair password and the emergency security code.

Ace chose Phantom, and I couldn't argue with that. Being Phantom girl was what brought me closer to Wren. It's given me all these new friends.

Plus, Specter and Phantom? How badass was that?

"You staying at home tonight?" Wren asked. "Want me to come stay with you?"

He did his best to sound casual, but I knew why he felt the need to ask. These days, I stayed in his apartment with him more times than not and it wasn't ever a conversation. It was just routine. I kept a toothbrush and fresh socks at his place for Pete's sake, but tonight was different. Because tomorrow morning I was going to wake up and attend my first day of college.

It took months and months and months for me to make the decision, but once I did, it felt like the weight of a thousand men was lifted off my entire body. I still wasn't sure what I wanted to study, but I knew I wanted to get an education. Brett and I signed up for classes at Trinity Washington together. I'll be taking general courses while he's diving head first back into biochemistry.

"Wren, I'm fine." I told him. "I was just gonna stay at your place like I always do. Brett's gonna meet me on campus in the morning."

"Oh, I'm going too."

"What for?"

He looked at me like I sprouted horns. "Because it's my girl's first day of college?"

"Are you gonna make me pose for pictures too?"

"Hell yes." He stood from his chair and palmed my face. "You know how proud I am of you, right?"

I kissed him. "Yeah. You tell me like every waking moment."

"I don't want you to forget."

"I'm not sure how I ever could."

In the time since I'd discovered Specter, I've managed to crack down barriers that held me back one by one. I still had my triggers, and there were moments I'd get thrust back in time and freeze up. Every once in a while, something would happen that rendered my mind and body immobile. But those moments were fewer and farther between than they'd ever been. I no longer screamed when somebody brushed against me. I no longer avoided restaurants like the plague. I didn't wake up screaming every other night.

For the first time since I'd met Julie, I actually believed I was healing. Although she was no longer my official counselor, I spoke to her weekly. She moved back to Florida to live with her mother after she'd been released from the hospital. She works in a center counseling patients who'd suffered physical trauma. She said it was an ode to her husband who had been desperate to get better but wasn't given the proper resources. I didn't reach out to her until over a month after she went back to Florida. I was still angry and she was still filled with guilt. Now, I'd consider her a friend.

My new counselor's name was Mandy. She wasn't Julie and there weren't any photos of the sun on her walls, but it didn't matter. Not when I had the sun sitting right next to me and holding my hand for the full hour I got all the hard questions hurled at me.

"Do you have everything you need? Notebooks? Pens? Highlighters? Calculator? Ruler? Protractor?"

"Protractor? Wren, I don't even have any math classes this semester."

"I was testing you."

I chuckled. "I'm going to be okay, Wren. I'm ready for this." I said it with so much confidence, it was impossible to miss how much I'd actually believed it.

"I know you are. And I'm glad Brett is going with you."

"I'm not!" Ace pouted, clearly eavesdropping on our conversation. "I'm gonna miss my big boo bear."

"Dude, you have got to stop calling him that."

Ace frowned. "I don't call him that to his face, Wilder. That'd be super weird."

"Are you crushing on my brother?" I faked a gag.

"Anybody with eyeballs that work properly is crushing on your brother." He wagged his eyebrows.

I rolled my eyes. Over the last few months, Ace and Brett had become incredibly tight. Wren joked his best friend status was getting taken away, but I knew as well as Ace did Wren was more than happy to welcome Brett. Aside from that, it was nice Brett and Ace got along so well. They'd even moved in together after Brett had come to conclusion he wanted to move out and Ace announced he had an extra room.

With those two always together, it was easier to ditch them so Wren and I could spend some time alone without one of them hovering and watching our every move due to boredom or so-called "big brother duties."

"The two of you are ridiculous." I declared. "We only have class three days a week. Besides, game night on Wednesdays will always be a thing."

"Yeah, and you two shitholes keep cheating!" Ace accused. "Brett and I have made a game plan. You bitches are going down."

"Don't call her a bitch!" Wren growled. "And there is

no game plan for MarioKart. You either win or you don't. In your case, you don't."

"Not all of us have girlfriends who lived as Princess Peach in another life."

"True." He sent me a smile I felt deep in my soul. "I'm pretty God damn lucky, huh?"

"I'd argue I'm just as lucky."

He cupped my face and kissed the ever loving shit out of me right in front of everybody. I pulled back and pushed him back in his seat, standing up. "Get back to work, Specter. I'll be up in the loft waiting for you."

He grabbed my wrist before I could take even one step. "Before you go, we got you something for your first day."

"We?"

"All of us!" August whooped, flying from his chair. "Guys?"

I watched in confusion as the entire circuit board rose from their chairs. Cruz included.

"What's going on?"

"We got you a little something." Wren grinned. "To show you how proud we all are of you. Something to make you feel safe." He palmed my hip. "Close your eyes and hold out your hands."

I obeyed because I knew without a doubt Wren was going to stay directly in front of me. As long as his hand was on my hip, I knew I was safe. "If somebody plops a spider or something equally gross and disgusting in my hands, I'm never bringing treats for you again."

"Nothing like that, Sunshine." Wren chuckled. "Just wait for it."

I waited for a few beats until something was plopped into my hand. Before I could feel it and try to figure out what exactly it was, another was plopped into my hand.

And then another. And another until I had two handfuls of long circular objects.

"Ready to see, babe?"

"Uhm, yes?"

Wren's lips hit my ear. "Open your eyes."

I opened my eyes and looked down. My stomach did a flip-flop. My heart turned over as I stared at a dozen cyan crayons cupped in my grasp.

"You are the biggest badass of them all, Sunshine." Wren grinned, adding one more crayon to my collection. "Saving you was the catalyst to the best day of my life."

A tear ran down my face but I didn't move to wipe it away. I didn't want to drop any of my badass crayons. "I love you."

"I love you too, Sage."

There were a few long years my mind refused to consider a future. I'd always had trouble making choices regarding my life past a day or two. As time went on, choices got easier to make and questions got easier to answer. But choosing Wren Wilder was the easiest choice I'd ever made. Because Wren wasn't just a regular choice. He was the one the universe made for me, and after spending so many years hating what it'd given me, all had been redeemed because I had Wren now. And life with him made all the darkness go dim.

He was the sun.

He was everything.

ACKNOWLEDGMENTS

Nina, thank you for always making time to read my novels and listening to me ramble about them.

Tristan, thank you for spending an hour helping me plot when I was stuck.

Lucas, thank you for telling me everything I needed to know about computers over drinks at a bar.

Monique, thank you for the numerous suggestions you provided and all the time and work you put into this novel. You are an essential piece in my writing process.

Mom, thank you for always reading my books cover to cover.

Thank you to the bloggers and bookstagrammers who have supported me nonstop. The love I feel from you all is profound.

As always, thank you to all the readers who continue to read my novels and express their love and interest. It means more to me than you'll ever know.

ABOUT THE AUTHOR

The best place to find Lacey is with her nose in a book. She's a sucker for a good love story and a happy ending that has her swooning. When she's not obsessing over giving her own characters a happy ending, you can find her in the dance studio empowering young dancers and giving out tons of stickers. Thanks to her mother's pizzeria, Lacey can make a delicious pizza.

When she's not putting on her dance shoes or inhaling a slice of pizza, she's in front of her computer binge watching romantic comedies and penning stories with love so powerful, it'll last a lifetime. As a recent graduate of Central Michigan University, Lacey intends to keep inspiring people through dance and lots and lots of words. She currently lives in Central Michigan surrounded by her family and unpredictable weather.

Connect with Lacey:

www.laceydaileyauthor.com

Made in the USA
Middletown, DE
21 December 2021